DARK DESTINY

M. J. Putney

 St. Martin's Griffin New York

This is a work of fiction. All of the characters, organizations, and events portrayed in this novel are either products of the author's imagination or are used fictitiously.

Printed in the United States of America. For information, address St. Martin's Press, 175 Fifth Avenue, New York, N.Y. 10010.

www.stmartins.com

Library of Congress Cataloging-in-Publication Data

Putney, Mary Jo.
Dark mirror / M. J. Putney.—1st ed.
p. cm.
Sequel to: Dark passage.
Summary: Tory and her friends receive an urgent summons, leading the young mages known as Merlin's Irregulars to ask Rebecca Weiss, an untrained telepath from 1940, to join them in 1804 and stop Napoleon from invading England.
ISBN 978-0-312-62286-2 (pbk.)
ISBN 978-1-250-02017-8 (e-book)
[1. Magic—Fiction. 2. Space and time—Fiction. 3. Boarding schools—Fiction. 4. Schools—Fiction. 5. London (England)—History—19th century—Fiction. 6. Great Britain—History—George III, 1760–1820—Fiction. 7. Napoleonic Wars, 1800–1815—Fiction. 8. France—History—1789–1815—Fiction.] I. Title.
PZ7.P98232Dar 2012
[Fic]—dc23

2012004624

First Edition: July 2012

10 9 8 7 6 5 4 3 2 1

DARK DESTINY

ALSO BY M. J. PUTNEY

Dark Mirror

Dark Passage

This book is dedicated to my great-nieces, Caroline and Marielle, because they're the right demographic for these stories!

ACKNOWLEDGMENTS

My thanks to all the usual suspects, most especially Pat Rice and Susan King for helping me bat this around.

A special thanks to my fellow Word Wench Nicola Cornick, whose wonderful blog post about "the last invasion of Britain" gave me so many ideas for the plot of *Dark Destiny.*

And more thanks to author Sarah Darer Littman for her advice on how Rebecca might have organized a gentile Shabbat.

Let us be masters of the Channel for six hours and we are masters of the world.

—Napoleon Bonaparte, while contemplating an invasion of Britain

I do not say, my Lords, that the French will not come. I say only they will not come by sea.

—Admiral Lord John Jervis, Earl of St. Vincent, when he was admiral of the Channel Fleet during the Napoleonic Wars

DARK DESTINY

CHAPTER I

Lackland, England, Autumn 1940

A fighter plane roared menacingly over the farmhouse just as Tory bent to blow out the candles on her birthday cake. She froze—she would *never* get used to destructive flying machines!

But she could pretend to be brave. She drew a deep breath and blew. The seventeen candles for her years were easily extinguished, but the one added for luck flickered persistently before guttering out. She hoped that wasn't an omen.

Her friends around the table applauded. Those who'd come from 1804 with Tory were enjoying the twentieth-century birthday customs. The five of them would return to their own time in the morning. She was glad to be heading home, but she'd miss her twentieth-century friends.

"Did you make a wish?" Polly asked. The youngest Rainford, she belonged to this house and this time. Though she was still weak from a bout with blood poisoning that had almost killed her, her mischievous smile had returned.

"Indeed I did," Tory replied. "And it was hard to decide what to wish for!"

Her life had changed so much since she turned sixteen a year ago. Then she had been the well-brought-up Lady Victoria Mansfield, youngest child of the Earl of Mansfield. Most of her thoughts had been turned toward her upcoming presentation to society, where she would look for the best possible husband.

In the year since, she'd become a mageling, an exile, and one of Merlin's Irregulars, sworn to use her magic to protect Britain. Not to mention being a traveler through time and an unsung heroine of Britain.

Best of all, she had fallen in love. Her gaze drifted to the young man who sat at her right, looking impossibly handsome. Justin Falkirk, Marquess of Allarde and her beloved. He gave her a smile full of the warmth and intimacy that had grown between them in the last months.

"Time to cut the cake!" Lady Cynthia Stanton, who was Tory's roommate back at the Lackland Abbey, was eyeing the dessert hungrily. "Mrs. R., if I come back for my birthday, will you make me a cake like this?"

"I will," Anne Rainford, their hostess, said cheerfully. "But give me some warning, please. This cake required almost a month's worth of our sugar rations. I'll need to save more coupons to create another cake this size."

"You won't want to take another beastly trip through the mirror just for a cake, Cynthia." Tory got to her feet so she could cut properly. "But you can have the first piece of this one."

The round cake had a thin layer of white icing, and "Happy Birthday, Tory!" was spelled out in rather uneven red letters. The same red icing had been used to draw little red rockets exploding around the edges.

Tory could have done without the explosions, but Polly had been pleased with herself for coming up with the idea. After all, war had drawn together this group of magelings from two different eras and forged lasting friendships.

Mrs. Rainford was sitting on Tory's left, and she held out a small plate to receive the first slice. "Here you are, Cynthia," Tory said as she set the wedge of dark fruitcake on the plate. Mrs. Rainford handed it across the table.

"I'm going to have trouble waiting until everyone is served!" Cynthia exclaimed. "I still haven't recovered from burning so much magic in France."

"As the birthday girl, I give you permission to eat now rather than wait for the rest of us," Tory said grandly. "We all need to eat to build up our strength for the return journey through the mirror."

Cynthia didn't hesitate to dig in her fork. After the first bite, she smiled blissfully. "This is wonderful, Mrs. R. If I didn't hate traveling through the mirror so much, I really would come back for my birthday. I'd even bring sugar so you could make the cake without using up your rations."

"That's not a bad idea!" Nick Rainford exclaimed. "Sending sugar, I mean. How hard would it be for you to throw sugar through the mirror?"

"We could do that," Elspeth replied. "Our sugar comes in big loaves that have to be broken into smaller pieces, but they'd throw very nicely."

"Tea and butter and bacon and all kinds of other things are

also rationed," Nick said thoughtfully. "If you can send them through the mirror, we could—"

"I will not have a black market operation run from my house," Mrs. Rainford said firmly. She handed another plate of cake to Rebecca Weiss, who was staying with the Rainfords to study magic. "But some sugar now and then would be nice."

"We can arrange that," Allarde said as he clasped Tory's hand under the table. She could feel his amusement.

She bit her lip, thinking how much she would miss this freedom to be together when they returned to Lackland Abbey. Male and female students were strictly separated in the abbey. Only in the Labyrinth, the maze of tunnels below the abbey buildings, could they work together as they secretly studied magic. And only there could she and Allarde have the privacy they craved.

"What is a black market?" Tory asked as she cut more slices.

"Illegally selling rationed goods, and Nick would dive right in if I let him," Mrs. Rainford said with a laugh.

She laid her hand on Tory's, but before she could continue, magic blazed from Mrs. Rainford through Tory to Allarde, kindling another blaze of magic from him. Allarde's hand clamped hard on Tory's and he exclaimed, *"No!"*

"Justin?" Tory said dizzily, shaking as she channeled power and shock between Allarde and her hostess. "What . . . what just happened?"

His gaze was unfocused. "I . . . I saw Napoleon invade England. Barges landing, soldiers pouring off. French soldiers marching past Westminster Abbey."

The Irregulars gasped with horror. The threat of invasion had been hanging over their heads for months as Napoleon Bonaparte assembled an army just across the English Channel from Lackland Abbey. Jack Rainford, one of the 1804 Irregulars, asked, "What makes you say that?"

Tory felt Allarde's effort to collect himself. "Mrs. Rainford and I both have foreteller talent, and Tory's ability to enhance magic seems to have triggered a vision of the future when the three of us were touching." He glanced at their hostess. "Did you see images of invasion?"

"I . . . I saw Napoleon in Westminster Abbey," Mrs. Rainford said unevenly. "But that was fear, not foretelling! We know from history that Napoleon never invaded."

Allarde shook his head. He was still gripping Tory's hand with bruising force. "I don't know about your history books. What I saw was an event that may well happen if we don't act. We need to return home immediately. If and when the invasion takes place, Lackland will be a major landing site." He swallowed again. "I saw French barges landing in Lackland harbor and soldiers pouring off. The village was burning."

Jack Rainford rose from his chair. "My family!"

"The French are *not* going to invade!" Mrs. Rainford repeated. "I'll get a history book and show you." She left the room, her steps quick.

Tory took a swallow of tea for her dry throat. Mrs. Rainford was a schoolteacher and well educated, but Allarde's magic was powerful. "Foretelling is what *might* happen, not necessarily what *will* happen, isn't it?"

Allarde eased his grip, though he still held her hand. "This felt very, very likely."

Mrs. Rainford returned with a textbook. As she thumbed through the pages, she said, "There's a chapter about how close Napoleon came to invading, but he didn't." She found the chapter she was looking for and caught her breath, her face turning white.

Tory peered at the book and saw that the letters on the page were twisting and flickering like live things. The words couldn't be read.

Mrs. Rainford said in a choked voice, "I remember what this chapter said, but . . . it doesn't say that anymore."

"The text being in flux here suggests that the history isn't set," Allarde said grimly. "Perhaps Napoleon just made the decision to launch and that's why we had the visions. If the Irregulars can do something to prevent the invasion, that might be why history records say that it didn't happen."

"If the past has changed, wouldn't the present also be different?" Rebecca, raised by two scientists, frowned as she tried to puzzle it out.

"Time travel is a mystery, and I don't pretend to understand how it works," Jack said, as grim as Allarde. "But there is danger at home and to my family. I can feel it like a gathering storm."

Elspeth, the fifth Irregular, rose. "We need to leave right away. We haven't much to pack."

Ever practical, not to mention hungry, Cynthia said, "We should take the rest of the cake. It will help us recover from the mirror passage."

Knowing that was true, Tory tried to eat her slice, but it tasted like straw. She and the other Irregulars had faced the dangers of war here in 1940, but her own time, her home and family, had not been threatened. Not until now.

"I'll pack the cake and some cheese," Polly said briskly.

As the party dissolved, Nick caught Tory's gaze and said with deadly seriousness, "You've done so much for England in my time.

If there is anything, *anything,* that I can do to help, send a message through the mirror and I'll come instantly."

"You saved my whole family," Rebecca said in her soft French accent. "I have only just discovered that I have magic, and I don't know how to use it. But I pledge everything within my power to your service."

Tory thanked them, but she realized with cold foreboding that even if all the Irregulars and their 1940 friends worked together, they were few and the French were many. The Irregulars might not be able to save England.

CHAPTER 2

Tory had come through the mirror with almost no possessions, so packing was quick. Allarde was waiting for her in the front hall of the Rainford farmhouse, his gray eyes haunted. Silently she took his hand, feeling how upset he was by his vision of invasion. Foretelling was not a comforting gift.

When the others joined them, they set off to the ruins of Lackland Abbey. Everyone came except Polly, who wasn't yet strong enough to walk that far. There was little talk. Jack and Cynthia also held hands. Since the village of Lackland was Jack's home and all his family was there, he was even more tense than the other Irregulars.

Here in 1940, it was autumn and darkness fell early. The cool night air carried the drone of distant engines as Nazi aircraft crossed the English Channel to bomb London. The attacks had been continuing for months and London hadn't broken yet, but Tory had seen pictures of the staggering destruction. Bombs had fallen here in Lackland, but only by accident, since a small fishing village wasn't a worthwhile target.

Weapons in her own time were not so devastating, but they were bad enough. Napoleon Bonaparte had become first consul of France and ruler of most of Europe because he was a brilliant and ruthless general. Tory shivered at the thought of France conquering England and Bonaparte swaggering through Westminster Abbey.

In Tory's time, Lackland Abbey was the school where Tory and her friends had been sent to be "cured" of their magical abilities. In this time, the abbey that she knew had been reduced to rubble by German bombs. Nick Rainford had had to dig a new entrance to the time portal they called Merlin's Mirror.

Once she descended belowground to the chalk tunnels they called the Labyrinth, Tory felt the tug of the mirror's powerful energy. She had a special affinity for the mirror's magic, so she acted as guide when she and her friends moved through the portal from one time to another. She brightened her mage light so she could pick her way through tunnels cluttered with fallen stones.

The group entered the chamber that held the mirror, and Tory mentally greeted it. The ancient, powerful energy had a kind of awareness, and it recognized her. She thought of it as a distant but rather benevolent uncle that approved of her efforts.

She drew a deep breath. "We need to go back to a time shortly after Jack and Cynthia and Elspeth came through the mirror. I think you said you came to join us two days after Nick and Allarde and I were pulled through?"

Elspeth nodded. "It was late at night, after a study session of all the Irregulars. You'll probably want to add half a day to be sure we return later than we left."

"Time to say our good-byes, then." Tory's smile was crooked. "I hate good-byes."

Her great gray eyes solemn, Rebecca gave Tory a swift, fierce hug. "To say thank you is not strong enough."

Tory hugged her back. They'd shared a perilous adventure in France that had brought them close. "When we've made it safely home, we'll send a message stone back to you here. Please send message stones about how your family is doing in Oxford. I know you'll miss them."

Rebecca stepped back. "I do, but they are safe and so are my father's research assistants and their families. They will work hard to help create the miracle medicine."

Anne Rainford gave the next hug. "Be careful, Tory. Don't let Allarde and Jack kill themselves by being too heroic."

Tory sighed. "I'll try, but they are both entirely too noble."

Nick hugged her last. He was her first friend in the twentieth century, the person who found her when she'd fallen through the mirror into another time and was alone and terrified. "If you need me, send a message and I'll be back." He grinned. "I'd like to visit 1804 and be able to leave the Labyrinth rather than stay there like a rat in a maze."

"If you're needed, we won't hesitate to call," she promised. "You owe me a considerable debt for hauling me through the mirror to France!"

"I do indeed." His glance touched Rebecca before moving back to Tory. "We all work well together. Surely we can stop a French invasion."

"I hope so." She squeezed his hand, then turned to the Irregulars. The farewells were finished and it was time to leave. Using her intuition to balance their energies, she said, "Jack, take my hand. Then Cynthia, Allarde, and Elspeth."

Silently they linked hands. Tory closed her eyes and tuned herself to the energies of her friends, feeling each like a distinct chord of music. Jack, teasing but utterly reliable, and the best weather mage in Britain. Cynthia, prickly and wounded, but healing. Allarde, whose power and strength were as deep as the earth. Elspeth, a wise, compassionate healer with the delicacy and silver blond hair of a fairy sprite.

When she was satisfied, Tory stretched her free hand to the mirror, visualizing the time she wanted to return to. A safe half day after her friends had followed them to France. Then she opened her mind to the deep, pulsing power of the mirror. It shimmered into burning silvery life. *"Now!"*

The mirror turned black and she led her friends into chaos.

As Tory prepared her friends for the journey, Rebecca shrank back against the cold chalk wall, instinctively recoiling from the fierce energy of the mirror. Her one passage through the portal had been short, from France to England without changing times, and it had still been fearsome. Like being ripped to pieces, then reassembled.

At that time, only a week earlier, Rebecca had just discovered that her odd abilities were magic, and she'd found the mirror travel profoundly disorienting. This time the energy was far more powerful, for it was taking her friends almost 140 years into the past.

Mrs. Rainford also retreated to the wall and put an arm around Rebecca's waist. Rebecca was grateful for the reassurance, but touching sharpened her awareness of the older woman's emotions.

Mrs. Rainford had foretelling ability, and she was very worried about what the Irregulars would find when they got home.

Nick stood closer to the mirror, his expression taut. Like Tory, he had mirror magic. He'd made his first passage in a blind, desperate attempt to find help after Tory had returned to her own time. Rebecca was awed by his courage. But he was worried, too; she could feel that even though they weren't touching.

She glanced away, wishing her magical gift were less uncomfortable. Being able to read people's emotions and sometimes even their thoughts was an invasion of privacy.

As soon as she'd arrived in England the week before, the Irregulars had begun to train her to use her power. The first thing she'd been taught was how to shield her mind so she wasn't overwhelmed by the emotions of others.

Though Elspeth said her talent was developing with lightning speed, Rebecca was still working on that lesson. It was particularly hard to block Nick, probably since she fancied him. And he fancied her, too. She could feel his intense interest whenever they were close to each other.

Luckily he hadn't yet said or done anything romantic. She wasn't looking forward to explaining why there could be nothing more than friendship between them.

Expression remote, Tory raised her hand and summoned the mirror from nothingness. It was a rectangle of menacing silver that faintly reflected the young people linked together in front of it.

Mrs. Rainford reached out and pulled Nick back to her other side. "I don't want you dragged through again," she said.

"Once was enough," he agreed as he wrapped an arm around his mother's shoulders. His fingers brushed Rebecca's arm with a tingle of magic and attraction.

He gave her a quick glance, then looked away when their gazes met. He was several inches taller than his mother, blond and broad-shouldered and altogether too good-looking in a very English way.

Then Tory invoked the power of the mirror and it turned blacker than night. The five Irregulars vanished in a blaze of stunning power.

Rebecca involuntarily pressed back into the wall. Silently she recited the Tefilat HaDerech, the Hebrew prayer for travelers. Might her friends arrive safely back in their own time and have the strength to do what must be done.

Then the passage was over, leaving the chamber empty and dark except for the small mage light that Nick had created. He brightened the light. "They'll be all right," he said as if trying to convince himself. "They're amazing."

"Yes," Mrs. Rainford said bleakly. Her arm tightened around Rebecca. "But I have a powerful feeling that the two of you are going to have to go to their time to help. And even all of you together might not be enough."

In a flash of absolute certainty, Rebecca realized that Mrs. Rainford was right: Rebecca and Nick would be called to the past to help their friends, and it would be very, very dangerous.

So be it. Rebecca had spent the last week absorbing Tory's shocking news that Rebecca had magical powers. The very idea ran counter to everything she'd ever learned from her scientist parents, yet it explained so much about how she was different from others. It was time to embrace her differences and learn to use them in ways that would help others.

The mirror flashed briefly as a small object flew through and clattered onto the floor. A message stone.

Nick scooped it up and unwrapped the piece of paper tied to

the rock. Smiling, he read, "Home safely, French not yet on our doorsteps, will send sugar. Allarde."

"That's good news," Mrs. Rainford said. "Now it's time for us to go home."

Silently they retraced their path through the tunnels and climbed up into the open air. It was full dark, a sliver of moon providing a bit of light. Rebecca had grown up in cities with lights all around, and she was always struck by how dark it was with the blackout rules requiring people to conceal all lights at night.

The night felt quiet and safe, far removed from war. But Rebecca had learned when she and her family were imprisoned in France that safety was an illusion. She could have died there. A bomb could drop on her head here. Since death was always a possibility, she tried not to worry about it.

She had been practicing her mental shielding to protect herself from random emotions. Now she cautiously lowered the shields and reached out to see what she could sense. Out here on the path along the cliffs that ran from the abbey to the village of Lackland, there were few human minds. But she found that when she made the effort, she could dimly sense the people in the houses along the road a quarter mile away.

She'd learned that magic followed thought. To create an effect, she needed to understand, then visualize, the result she wanted. She told her mind to ignore routine emotions, and her awareness from the nearby homes faded away.

As they neared the Rainford farmhouse, Mrs. Rainford said, "Now that you're settled in, Rebecca, it's time to start school."

"I'll be glad to return to my studies," Rebecca said. "After being imprisoned for almost a year, I must be far behind in all my subjects."

Nick laughed. "Few of my friends would be so keen to return to school."

Perhaps not. But they hadn't been jammed in a stone cell for many months with the threat of death always present. Rebecca welcomed a return to normality.

"Your mother told me that she tutored you and the other children while you were locked up?" Mrs. Rainford said, her voice questioning.

"Yes, but the lessons were not well organized," Rebecca explained. "To be accepted to a medical school will require certain courses."

"You have several years to get caught up, and the Lackland Girls Grammar School is quite good," Mrs. Rainford said. "If necessary, we can arrange for extra tutoring for you."

Since Mrs. Rainford taught at the school, Rebecca thought the teachers would be helpful to a new girl who was under the Rainford wing. She wasn't as sure about the other students. Polly Rainford attended the LGG, but she was three years younger.

Rebecca had been in England for only a week, but she'd seen fair English coloring all around her. All the Rainfords were blond. Rebecca was dark-haired, foreign, and Jewish. She asked hesitantly, "How will the other girls feel about someone who is different, like me?"

"They'll think you're really interesting," Nick offered.

"She is," Mrs. Rainford agreed. "But this has been a peaceful little fishing village where anyone from more than twenty miles away was thought of as a foreigner. There will be some students who won't quite know what to make of you at first."

"The war has changed many things," Nick added. "Both the boys and the girls grammar schools have students who were evacuated from London when the bombing started. Everyone has heard of the refugees who came from the Continent to escape the Nazis, so Rebecca won't seem as unusual as she would have two or three years ago."

"Fortunately, you speak lovely English," Mrs. Rainford said encouragingly. "It won't take long for people to accept you."

Rebecca hoped the Rainfords were right, but she suspected they were being optimistic. Ah, well, the school was for education. She would be quiet as a mouse and learn her maths and science—and would study magic outside the school.

She resumed the search for emotions and people that were in any way out of place. She sensed nothing until they came in sight of the Rainfords' rambling stone farmhouse. The house was over two hundred years old and solidly built on a bluff overlooking the English Channel.

On a clear day, Rebecca could see her homeland, now conquered by the Nazis. Every day she prayed for many things, and among them were prayers for France.

As they neared the house, she became aware of . . . an unknown presence inside. "You have a visitor," she said.

"You can sense someone this far away?" Nick asked.

She nodded. "I've been practicing and my range is getting better."

"Polly is all right?" Mrs. Rainford asked.

Rebecca focused her attention on the wispy traces of energy she was feeling. "Yes, and she's happy. Perhaps Captain Rainford is home for a brief visit?"

Mrs. Rainford's pace quickened. "Oh, I hope so!"

They entered through the kitchen door, moving quickly so no light would escape. Polly's voice called out, "Look who's here!"

A lean young man was sitting at the kitchen table opposite Polly and wolfing down a bowl of soup. Mrs. Rainford cried, "Joe!"

Rebecca had heard of Joe, the eldest of the three Rainford children and a fighter pilot in the RAF. With German aircraft pounding Britain daily in the assault known as the Blitz, being a pilot was one of the most dangerous occupations imaginable.

Joe rose and hugged his mother hard. "I have a forty-eight-hour pass, so here I am, Mum. Hungry and craving some home cooking."

Mrs. Rainford laughed. "Rationing means I can't make some of your favorite dishes, but I promise you won't go hungry."

"Leave it to a pilot to just drop in without warning," Nick said as he clapped his brother's shoulder. As they stood next to each other, it was clear they were brothers, with the fair Rainford coloring and blue eyes.

Joe's glance moved past his mother and he saw Rebecca. "Who's this? Have you acquired a girlfriend, Nick?"

Nick blushed, but his voice was steady when he said, "This is Rebecca Weiss. Her parents are scientists working in Oxford, but she's staying with us for a while."

"Are you tutoring her in English, Mum?" Laughing, Joe offered Rebecca his hand. "Or magic?"

Magic sparked when they touched, and Rebecca had a disorienting moment of double vision. Joe Rainford stood in front of her, his handsome face smiling as if he didn't have a care in the world. Yet at the same time, she saw him as a young man strained almost to the breaking point.

Something bad had just happened, she realized, though Joe wouldn't talk about it to his family. She sucked in her breath when an image flashed through her mind of his plane being shot down over the Channel just the day before.

Joe had escaped with only bruises. But a close friend of his had been shot down at the same time and died. Their commanding officer had given Joe leave so he could come home and unwind before he shattered.

All of that passed through her mind in an instant. Wrenching herself back to the moment, she said gravely, "I speak English well. I am here to study magic."

"Joe doesn't quite believe in magic yet," Nick said. "Perhaps he will after we tell him about our journey to France."

Joe blinked. "France? Surely that's a joke?"

"It was no joke." Nick glanced at the pot of hearty bean soup on the stove. "That looks like enough soup for all of us, so let's eat while we talk."

With a shuffling of chairs and a clattering of bowls, the five of them settled down around the table for bread and soup and cheese. As always, Nick managed to be sitting next to Rebecca. She liked having him close even as she told herself that it would be wiser to keep him at a distance.

Rebecca wondered if Joe knew that he had magical ability, and that that power was keeping him alive. She hoped it never failed.

CHAPTER 3

Lackland, England, 1804

Tory had thought the mirror transits were becoming easier, but this trip disproved that theory. Chaos and dissolution and formlessness tore at mind and body before she returned to normal awareness in a jarring collapse onto a chalk floor. She felt like a squashed bug.

Her first attempt at speech failed. She tried again. "Is everyone all right?"

Jack squeezed her hand, then released it. "I'm well enough. Cynthia?"

"Still breathing," she said grumpily. "Which makes this a better trip than some."

A mage light flickered on, held aloft by Allarde. Beyond him, Elspeth sat up, looking even paler than usual. Jack had an arm around Cynthia. She leaned into him, her eyes looking bruised. She'd always had more trouble with mirror passages than anyone else, but she was doing better now.

Tory created another mage light and tossed it up to hover above them. Then she rose creakily to her feet. "Now to find if we're back in our right time."

"I hope so. I want to sleep in my own bed," Elspeth said with a sigh.

"We're not going to go aboveground and find French troops in Lackland, are we?" Jack said as he helped Cynthia up.

Allarde hesitated, as if listening to voices only he could hear. "Not yet," he said. "But soon. Invading across the English Channel is devilish difficult and hasn't been done successfully since William the Conqueror in 1066. That's why Napoleon has been hesitating for so long, building an army and a flotilla just across the Channel, but never giving the order to invade. Now he's made up his mind, and will launch the invasion as soon as he can."

"I wonder if we can deduce what made Napoleon decide to invade?" Tory said slowly. "If we can, perhaps there is some way of countering that decision."

"We can try a clairvoyant circle with all of us working together," Elspeth said. "We need to talk to Miss Wheaton and Mr. Stephens. They're also in touch with mages outside the school. A threat like this will bring all the mages in Britain together."

It was comforting to remember that they weren't alone. "If I calculated correctly, it should be very early in the morning several hours after you and Jack and Cynthia followed us to France." Tory covered a yawn. "Time to get some sleep. We can take this up with Miss Wheaton and Mr. Stephens tomorrow."

"Who has the cake?" Cynthia asked.

"I do." Allarde opened the bag that was slung over his shoulder and brought out a bulging paper sack. As he handed out pieces of cake, he said, "Polly was generous."

Traveling through the mirror always left Tory ravenous, so she bit into the rich fruitcake immediately. The others did the same. Her birthday party might have ended badly, but the cake was a blessing.

"There's enough for each person to have a bit more." Allarde opened the bag and broke the remaining chunk into five pieces so he could pass them around. Nibbling as she walked, Tory took his arm as they headed toward the center of the Labyrinth.

Their tunnel curved just before reaching the central area. "Odd," Jack said as they approached. "Mage lights. Any study sessions should be over by now."

"Unless I didn't get the time right," Tory said.

"Since everyone knows we're gone, maybe they left a light to welcome us home," Elspeth suggested.

They turned the last bend in the tunnel and stepped into the wide central area. The room was furnished with worn but comfortable chairs and sofas as well as tables and kitchen equipment. A handful of mage lights clung to the low ceiling, and they illuminated a pair of half-naked bodies entwined on a sofa.

Tory almost choked on the last bite of cake when she recognized that the couple was Miss Wheaton and Mr. Stephens. Miss Wheaton's soft brown hair was loose and she looked younger and much prettier than when she was teaching. Swearing under his breath, Mr. Stephens sat up, yanking the blanket over Miss Wheaton.

Not missing a beat, Allarde asked, "Have the French invaded yet?"

As he pulled on his jacket, Mr. Stephens said, "Not yet, but very soon."

Wrapping the blanket around her shoulders, Miss Wheaton also sat up. "Sorry!" she said ruefully. "We thought we were alone."

"Everyone knows the two of you are in love," Cynthia said with a shrug. "The energy between you is very clear whenever you're together."

The teachers exchanged a glance, as if silently conferring about what to say. A bond of blazing light flared between them. Startled by her intuition, Tory exclaimed, "You're not just in love. You're married, aren't you?"

Miss Wheaton nodded. "We've been secretly married since we were released from Lackland Abbey after our twenty-first birthdays."

Mr. Stephens continued, "Teachers of magical control are always recent Lackland Abbey graduates who were also Irregulars. Usually people teach for a few years, then leave to build lives elsewhere. Before that happens, they find new teachers among the oldest Irregulars and recommend them to the school's board of directors. That way, the tradition of teaching students who want to develop their powers rather than be 'cured' has been passed down through the years."

Miss Wheaton—Tory supposed she was really Mrs. Stephens—took her husband's hand. "It's not uncommon for the male and female teachers to be a married couple, but the school insists teachers be single, so marriages must be concealed."

"Waiting until you can be together must be difficult," Elspeth said softly.

"It is," Mr. Stephens said, his voice terse. "But great danger threatens Britain. We've sworn to stay until that's resolved since

Beth and I are part of a network of mages who maintain magical wards to protect this coast from invasion."

Jack blinked. "I've never heard of magical wards here. What do you do?"

"We visualize an impenetrable wall in the English Channel and send the command *You cannot cross the sea,*" Miss Wheaton explained. "This runs in the back of our minds rather than something we have to think about all the time, but it does take power and some attention. Luckily magic is enhanced here in the Labyrinth."

"Since I'm good with stealth magic, I also monitor the French ports in case they use stealth spells to slip ships through the British blockade," Mr. Stephens explained.

"Is magic used much in warfare?" Allarde asked. "Except for weather magic, most powers are small scale and local, like healing or lifting or warming a house."

Miss Wheaton looked rueful. "We don't really know how much magic is used, or how effective it is. I believe that the wards help us, and that stealth magic helps keep our activities out of sight of the enemy. But the French have mages, and surely they also use their talents to serve their country. Weather magic, stealth magic, scrying—all can be useful in war. And we have very little idea what the enemy is doing."

Mr. Stephens nodded. "It's much easier for me to practice stealth magic than it is to detect when someone else is using it. Several times I've detected attempts to break through the blockade. We have ways of getting that information to the Channel Fleet so they could head off the French when that happens."

"Have any foretellers seen more about a French invasion?" Allarde asked.

"Not much," the teacher replied. "What have you seen?"

Allarde grimaced. "No details yet. I felt as if a switch was thrown in my mind and invasion went from a possibility to a certainty. We returned immediately."

"Was your mission successful?" Miss Wheaton asked.

"It was." Allarde put his arm around Tory, who was wilting with fatigue. "But if the situation isn't critical yet, I suggest we all get some rest and meet here tomorrow night. We'll tell you about our mission, and you can tell us everything you know about French invasion plans."

After everyone agreed, they split and moved in different directions. Allarde said, "I'll send a message stone back to say that we arrived safely."

Which was a good excuse for the two of them to have some private time. After they returned to the mirror, holding hands, Allarde scribbled a message on a stone and Tory tossed it back to their friends.

Then they turned into each other's arms. "This is the part I hate about returning home," Allarde murmured. "The fact that we can't be together."

She nodded mutely as she wrapped herself around him and raised her face for a kiss. They were both stronger when they were together, nurturing each other on some deep level that blended souls and passions.

She tried not to think about the future. Even though Allarde was willing to forfeit his inheritance to be with her, there were too many things that could go wrong before they'd ever stand together at the church altar.

Reluctantly moving out of his embrace, she said, "Even when we're apart, I feel your presence with me always."

Tenderly he brushed back her wayward dark hair. "You're in my mind, too. But actual touching is better."

She caught his hand and pressed it against her cheek. "Yes. But I'll see you tomorrow evening. Or given how late it is, this evening."

Arms around each other, they returned to the central hall, then divided to return to their schools. Elspeth was about to leave, but she waited for Tory so they could walk back together. Since they were both tired, they took the shortest route. As they entered the tunnel, Tory asked, "Have you recovered yet from all the healing work you did?"

"No, but soon. The power here in the Labyrinth is energizing." Elspeth made a face. "I hate knowing that the suppression spell will hit as soon as we leave the tunnel."

"So do I." Tory continued another dozen steps before adding, "I'm amazed that Miss Wheaton and Mr. Stephens are willing to stay and teach here even though it means being apart and spending years more under the suppression spells."

"We must be grateful for their sense of duty," Elspeth observed. "When I first started here, the teachers who taught magical control in the schools weren't as good at training the Irregulars. I've learned much more since Miss Wheaton took over."

"You've been at Lackland longer than any of the other girls. Have you ever felt like walking out of the Labyrinth and never coming back?"

"Often," her friend said with a sigh as they started up the steps that led into the cellar of the refectory. "But I've had a strong feeling that this is where I should be. It won't be forever, even if sometimes it seems that way."

"Do you think you might meet someone here? A future husband?" Tory asked, wondering if her friend minded the fact that Tory and Cynthia had found partners among the Irregulars.

Elspeth shook her head emphatically. "It's duty that keeps me here, not future romance. There is someone out there for me. But not yet."

Irregulars didn't question friends' intuition. Tory said, "I'm grateful you're here, since you heal us when we need it. If not for you, Jack would surely have lost his eye."

"I knew I'd be needed, though not who would be injured." She smiled. "I'm sure Jack would look very dashing with an eye patch, but better to have two eyes."

"What will you do when you leave here? Healing is the most valuable magical talent, so you should be able to find work and support yourself anywhere."

Her friend shrugged. "I'm not sure. Perhaps I'll settle in London. I've only visited there once, but I really enjoyed the variety and liveliness of the city."

Tory realized that she had no idea where she and Allarde would go when they left Lackland. They'd only recently made a private commitment to each other, and she'd been too busy dodging Nazis and bullets to think about the future.

She hated knowing that marrying a girl with magic meant that Allarde's father would feel obligated to disinherit his only son. It wasn't so much that Allarde wouldn't become a duke, but that he would lose Kemperton. The estate had been in his family for generations, and Allarde was deeply connected to the land.

She guessed that he would be welcome at Kemperton even after his father officially disinherited him, because he and his parents loved each other. But his father was very old, and after he died and the dukedom and estate passed to a cousin, Allarde would probably no longer be welcome in his home.

He said that Tory meant more to him than Kemperton, which was very moving, but she still hated to be the cause of his losing so much. She'd tried being noble and ending the relationship. She was glad it hadn't worked, but their reconciliation was a bittersweet lesson in not being able to have everything one wanted.

They reached the steps that led to the basement of the refectory building. Tory said, "After our first mission, we came back with increased powers. I wonder if that will be true again. We all worked a huge amount of magic in France."

Elspeth yawned. "Tomorrow we'll find out, but tonight, I'll sleep."

Side by side, they climbed the steps. Tory touched the magical spot that opened the door, and it silently swung aside. Instantly the Lackland suppression spell engulfed her like a smothering blanket.

She drew a deep breath, then started through the cellar. The horrible spell was why the abbey had been chosen for the school. The Lackland school governors had no idea that the magic was driven from the abbey and into the chalk tunnels below. That made the Labyrinth an ideal place for studying magic, but Tory never got over the shock of moving from an area rich with magic into the school's magical dead zone.

As Tory and Elspeth emerged from the cellar, they dug their stealth stones from their pockets to make it less likely that anyone would notice them. Not that any sane person would be awake at this hour.

Tory's hand closed around the smooth white stone with its low buzz of magic. Mr. Stephens was the mage who charged all the stealth stones with energy to make it less likely that students would be noticed when they slipped down to the Labyrinth to study. She'd taken the stone for granted after the first few times she'd used it, but now she saw the broader applications for the teacher's talent for concealing people and things.

When they reached the girls' dormitory, Tory whispered a

goodnight and returned to her room. Cynthia hadn't returned yet. She and Jack were probably kissing in one of the tunnels and had lost track of the time.

Tory was so tired that she barely had the energy to change into her nightgown. She was asleep almost as soon as she crawled into her bed.

Being a heroine was very tiring. But tomorrow would be another day, and one way or another, the Irregulars would find a way to stop Napoleon.

CHAPTER 4

Tory was awoke by soft, stealthy footsteps. Opening her eyes to slits, she saw Cynthia silhouetted against the dawn-lit window as she tiptoed into the room. It must be almost time for the wake-up bell. "Where have you been?" Tory asked sleepily. "Or shouldn't I ask?"

Cynthia skinned out of her gown, which had taken a beating in the last days. When she emerged from the fabric, she said, "Jack was worried about the possibility of the French invading since Lackland could easily be a landing site. I thought I should stay with him until he was sure his home was safe, so I walked back to the grange with him."

Tory chuckled. "Careful. If you get caught being sensitive and supportive, no one will recognize you."

Cynthia threw her pillow at Tory. "I was also worried and wanted to see Mrs. Rainford. Jack woke her up. She hadn't realized yet that Jack had been gone since you brought us back so close to the time we left."

"Perhaps it would be better if she hadn't known about this little adventure, given that Jack was almost killed."

In the increasing brightness, Cynthia unpinned her hair and began brushing it out. "They're too close for him to keep important things from her. Remember that she was also an Irregular when she was at Lackland, so she understands. Not that she was happy to hear what happened to Jack."

"Did she have information about a possible invasion?"

"She's worried—she can feel that danger is in the air. But she has no more knowledge than we do."

The wake-up bell sounded, loud enough to wake the dead, or at least the seriously drunk. Tory winced, then swung out of the bed. "You're going to be exhausted since you didn't get any sleep."

"I fell asleep on the sofa when Jack was telling his mother all that happened. Mrs. Rainford put a blanket over me, then walked me back here so she didn't have to wake Jack." In a small voice, Cynthia added, "She's wonderful. Like my own mother."

"Perhaps someday she will be your mother, or at least your mother-in-law," Tory said, interested in what Cynthia might say.

Her roommate pulled on a fresh gown. "Jack says we belong together."

"Do you agree?"

Cynthia laughed. "Maybe he's right. Who else would put up with me?"

"No one," Tory said promptly, then ducked as another pillow came flying at her. She threw her own pillow back.

A friendly pillow fight wasn't a bad way to start the day.

Tory had missed several days of classes since she had been on the other side of the mirror longer than Cynthia, Jack, and Elspeth. Cynthia had told the headmistress that Tory wasn't well and needed rest, so now her friends welcomed her return to health. Tory disliked the deception, but life would be far more complicated if the headmistress ever realized that some students were slipping away from the abbey for days at a time.

The chapel was still cold during the morning service and the breakfast porridge was still boring, and Tory still disliked the way the girls broke into groups, with Elspeth and the others who embraced their magic being ostracized. But it was nice being back in a place where she didn't have to dodge bullets.

At least, not yet. If the French invaded England. . . . She suppressed the thought as she headed for her first class.

The night before, she'd wondered if her magical power had been increased by her mission to France. Very quickly she learned the answer: Yes, it had.

She made her discovery during her Italian class with the horrible Miss Macklin. No sooner had Tory taken her seat when Miss Macklin sneered, "You look very healthy for a girl who was supposed to be sick in bed, Miss Mansfield."

She marched down the aisle toward Tory's seat. "I think you were malingering to avoid work. Put your hands out!"

Knowing what was coming, Tory reluctantly obeyed. Miss Macklin loved any excuse to smash her brass ruler across the hands of students, and it was Tory's turn again. The last time, she'd cracked a bone in Tory's finger. If Elspeth hadn't healed the break, she'd have been in agony for days.

Tory's mouth tightened. This time she was not going to tamely accept unjust punishment. As Miss Macklin slashed the ruler downward, Tory channeled power to slow the ruler so it wouldn't hit so hard.

A startling amount of magic rushed through her. Before she could reduce it, the ruler flew out of Miss Macklin's hands, spun across the room, crashed through the window, and disappeared.

The teacher gasped, her eyes round with shock. "What did you do, you dreadful girl?" she hissed. "What evil magic did you practice on me?"

Startled, Tory donned her most innocent expression. "How could I do magic, Miss Macklin? You know it doesn't work here in the school. Perhaps you were striking with such force that it spun out of your hand."

The teacher hesitated, unsure how to respond, then pivoted and walked back to the front of the room. The other students looked around at each other. They knew that someone had done magic, but who?

Tory continued looking innocent, but inside, she was exultant. If her power had increased, the same was probably true of the others who went through the mirror.

And that was good, because they were going to need all the power they had if they were to have a chance of stopping the French.

The gathering that evening in the Labyrinth was somber. Besides the Irregulars just returned from the twentieth century and the two teachers, Jack's mother had also come. Though her talents weren't likely to be directly relevant to the invasion, she was a strong mage and a soothing presence.

When the greetings were over, Mr. Stephens said, "Allarde, what was in your foretelling about the invasion?"

"Nothing specific, I'm afraid. Just a strong feeling that a definite decision was made to go ahead. Preparations have been underway for many months. Now Napoleon is ready to move," Allarde replied. "We need to combine our power in a circle to try to learn more. We need more information before we can decide on a course of action."

Allarde continued, "Elspeth, you have the most scrying ability, don't you? You should take the lead since we want to find out what is happening now."

Elspeth glanced around at the others, evaluating the range of abilities. "I think so, though I'm not brilliant at it."

"You might find that you're better than you were," Tory said. "I found earlier today that my adventures in France increased my power. I tried to reduce the power of Miss Macklin's brass ruler, and accidentally tossed it through the window. I don't think the increase is as much as when we worked together at Dunkirk, but a definite increase."

The other Irregulars silently tested their abilities, then gave nods of agreement. "With this group, we should be able to do some powerful scrying," Elspeth said. "I'll get a bowl of water for viewing the images. Allarde, since we'll also need your foretelling, be prepared to take the lead when I've seen as much as I can."

With a shuffling of chairs, the mages sorted themselves out. Using her intuition, Tory told everyone where to sit since she was best at balancing and enhancing energy. She chose a circular table which was the right size for the group to sit around and gave Elspeth a place to set her scrying bowl.

Elspeth cupped the bowl between her palms while her neighbors, Miss Wheaton and Jack, each clasped one of her wrists.

Everyone else held hands. Tory, who held Allarde's hand on one side and Cynthia's on the other, closed her eyes and tuned herself to the energies of her friends.

The teachers always participated in the closing circles at the end of a study session, so she knew their energies well, but she'd never been in a circle with Jack's mother. Mrs. Rainford brought a rich warmth to the blending of magic. "Let us begin . . . ," Tory said after she'd collected and balanced the energies. "Elspeth, lead on."

Elspeth gazed into the water with unfocused eyes, looking for images of what was happening elsewhere. "I'm seeing a rough map of France," she said. "The French have been building boats in several places, not just Boulogne. Montreuil, other ports in France and the Low Countries. They're gathering the ships in Boulogne and . . . and Brest, I think. So many ships! Sloops and gunboats and barges to carry troops."

"How large is the Army of Boulogne?" Mr. Stephens asked.

"Vast," Elspeth said, her voice tight. "Beyond counting."

"The number two hundred thousand comes to my mind," Mrs. Rainford said. "Is such an army possible?"

"I'm afraid so," Elspeth said grimly. "Heavens, there seems to be a victory column in the center of the camp in Boulogne, as if they're sure they'll be successful!"

"The more fools they," Jack growled.

Elspeth sucked in her breath. "A fleet of French ships is approaching Ireland! They broke out of the harbor at Brest and managed to evade the British blockade."

Allarde gave a low whistle, while Mr. Stephens swore under his breath, using words Tory had never heard him use before. "They used stealth magic to get past the blockade," the teacher muttered. "I should have seen that!"

"As good as you are, James, detecting stealth magic all the way over in Brest is almost impossible," Miss Wheaton said. "Elspeth, do you think they're planning to land in western Britain or in Ireland?"

"I think Ireland." Elspeth frowned as she gazed into her bowl of water. "They want to join with Irish rebels for an uprising to drive out the English."

"Then the Irish will have to worry about driving out the French," Jack said with dark humor. "But this is big trouble for us. We need to call some weather down on this fleet. How far are they from landfall, Elspeth?"

"I'm not sure. Not too far." Elspeth gasped. "The fleet heading toward Ireland is very large, perhaps thirty ships or more, but there's also a much smaller squadron heading toward England! Tory, can you blend my scrying power with Allarde's foretelling ability so we can learn more about where they're heading?"

Tory murmured assent and closed her eyes. The individual energies of the mages in the circle pulsed through her like silken cords of different colors. Mentally she braided together Elspeth's bright silver and Allarde's deep, rich power to produce a magic that might be able to see both present and future.

When the energies were blended, Allarde said, "The Irish fleet is heading toward a place called Bantry Bay and I'd say it's half a day's sail away. The smaller squadron, perhaps four or five ships, is heading toward . . . Bristol? I think Bristol. As the largest port in the west of England, it will be a good target if they could strike without warning."

"With thirty or so ships, the Irish fleet must be carrying more than ten thousand troops," Mr. Stephens said tightly. "Even the small squadron could transport over a thousand men."

Tory sucked in her breath. "We've all seen the defense preparations here in the southeast, where invasion is most likely. Militia units and Martello towers and all sorts of fortifications. Even the magical wards are concentrated here. A successful attack in the west, where there are fewer defenses, will create panic all over Britain."

Mr. Stephens nodded grimly. "If the French attack in areas that feel safe, there will be a firestorm of reaction. Perhaps to the point where the population will demand a peace treaty with France."

Fairmount Hall, Tory's family home, was built on the Somersetshire coast in southwest England. There were local militia units, of course, but their coast had none of the fortifications found around the Kentish coast, where Lackland was located. The thought of French troops landing near her home, perhaps burning Fairmount Hall . . . She shuddered at the stark knowledge that such a thing could happen.

"If the French invade, some people might want peace, but many others will fight," Jack said firmly. "Since we can't be sure of their strategy, let's just blast those ships away from their goal with weather magic."

No more discussion was needed—Tory felt the assent of everyone in the circle. Jack and Cynthia, the weather mages, were so much in harmony that they needed no blending of energies. Tory had only to channel the power in the circle to them.

She smiled with grim satisfaction to know that the French ships would be in trouble very soon.

CHAPTER 5

Cynthia squeezed Jack's hand as the combined magic was channeled to the two weather mages. Cynthia and Jack had always worked well together, even when she couldn't stand him. Since becoming a couple, they'd become an even better magical team. She loved his kisses, but she loved the emotional intimacy when they worked closely together just as much.

She let Jack take the lead as he searched for a storm system that they could move toward the French ships. He had more raw power and range than she, but she was better at sending weather exactly where they wanted it to go.

She felt his mental frown through their magical bond. "There isn't much weather to work with," he said aloud. "The French ships have a good wind, and there aren't any major storms for hundreds of miles, which is unusual. We'll have to pull a storm from quite a distance if we want something strong enough to disrupt the fleet."

"Try the Arctic regions. One can usually find some good storms there," Cynthia suggested.

After a pause while Jack searched through enormously complex weather patterns for hundreds of miles, he replied, "I've found a fine storm west of Norway. We can drive it down over the North Sea. That will take time, so we need to displace the good winds the French have now so they'll be becalmed."

Cynthia nodded. "First the winds. Then we can bring on the storm! I'll aim the heart of it at the fleet heading toward Ireland, but the storm is large enough that it will blast the smaller group of ships as well."

Jack joined his magic with hers as smoothly as a kiss, and they easily shifted the moderate winds away from the French fleet. Elspeth reported, "Well done! The French sails are flapping and the ships are almost dead in the water."

"Now for that Arctic storm . . ." Jack reached north through the night.

Cynthia laughed with exhilaration as she discovered what a large, lively tempest he'd found. She loved working with storms. Wind and rain, thunder and lightning, yes!

She felt like a magical otter, diving into the storm's power and playing in the winds just as real otters played in the water. When she and Jack did major weather work, they became a pair of otters playing together. It was very romantic, in a way that could be experienced only by two weather mages.

Using the combined magic of the other magelings made this weather working particularly enjoyable. She and Jack started herding the storm south across the North Sea. He did most of the heavy work of changing the storm's course, while Cynthia coaxed it into exactly the right track to sweep it through the French fleet.

She didn't really want the ships to sink and the sailors to drown. But she wanted the masts broken, the sails torn, the ships left helpless in the water a good safe distance from Britain. Then the French sailors could be captured by the Royal Navy and imprisoned until the war was over.

She exhaled with satisfaction when she had the storm moving exactly where she wanted it to go. Weather never wanted to behave, so a bit of tweaking would probably be required later, but for the next hours, no more work would be required.

Jack said, "Now that we've done that, I'm ravenous and ready to find what was in the food basket my mother packed for us. Does anyone want to use the circle energies before we close? Elspeth—"

Before he could finish the sentence, a gigantic fist of power slammed into the circle, battering and bruising minds and magic. There were gasps of shock, and the ring of magic shattered painfully as clasped hands were torn apart. Cynthia felt as if she were being hurled from a high place, plunging down, down, *down* into a drowning sea.

"French mages trying to stop us!" Jack gasped. As soon as he recognized the attack, he launched his power at the enemy.

Cynthia sensed him blocking and deflecting the destructive energy, as if he were a lightning rod drawing off a searing bolt. As the enemy attack shifted away, her mind cleared and she no longer felt as if she were falling out of control.

But all around her was chaos as the Irregulars struggled to recover from the assault. And Jack . . .

He collapsed, knocking over his chair as he crumpled to the

floor and his hand dragged out of Cynthia's. She cried out as she realized that Jack's mind and magic were being torn apart by the attackers. He was sacrificing himself to protect them.

Scorching rage blazed through her. Recklessly she followed the fearsome energy back to the mages who were creating it. They were in France, eight or ten of them joined in a circle much like hers. They'd been keeping bad weather away from the French fleet and supplying fast, steady winds until the Irregulars had thwarted them.

Now the French devils wanted revenge.

An enemy mage sensed Cynthia and struck at her, but she parried the blow and called out to her friends, "Join hands again and send me all the power you have!"

"What are you going to do?" Miss Wheaton asked in a thin, ragged voice.

"I'm going to *burn* them!" Cynthia hissed. She'd lost her grip on Tory's hand during the attack, so she reached out. Tory's fingers locked around hers again.

Cynthia felt a solid pulse of power that became stronger and stronger as the circle regrouped. Allarde's deep, smooth energy. The experienced power of Miss Wheaton and Mr. Stephens. Mrs. Rainford, burning with an anger to match Cynthia's.

Elspeth reached across Jack's empty place to clasp Cynthia's hand. Cynthia wanted to wail with anguish, but there was no time to check Jack's condition now. The enemy must be stopped before all the Irregulars were damaged beyond repair.

As Tory channeled the combined magic, Cynthia forged it into a flaming spear of furious power. When she'd gathered and focused all her friends' energy, she hurled her magical weapon into the heart of the enemy circle.

The raging power blasted through the French mages like wildfire, draining their magic and hammering their minds. Cynthia could hear their wordless, agonized screams, but ruthlessly she continued her assault, engulfing her enemies in burning power until the last spark of magic had been smashed.

Then she slid dizzily into darkness.

The aftermath of the magical battle left Tory shaking. She was also, she realized, wrapped in Allarde's arms. He'd been sitting to her right, and in the cacophony of the magical attack they'd instinctively turned to each other. His heart was hammering under her ear and his breathing was as ragged as hers, but in his embrace she felt safe.

When the world steadied, she straightened, though still holding on to him. "Are you all right, Justin?"

"I feel like I've been swept over a waterfall and crashed into the rocks below, but there's no permanent damage done," he said wryly.

She glanced around the circle. Others were stirring. Elspeth was bent over, her face buried in her hands, while Mrs. Rainford's fists were clenched and her eyes were screwed shut. Mr. Stephens held Miss Wheaton and his face was buried in her soft brown hair. Cynthia had folded over onto the table and her head rested on her crossed arms as she gulped for air.

Jack was missing. Terrified, Tory shot to her feet and saw that his chair had tipped over and he lay sprawled on the floor. Dear God, he wasn't breathing!

In an instant, she closed the distance between them and knelt beside his limp body. She gave thanks when she saw a pulse beating in his throat, but he still wasn't breathing. "Elspeth, Miss Wheaton, Jack needs healing energy *now*!"

Elspeth had been sitting on Jack's other side, so she slipped from her chair to kneel beside him and flatten her palms on his chest. As she closed her eyes and sent healing energy, she was joined by Miss Wheaton. The teacher rested her hands on Jack's temples and murmured, "Breathe for me, Jack. *Breathe!*"

Mrs. Rainford joined them, tears glinting in her eyes as she took her son's hand. "Don't you *dare* die, Jack!" she said, her voice shaking. "I will not permit it!"

Tory rested one hand on Elspeth's shoulder and the other on Miss Wheaton's shoulder so she could use her talent for enhancing the magic of others. Despite the three of them working together, the flow of energy was worrisomely low even when Allarde and Mr. Stephens rested hands on her shoulder to add their power.

After what seemed like an eternity of anxiety, Jack gasped and began breathing again, though his eyes remained closed. Mrs. Rainford sighed with relief, her lips moving silently in a prayer of thanks. Then she rose and collected a blanket and pillow from a sofa and made Jack comfortable, staying beside him as he rested quietly.

As Elspeth wearily returned to her chair and began helping Cynthia, Allarde offered a hand to help Tory from the floor. "Apart from Jack, everyone seems to be more or less all right," he said. "Did anyone suffer burnout of their magic?"

Mr. Stephens frowned as he evaluated his power. "I'm not burned out, but I am very drained. It will be several days before I'm back to normal." He ran stiff fingers through his hair, his expression haggard. "We need to discuss what happened."

"First we need to eat. Burning so much magic has addled everyone." Allarde retrieved the basket of food the Rainfords had brought and began passing out meat pies. Since Cynthia was still dazed, Tory took pies and a teapot to Mrs. Rainford, who was a powerful hearth witch and could heat the food and tea water. The heating took longer than usual, more proof of how depleted everyone had become.

Tory was so ravenous that she fell on her beef-and-onion pie like a starving wolf. As she went back for a second, Jack's eyes opened. He was silent instead of making his usual teasing comments, but he managed to get to his feet and sit between Cynthia and his mother. After eating his way through five meat pies and a slab of cheese, he began to look almost normal.

"We're down to a handsome fruitcake. Your kitchen is wondrous, Mrs. Rainford." Allarde carefully cut the dense cake into eight pieces and passed them out. "Which reminds me. Could you buy two large sugar loaves for us to send forward to our friends in 1940?"

"It will be my pleasure," she said dryly. "In my experience, magelings couldn't survive without sugar."

Perhaps Mrs. Rainford was right, because after burning large amounts of magic, Tory was ready to eat her own weight in sweet cakes. She made a point of consuming her fruitcake slowly, savoring the sweetness of the dried fruit and the crunch of the nuts as she washed each bite down with her third cup of tea.

After polishing off the last crumbs, she said, "Now that good food has restored our wits, if not our magic—what happened? I gather that a circle of French mages were helping their ships break out and attack Ireland and Britain?"

Jack nodded, his hands clasped around his tea mug. "There were nine of them, I think. All men and older than we are. I don't think they had as much individual magic, but they were very experienced. They knew how to use their power as a weapon."

"We seem to have learned that very quickly," Allarde said

dryly. "Cynthia, I'm almost afraid to ask what you did after saying you'd burn them."

"I didn't kill them, if that's what you're wondering, though I might have if I'd been able to." Cynthia's eyes narrowed like an angry cat's. "But I did manage to burn out their power. It will be days, at least, probably weeks, before they can do much to help Napoleon again."

Jack frowned. "We temporarily burned out that circle, but I had the sense that it was just one group within a larger organization of mages. This group was made up of weather mages, but there must be other sorts of magic workers."

"A depressing thought," Allarde said, "but at least most forms of magic don't work over distances the way weather magic does."

"Jack and Cynthia, I'd like to have a medal struck in thanks for what you two did to protect us," Mr. Stephens said. "Can you still work weather? I'm guessing not."

Jack and Cynthia shared a glance. She said, "My power is down, but I should be able to tweak our storm if needed."

"I doubt I'll be able to do major weather work for a few days," Jack admitted. "But I'm not completely burned."

"We'll have to hope the French squadrons don't recover and make it to land before we can stop them," Allarde said soberly. "But for now, we all need to rest. Shall we meet again in two nights?"

After nods of agreement, the Irregulars did a brief closing circle to smooth out their ruffled energy. Tory guessed that most of the magelings were at about a quarter of their usual power, with Jack very close to burnout. She gave a silent prayer that they would recover quickly enough to prevent the horror of a French invasion.

When the circle ended, Allarde said, "I'm going to check to

see if any messages have come through Merlin's Mirror. Will you join me, Tory?"

She never turned down an opportunity to be alone with him. Taking his arm, she accompanied him into the tunnel that led back to the time portal. As soon as they were out of sight of the others, Allarde's arm came around Tory's shoulders to tuck her close to his side. Usually his energy seemed limitless, but tonight even he seemed tired.

There were no messages at the mirror. Tory turned and linked her hands around his neck. "I assume you have other reasons for coming back here."

He laughed. "Indeed I do." He bent into a kiss that made her pulse quicken and her energy rise. He murmured, "You are the best cure for burnout imaginable."

"I try," she said modestly.

He caught her gaze with his, his eyes serious. "I'm writing the letter to my father to inform him that I choose you over my inheritance. It's . . . taking time."

"Finding the right words must be terribly difficult," she said, her heart aching for him. "I hope you never regret your choice."

"I won't." He smiled with a warmth that curled her toes. "And now for one more kiss to remind me why I'll have no regrets!"

CHAPTER 6

Lackland, 1940

Rebecca's first day of school arrived, and she dressed carefully in the Lackland school uniform that Mrs. Rainford had provided. The straight gray skirt, white shirt, and navy blue jacket looked crisp and serious, and a dark red tie added a dash of brightness. All she needed now was to fill the empty leather book bag Mrs. Rainford had given her.

After tying her dark hair back neatly, she examined herself in the mirror. It was such a relief to look like a proper schoolgirl again. She'd worn the same dress day and night for months when imprisoned in France. After reaching England, she and her family had ceremonially burned the clothing they'd worn in captivity.

Polly wasn't yet recovered enough from her blood poisoning to go to school, so Rebecca and Mrs. Rainford walked together to the village. Nick had already left for his school. As she walked down the footpath, Rebecca had a clear view of the harbor and the English Channel beyond. She'd grown up inland in France, but she realized that she loved the sea. She hoped she could always live near it.

The Lackland Girls Grammar School was a wide brick building with playing fields behind it. Rebecca guessed that it had been built sometime in the late nineteenth century, and many, many students had passed through it.

As they approached, Mrs. Rainford said, "How is your ability to read emotions and minds coming along? It will surely be useful when starting at a new school."

"I can already feel the students in the building," Rebecca admitted. "I've been learning how to ignore routine emotions and notice only what is unusual." She gestured at the school. "I feel what one would expect. Thoughts about classes and exams and friends and family." She smiled. "And boys."

Mrs. Rainford laughed. "Rather a lot of thoughts of boys, I'm sure. Nick's school is only a block away." As they climbed the steps to the front door, she added, "I don't want to hover too closely since that might make you the target of resentment from some students. But if you need help, I'm never far away."

Rebecca nodded her thanks. But even after that reassurance, her palms were damp as they entered the school. She'd led a protected life until the Nazis came to arrest her family.

The halls were empty, though Rebecca could feel a low churn of emotions in the classrooms. The headmistress's office was near the front door. Mrs. Rainford led the way in, introducing Rebecca to the school secretary before taking her into the headmistress's private office. As they walked in, Mrs. Rainford said, "Good morning, Miss Smythe. This is Rebecca Weiss, the student I told you about."

The headmistress had white hair and shrewd eyes that studied Rebecca with interest. Offering her hand, she said, "It's a pleasure to meet you, Miss Weiss. Anne, you go along to your classroom while I discuss the proposed schedule. I understand that you want a heavy course load of math and sciences, Miss Weiss?"

Rebecca nodded. "Yes, ma'am. I am behind in my studies and wish to catch up."

The headmistress handed her a copy of the proposed schedule. "Since you're French, you needn't take the French class, so I'm putting you into chemistry as well as biology, mathematics, history, English, and Latin. It's a demanding schedule, so after a fortnight, we can decide if adjustments need to be made."

Rebecca studied the schedule, thinking that her lessons in magic must be added to this. But she was determined to make up the time lost in captivity and to master magic in case her friends in the past needed her particular talents.

Miss Smythe rang a small bell on her desk. "I've arranged for a student guide to help you until you settle in."

Rebecca was surprised when a dark-haired, dark-eyed, un-English-looking girl around her own age entered the room. It was a relief to find that not every student in the school was blond.

"Miss Weiss, this is Miss Demetrios, who has also had the experience of starting here as a new student during a term. Miss Demetrios, Miss Weiss is recently arrived from France." The headmistress made a shooing gesture with her hand. "Now off with you both. Take a bit of time to become acquainted, then on to your next class."

As they left the office, Rebecca said, "You're Greek, Miss Demetrios?"

"My parents are," the other girl said with a distinct London accent. "Me, I'm a Cockney, born within the sound of Bow bells. My name is Andromeda."

"Andromeda is a wonderful name!"

The girl made a face as they passed through the secretary's office and into the hallway. "It confused everyone here at first. That's why I go by Andy."

"My name is Rebecca. I see why you were chosen as my guide."

"Miss Smythe is a shrewd old duck," Andy agreed. "You're French and Jewish? Escaping from France must have been exciting!"

"Too exciting," Rebecca said wryly. "I look forward to quiet days in school."

"Your English is excellent. You have hardly any French accent." Andy pushed open a door into the washroom. "We can get acquainted here, where it's private."

"How did you come down from London?" Rebecca asked curiously.

"My parents wanted to get my little brother and me away from the bombing," Andy explained. "My uncle has a small café in Lackland and he volunteered to take us. It's not the safest place in England with German aircraft flying overhead every day, but better than London's East End. It's nicer to be with family than a house full of strangers, and my brother and I can help out in the café."

Rebecca had heard that huge numbers of children had been evacuated to the countryside when the Blitz started. Despite being safer in the country, many couldn't wait to return to their London homes.

Andy crossed her arms and leaned back against a sink. "This is a good school and most of the girls are nice, though there are exceptions. There's a lot of competition for grades because most students hope to get places at a university. There's a good solid air-raid shelter under the school if we need it. Do you have any questions of the sort you can't ask a headmistress?"

Rebecca laughed. "You're very efficient! I don't know what else to ask."

Andy cocked her head to one side. "Do you want to go to university?"

Rebecca nodded. "Both my parents are doctors, and I want to become one also."

The other girl's dark eyes rounded. "A doctor father is good, but a doctor mother is even better! What kind of physician do you want to become?"

Though Rebecca had always known that she wanted to become a doctor, she'd never thought much about what kind, but her reply was instant. "A psychiatrist. A doctor of the mind." Knowing that she had magical ability was so new that she hadn't thought how it would fit with her ambitions, but Andy's questions made her realize that her talents could be used to heal minds and emotions.

"I know nothing about being a psychiatrist, but I'm sure that it's needed." Andy sighed. "And will be needed even more after the war is over."

"Do you also want to go to university?"

"Yes, I want to study mathematics." The other girl smiled shyly. "No one in my family has ever gone to university, but Miss Smythe thinks I can win a place. Perhaps even at Oxford or Cambridge."

"How wonderful that would be!" Rebecca exclaimed, even more impressed with how well Miss Smythe had chosen a guide. "My parents and brother are in Oxford now. Both my parents are researchers at a medical laboratory."

"Then they made it out of France, too! I'm glad to know that." Andy sighed. "Almost everyone here has family serving in the army or navy or RAF. It's considered polite to wait for people to volunteer rather than asking about family."

So Andy had been wondering if Rebecca was orphaned or alone but had been too tactful to ask. "We were very lucky to escape. I'm staying with the Rainfords for a while. They're friends of the family and Mrs. Rainford volunteered to help me adjust to an English school and give me extra tutoring if I need it." It was the explanation they'd all agreed on and was also the truth, if not the whole truth.

"Mrs. Rainford is lovely. One of my favorite teachers."

The conversation ended when a raucous bell blasted through the school. As Rebecca jumped, startled, Andy said, "First period is over, and I thank you for getting me out of most of it. Now it's time for history. The teacher, Mrs. Rigley, is a right bear."

"Every school has a few bears," Rebecca said philosophically.

Girls began pouring into the washroom during the short break between classes. Because Rebecca was wearing the school uniform, she was obviously a new student and she attracted curious glances. Luckily, Andy was there to make introductions, and she seemed to be well liked.

As the day progressed, Rebecca sat quietly in each class, taking notes and studying the teachers and students. There was no hostility toward her foreignness—except once, when she felt a stab of revulsion from another student while changing classes. The hallway was crowded so she couldn't identify the source, but she found the ugly emotion so upsetting that she shut down her magical abilities for a time.

But she was favorably impressed with the school. The teachers were good and the subjects challenging. She was intrigued to have a history textbook written from an English point of view rather than French. In Mrs. Rainford's English class, students were reading and discussing a play by Shakespeare, *King Lear,* which was interesting even though the archaic language was confusing.

But she found it eerie to be in a school again, as if the months in a cramped cell waiting for death had never happened. Prison was where Rebecca had started sensing the emotions around her. She'd felt resignation and fear from her fellow prisoners, who were women and children of all ages, from a white-haired grandmother down to an infant not six months old.

The guards were a more mixed lot. A few were compassionate and might provide small comforts to ease captivity. Most were businesslike, intent on doing their jobs; some had ugly, lustful thoughts about the younger prisoners like Rebecca—and a few despised all Jews, thinking of them as greedy swine who oppressed good Christians and deserved to die ugly deaths.

She shuddered at the memory. She'd known the commandant had them marked for death and had not dared speak of it to anyone, even her mother, because that would have meant the end of all hope for everyone in the cell. At least, if she'd been believed.

Her last class of the day was biology. Behind the usual desks was a laboratory. Andy led her in and they walked to the front of the room, where the bald, elderly teacher was studying notes at his desk.

Andy said, "Dr. Gordon is a retired doctor who was brought in to teach because our last science master went into the army. Sir, this is a new student, Rebecca Weiss."

The science master stood and peered at Rebecca over his spectacles, his faded blue eyes amiable. "Weiss. You are German?"

"My father's parents were, but I'm French, sir."

"Then it's good that you are here, not there. Take the empty desk beside Miss Demetrios. After class, we can discuss what you learned at your school in France."

Rebecca nodded and followed Andy to the seats near the door. As other students filed in, she felt the same sting of revulsion she'd experienced earlier in the hallway. She studied the other girls and saw that one was frowning at her. She was tall and sharp-faced and had a tight, angry-looking mouth.

"Who is that tall girl?" she asked Andy in a whisper.

"Sylvia Crandall," Andy replied in a matching whisper. "She's the top student in the school, but a bad-tempered snob."

Even in the standard school uniform, Sylvia looked as if she came from a home with money. Not only did she have expensive shoes and a gold barrette in her hair, but her uniform looked as if it had been carefully ironed by a maid, and she had an irritating air of superiority.

Rebecca's musings were interrupted when Dr. Gordon called the class to order and announced, "To keep you lovely young ladies alert, today we'll start with a test on what we've learned so far this term."

There were quiet groans as he started handing out duplicated sheets of questions. Rebecca thought gloomily that it was a bad way to start a new class. But the examination turned out to be simple, just two pages of multiple-choice questions. She marked the answers as fast as she could read through the test, then sat quietly. Other students seemed to be having much more trouble.

"Time!" Dr. Gordon said. "Exchange papers with students across the aisle so you can grade each other."

Rebecca's exam went to a freckled girl on her right who exchanged papers with a shy smile. "I'm Mary Hampton. Welcome to LGG."

"I'm Rebecca," she said, returning the smile. As Andy had said, most of the students were nice.

Dr. Gordon read through the questions, using each as an opportunity to discuss the subject while the girls graded the papers. The teacher called on students to talk and encouraged more questions. At the end, he said, "Did anyone have a perfect score?"

Mary raised her hand. "Miss Weiss did."

"You are well taught, Miss Weiss!" Dr. Gordon said with a smile. "You shall be an asset to this class."

Rebecca shrank back in her chair, pleased but embarrassed as all eyes turned to her with curiosity and approval. But buried within those emotions was a sharp thorn of resentful fury from Sylvia Crandall. Andy had said the school was very competitive, and Sylvia now saw her as a rival.

"Maybe Sylvia will have competition for top student," someone whispered cattily in a voice too low for the master to hear.

"Now, how many had only one question wrong?" Dr. Gordon asked.

Andy and Sylvia Crandall fell into that group. No one in the class missed more than five questions. The students had been paying attention to their lessons.

Though the rest of the class was uneventful, Rebecca could feel anger and resentment simmering in Sylvia the whole time. It was a relief when the bell rang, ending the class and the school day.

"You must be ready to go home and collapse," Andy said sympathetically as she stood up from her desk. "That's how I felt after the first day here. Too much newness."

"Tomorrow should be easier." Rebecca stood and tucked her notebook into her book bag as other students streamed by her to the door. Sylvia was approaching, expression tight, when Andy stepped into the aisle between the desks and said sweetly, "Sylvia, have you met Rebecca Weiss? This is her first day."

Aloud, Sylvia said brusquely, "I know who she is," as she pushed past. But in her mind were the words *Filthy Jew!*

The hateful insult blasted into Rebecca's mind as her arm brushed Sylvia's. The vicious thought literally knocked her off balance. Instinctively she reached out to save herself from falling and caught Sylvia's arm. A flood of new images and emotions cascaded through her.

Sylvia's mother drank too much. Her father doted on her younger brother and her pretty older sister. He'd cursed when Sylvia was born because he didn't want a second daughter, especially not such an ugly baby. He was fiercely anti-Semitic, despising all Jews. Sylvia studied ferociously hard to make her father proud of her, and she'd taken on his many prejudices.

Sylvia's bitterness and lonely pain were so intense that they triggered Rebecca's instinctive sympathy. A white current of magical energy flowed from her into the other girl. It was over in an instant, leaving Rebecca shocked and shaking. Having no idea what had just happened, she released Sylvia's arm and stepped back. "I'm so sorry! I trip over my own feet sometimes."

Sylvia stared at her, as disoriented as Rebecca. After a moment, she said in a tentative voice, as if uncertain how to act, "I do that, too, sometimes."

Wanting to know more about the other girl's state of mind, Rebecca offered her hand. "I'm pleased to meet you. Andy says you're the best student in the school."

"In most subjects," Sylvia said stiffly as she took Rebecca's hand. "Andy is better in mathematics, and you may be better in biology."

"One test doesn't prove that." As they shook hands, Rebecca

sensed that some of the darkness of Sylvia's spirit was gone. The other girl had always bitterly resented that her family never acknowledged or respected her intelligence or hard work. If Rebecca was reading Sylvia correctly, much of that resentment had dissolved, leaving more acceptance of her situation.

Not at all sure what she'd done, Rebecca imagined more light flowing into the other girl until the handshake ended. She didn't think healing light could do any damage.

"There was an odd number of students in this class, and I was the one who didn't have a laboratory partner, so you'll be paired off with me." Sylvia's expression was wary. Rebecca had the sense that in the past, no one wanted to work with her.

"Excellent! Since I'm new, I need to work with someone who is skilled," Rebecca said with a warm smile. "We'll be the best pair in the class."

Sylvia looked startled, then smiled uncertainly, as if she didn't know quite how it was done. "That's settled, then. I'll see you in class."

When the other girl was gone, Andy asked with amazement, "What did you do to Sylvia? She was practically civil!"

"Maybe she's tired of being bad-tempered." Rebecca pressed a hand to her midriff. Apparently she had made changes in Sylvia's mind so the other girl was less unhappy, though she didn't know how she'd done it.

She didn't know whether to be proud of herself or horrified.

CHAPTER 7

Lackland, 1804

"I wonder what our storm has done to the French squadrons?" Jack asked in an overhearty voice as the Irregulars gathered around the circular table.

"Let's join hands and find out." Tory kept her voice light as she sorted out her friends and they built another circle. As she'd suspected, Jack was trying to conceal the fact that two days of rest had only partially restored his magical power. The rest of the Irregulars, including her, were close to normal, but Jack had been drained the most, and he was still well short of his usual ability.

"And so we begin . . . ," she intoned as energy flowed through their clasped hands, creating a power that was greater than the sum of the individuals. Once more Elspeth used a bowl of water to scry, and Tory enhanced the images to help others see them.

"The storm struck the fleet full-on," Elspeth said with approval. "You did a good job of aiming it, Cynthia. Most of the ships have lost sails and masts, and several seem to have crashed on shoals south of Ireland. The storm is passing now. Some Royal Navy ships are pursuing them, and they should be able to capture the remaining vessels once the weather clears."

Relief ran through the circle. "What about the smaller group of ships that left Brest later?" Tory asked. "Were they also stopped by the storm?"

"Let me see . . ." Elspeth cleared her mind, then sought the smaller group of ships.

Suddenly she gasped. "Dear God, the French are landing in Wales *right now*!" Her horrified words were accompanied by images of ships moored in a protected cove and small boats transferring soldiers to the shore.

Shock seared through the circle as everyone saw the grim evidence of invasion. Jack growled, "They were too far from the center of the storm to be badly damaged. Where are they landing?"

"Instead of Bristol, they've landed . . . somewhere near Carmarthen, I think," Miss Wheaton said tautly. "I doubt there are many coastal defenses in that area. If the French ships are carrying a thousand or more trained troops, they can easily take control of a sizable area before British troops can be mustered to fight them."

"Can weather magic be used to damage the ships?" Mr. Stephens asked.

Cynthia shook her head. "It's too late. By the time we could bring in another storm, all the soldiers and weapons will have landed."

Jack swore under his breath. "Is there anything we can do to stop them before they get a foothold?"

An idea struck Tory. She closed her eyes and visualized the network of portals connected by Merlin's Mirror. "The legends say that Merlin was born in a cave near Carmarthen. One of the mirror portals is very near there."

"Then we go *now*!" Cynthia said firmly. "Our only distance weapon is weather, but if several of us are there on the spot, there is much we could do to foil the invasion."

Silence fell at her words. Tory shivered at the thought of going on another mission when she'd just returned from their perilous sojourn to occupied France.

But this was her own time that was being threatened. "We'll need to make a few preparations, but I agree that we must go as quickly as possible. Tonight."

Mrs. Rainford shuddered and closed her eyes. "It's so dangerous! By the grace of God, you've all survived two hazardous missions, but luck and talent won't last forever."

"We can't play coward this time, Mum," Jack said. "It was bad enough that Britain is being attacked in the future, but this is here and now. I'm not going to stand by and let an invasion happen when I might be able to make a difference."

"I'll go, too." Allarde looked thoughtful. "When I was at Eton, I knew a pair of brothers, Blakesley Major and Blakesley Minor. They're from a military family and they lived near Carmarthen. I have a feeling that working with them could make a real difference in stopping the French."

"I'll go," Tory said. "I'm best at taking people through the mirror."

"I'm coming, too," Elspeth said. "Where there is fighting, healers are needed."

Cynthia gave a smile that was all teeth. "I am remembering that I am descended from warriors. How *dare* the French invade my land!"

Mr. Stephens looked torn. "I should go, too."

Miss Wheaton shook her head. "We're needed here to maintain the coastal wards. One group of French mages have been burned out, but they have more. If the wards weaken, the French navy may be able to elude the blockade and attack this coast."

"I wasn't able to detect this lot!" he said bitterly.

"Brest is a long way off," his wife pointed out. "Now that we know they've used mages with strong stealth magic to elude the British blockade outside Brest, we can see about sending a good stealth mage to the Channel Isles, which are much closer to Brest than we are. You've done an excellent job of detecting attempts to evade the blockade from the nearer ports."

His mouth twisted. "I suppose. But it feels wrong to allow students to fight our battles!"

Understanding how he must feel, Tory said, "We're all mages working for a common goal. You are more needed here in Lackland."

"Besides the work we've been doing," Miss Wheaton said, "we need to start enlisting other Irregulars to strengthen the wards. None are as powerful as you five are, but together, they can make a real difference."

"I don't have stealth magic, but I have a fair amount of power," Mrs. Rainford said hesitantly. "Can I join the network of mages that maintain the wards?"

"Absolutely!" Mr. Stephens replied. "With the threat of invasion imminent, we're recruiting as many trained mages as we can find to augment our magical defenses."

"I can connect you with the strongest mages in the Lackland

area." Mrs. Rainford smiled wryly. "Traditionally mages are an independent lot, so we don't usually work together. That must change."

"Cynthia, I'm thinking that this is the sort of adventure where it will be useful for me to wear my boy's trousers," Tory said. "Can you alter my appearance enough so that I'll seem to be wearing a dress, but I can be agile as a boy?"

Cynthia thought a moment. "After I set up the illusion spell, it can be powered mostly by your energy so it won't use too much of my magic. I'll wear trousers also, having learned to my cost that skirts and adventures don't go together."

"I'd like you to spell me the same way," Elspeth said.

After Cynthia nodded, Tory said, "It's time to close the circle." She tightened her clasp on her neighbors' hands. "Then we'll prepare for a swift journey to Wales!"

After the circle closed and the magelings separated to prepare for the trip, Cynthia cornered Jack, latched on to his wrist, and hauled him into a private side passage. He grinned at her when they were alone. "Am I here for kissing or a lecture?"

She scowled at him. "Both, but the lecture first. Your power is still far below normal, Jack. Maybe you should stay here rather than go to Wales. If you're in trouble and reach for your magic and it isn't there . . ." She shook her head, not wanting to think of all the ways disaster might result.

His blond brows arched. "Do you really think I'll stay here when the rest of you are headed off to battle?"

"No." Her throat tightened. "But I had to ask. I came so close to losing you in France! I've been having nightmares ever since."

He pulled her into a hug, his warm arms around her waist. "That was bad, but we all got out safely. We will again."

She hid her face against his throat, feeling the warm beat of his blood. "You can't know that. We've been lucky before, but luck can run out at any time."

"Don't forget that the Irregulars are talented and clever as well, but you're right. We've been lucky so far, and we can't count on that to always be the case." His embrace tightened as he spoke without his usual lightness. "The stakes are too high to stand aside and let others take the risks, Cinders. If my luck had run out when we were in France, it would have been hard on my family and friends, but there wouldn't have been serious consequences."

"Breaking your mother's heart isn't a serious consequence?" she snapped as she blinked back tears. Her heart would be broken, too. No one had ever cared for her as much as Jack did, and she had the horrible feeling no one else ever would.

"Of course I don't want that to happen. I enjoy life and want a lot more years of enjoying it. But this mission is different. There are French troops on British soil, damn it! We all die eventually. If I fall while defending my homeland . . . well, there are worse ways to go." He stroked his hand down her spine, sending shivers through her. "Don't pretend that you don't feel exactly the same way, my warrior princess."

"I do feel the same way," she whispered. "But if something happened to me, I wouldn't be missed much."

"You are so wrong, Cynthia!" He lifted her chin and kissed her hard, his blue eyes intense. "You're brave and beautiful and delightfully prickly, and there is no one else like you. So don't you *dare* get yourself killed in Wales!"

She gave him a crooked smile. "Then I guess we'd better survive or go down together so one of us isn't left alone."

"We'll survive together," Jack said firmly. "And now that the lecture is over, it's time for the kissing!"

CHAPTER 8

Lackland, 1940

After her shocking interaction with Sylvia Crandall, Rebecca managed to pull herself together enough to talk with Dr. Gordon about her past studies. He was pleased with her desire to be a doctor, and after asking her a variety of questions, he declared that her education so far had laid an excellent foundation for future studies.

She thanked him for his offer to help if she needed it and made her escape. The school was almost empty since the students had left for the day. Because Mrs. Rainford needed to stay late for a meeting, Rebecca would walk home alone.

She was surprised and pleased to find Nick waiting on the

steps outside. Closing his book, he got to his feet and reached for her book bag. "How did your first day go?"

Rebecca was tired enough to hand over the heavy book bag gratefully. "Reasonably well, but one thing was . . . upsetting." She looked around, but the street was empty. Nonetheless, she dropped her voice to a whisper. "I . . . I entered someone's mind and changed her."

Nick stopped short and stared, his blue eyes searching. "With your mind magic? What exactly happened?"

Rebecca described the flashes of hostility she'd experienced. When she mentioned Sylvia Crandall, Nick made a face. "She's clever, but the meanest girl in the school. Polly always avoids her. I'm not surprised to hear Sylvia was thinking evil thoughts in your direction."

"Prejudice against my people is not uncommon. The real shock was the way her feelings and experience blazed through me like a bonfire when we touched." Rebecca shuddered at the memory and started walking again. "Her parents are dreadful, and she burned with anger and resentment toward the world."

"Being swamped with Sylvia's nastiness must have been grim," he said sympathetically.

"It was, but I also felt so sorry for her. She has known little kindness and has no friends. All she has is her intelligence and her sharp tongue." Rebecca swallowed hard. "I don't really understand what happened, but it seemed as if the magic poured from me and into her and *changed* her!"

"She needed changing," Nick said, startled. "But this is beyond any magic I've ever heard of. Did she behave differently afterward?"

"She was civil, and it felt as if most of her bitterness was gone." Rebecca frowned. "Her essence didn't change, but she seemed like a better version of herself. She said she was pleased to meet me and we decided to be laboratory partners in biology. Not only was she civil, but she smiled, though she wasn't very good at it."

"That's miraculous!" Nick exclaimed.

Rebecca shook her head vehemently as she recognized the full horror of what she'd done. "I committed a crime, Nick! I assaulted Sylvia's spirit and changed her without her knowledge or consent! My parents would be so ashamed of me." She felt ready to weep. "It is more evil to steal a soul than to kill a body."

"Whoa, Rebecca!" Nick shifted both book bags to his left shoulder and rested his right arm over her shoulders. To an onlooker, it would have looked casual, but his warmth and strength and steadiness flowed into her.

Nick continued, "If you feel that you did that, of course you're upset. But did you steal her soul and her free will? Or did you remove some of her pain?"

Grateful for his calm, Rebecca tried to think clearly about that swift, improbable interchange. "I removed her pain, at least for now. I don't know if the change is permanent, but there's a good chance that in the future she'll be able to shrug off her family's flaws rather than allow them to poison her."

"So you didn't steal her soul, you did a healing," Nick said thoughtfully. "Not of the body, as Elspeth does, but of the mind. Like a psychiatrist removes pain, but you did it much more quickly and efficiently. Is that such a terrible thing?"

She gave him a sharp look. Though he knew she wanted to be a doctor, she'd never mentioned psychiatry. She hadn't recognized that herself until she was talking with Andy. "That doesn't sound so bad," she agreed. "But it was done without Sylvia's consent, and without control on my part. It left me exhausted, too!"

"Major magic is vastly tiring. I'll need to feed you up when we get home," he said. "I agree that you shouldn't make a habit of rearranging people's minds without their consent, and as with any kind of magic, you must learn discipline and control. But this is a wonderful gift you have, Rebecca! Several of our friends from the past have some ability to soothe a person's pain, but not the ability to go inside a tormented mind to remove deeply rooted damage."

"It feels like more power than anyone should have," she said fiercely. "I am not fit to take such responsibility!"

"Then learn how to be fit," Nick said flatly. "You have a conscience, so you're already well on your way."

"I hope you're right," she said with a sigh. "It's frightening to have done something so profound without even intending it."

He smiled teasingly. "Maybe the effects of your treatment will pass and she'll be her mean old self tomorrow."

Rebecca shook her head. "I hope not. Not when she's my new lab partner!"

Their walking had taken them out of the village. They were climbing the hill when Nick said soberly, "We need to send a message about this to our friends in the past. Your talents could be useful."

"You think I should go back and forcibly change minds?" she asked, aghast.

"You can do things no one else can. That could make you very useful in their struggle to block a French invasion." He glanced down at her, his blue eyes serious. "You promised to help in any way you could."

She swallowed. "I did, and I meant it. But I don't know what I can do. It's all too new. I had to be touching Sylvia to affect her, and I don't think that's very practical when dealing with an invading army."

They reached the top of the road and turned onto the footpath that ran along the cliffs toward the Rainford house. "If you join an energy circle with the others, you might be able to magnify your power enough to affect someone over a distance," Nick said. "I'm only guessing. I do know that our friends need to hear of this ability since it's different from anything they have. Think about what happened, talk it over with my mother, then write it up and we'll send a message stone through. You might want to wait a day or two to see if anything similar happens."

"I'll do that." Nick's arm was still around her shoulders, so she moved away.

He caught her wrist. "Rebecca," he said, his blue eyes blazing with intensity. "Since you can read people through touch, you must know how I feel about you."

His emotions flooded through her. Liking. Respect. Desire. And something deeper that was too powerful and frightening to name.

She blushed violently. Though she'd sensed attraction from him, she hadn't fully believed that a boy as handsome and talented and generally marvelous as Nick really cared for her. Now it was blindingly clear that her imagination hadn't misled her.

Heart hammering with delight and despair, she yanked her wrist away. "I thought you might be interested in me, but I've been doing my best to pretend that wasn't so."

Pain showed in his eyes. "I haven't wanted to rush you, not after all you've gone through, and you living under my parents' roof. But from the moment we met, I've felt that . . . we belong together. It's not just that you're really pretty, but that you have intelligence, warmth, and honor. Though I don't have your ability for reading people, I've sensed that you care about me, too."

She drew a shaky breath, knowing she owed him an explanation. "I do care, Nick. Your courage saved my whole family from the Nazis, and you're also the most attractive boy I've ever met. But we can't be together. Trying would be too painful."

He frowned. "Why? I haven't been able to figure out why you've kept your distance from the start. Is it something I've done? I can change if you tell me what's wrong, but I have to know!"

Throat tight, she gazed out to the gray waves of the sea below. "How can you not know when it's so simple? I'm Jewish. You're Christian. It's a huge gulf. Impassable, at least for me."

"It's hardly unknown for people from different religions to marry," he retorted. "My friend Bobby's father is Catholic, his mother Church of England. Bobby says they had some difficulties in earlier years, but they've worked it out. The children go to both churches and his parents dote on each other."

"They were both Christian. To me, Catholics and Anglicans are hardly different at all. Judaism is *different.*" Seeing that he still didn't understand, she said with exasperation, "Nick, when Jewish children marry goyim, Christians, sometimes their parents declare them *dead*! They are no longer part of the family. Can you imagine how dreadful that would be?"

Shocked, he said, "How can they? My parents would never do that!"

"Probably your parents wouldn't," she admitted. "But parents have cut off their children for lesser reasons. We Jews—there are not so many of us. When we marry outside our faith, we make Judaism weaker. I will not turn away from my people."

"Would your parents declare you dead?"

She thought of her kind, tolerant mother and father. Both were scientists and broad-minded, but they were also proud of their Jewish history and identity. "They wouldn't declare me dead, but they would be deeply grieved."

"Of course you don't want that. Neither do I," he said quietly.

"But we are Nicholas Rainford and Rebecca Weiss. We are individuals, not defined only by the religions we were raised in. Can't we at least try to build a bridge across that gulf?"

She wanted to believe that would be possible, but maybe she was deluding herself because she was so attracted to him. "I don't know, Nick. The gulf is wide."

"Since you were raised in a mostly Christian nation, you probably know quite a bit about Christianity," he said. "I'm not sure there's a Jewish family in the whole of Kent, so I'm far too ignorant about your faith. What could I do to convince you that I'm trying to understand better?"

"You could start by reading about Judaism. Our history, our traditions, our festivals." She offered a fleeting smile. "Our food. You may have noticed that I don't eat pork or shellfish because they aren't kosher. Not permitted."

He began walking along the cliff path again, and she fell into step beside him. "I looked up kosher food in an encyclopedia, and it's much more complicated than avoiding pork and shellfish. Special dishes are used, no mixing of meat and dairy," he said. "All kinds of complicated rules. You don't seem to follow most of them."

She felt absurdly touched that he'd already made some effort to understand what it meant to be Jewish. "In my family, when we're out in the gentile world we compromise by avoiding what we can and accepting the rest. I couldn't live with your family if I insisted on a kosher kitchen, but I need to be here to learn more about my magic." She waved a hand. "So no bacon or clams or mussels."

He smiled mischievously. "Compromise. I like that word. If we both try, maybe we can build that bridge. I'll see what books the library has on Judaism."

She thought of the tiny Lackland public library. "Probably not much. The bookstores in Oxford will be much better. I'll ask my mother to send some books."

"Will she suspect there is a reason why I want to study Judaism?"

"Perhaps," Rebecca said noncommittally, thinking such a suspicion might prepare her parents for a possible future with a goy in the family.

His chuckle told her that he understood what she hadn't said. She glanced at him out of the corner of her eye, admiring his strong profile. She'd love to run her fingers through his blond hair, which was in need of a cut. She forced herself to look away and concentrate on her footing along the path.

"Let's take it day to day," he said. "There's a war going on. The world is being disrupted as never before. Maybe in time the gulf between your people and mine won't seem impassably wide." As he spoke, he quietly took her hand.

Warmth rushed through her when he laced his fingers between hers, and it wasn't only her melting attraction. Might magelings have a special ability to connect swiftly and deeply with others? She had the impression that Tory Mansfield and Lord Allarde had experienced that kind of silent, immediate connection when they met.

Though she'd tried to deny it, she'd felt a connection with Nick from the first moment she saw him. Perhaps what was between them might be strong enough to build bridges.

She squeezed his hand, and allowed herself a glimmer of hope.

CHAPTER 9

Lackland, 1804

Back in her room, Tory changed quickly, tossed a few extra garments in her shoulder-slung bag, and returned to the Labyrinth. She immediately went to Merlin's Mirror to spend some time communing with it privately.

She closed her eyes as she stood in front of the burning power and reached out with her mind. No one knew if the portals had really been created by Merlin and his associates, but the creators had been ancient British mages. Surely they would approve of defending their country.

We're going to a portal we've never used before, and it's in our time, not the future. This is very, very important because we want to protect Britain from this horrible invasion. We need all the help we can get!

It took several minutes to clear her mind and tune her energy to that of the mirror, but when she did, she sensed that the mirror approved of her and her mission. She thanked the mirror and withdrew into her own consciousness.

As she did, she heard a small sound behind her, and warm hands came to rest on her shoulders. Allarde. "I don't suppose you're interested in my suggestion that you shouldn't go into the middle of a French invasion," he said wryly.

She laughed and rested her hand on his. "I'm no more likely to hide here in safety than you are."

"I know. But I had to ask. It's what males do." He brushed a quick kiss on the back of her hand. "Even when the female is as intrepid as you."

She leaned back against him, her back resting against his warm chest. "We're in this together, Justin. For better and worse." Then she wished that didn't make her think of the next line in the marriage service, *till death do us part*.

Hearing the sound of approaching feet, she turned and put a discreet distance between herself and Allarde. The three adults entered the mirror chamber first, followed by the other Irregulars.

All three girls wore their trousers. Tory and Elspeth were small enough to pass as boys from a distance if their hair was concealed, but that wouldn't work for Cynthia, who was too tall and curvy to be a convincing boy. Over her shirt and trousers, she wore a loose jacket that probably had belonged to Jack, but nothing short of illusion magic would make her look male.

Cynthia reached into a pocket and produced two small, polished black pebbles and handed one each to Tory and Elspeth. "I've been working on a new illusion trick. These pebbles are charged with illusion energy. What do you look like to each other?"

Illusion magic didn't change how one saw oneself, so Tory clasped her pebble in her palm and examined Elspeth. Her friend looked like a modestly dressed young girl instead of a trousered hoyden. Cynthia had also designed the spell to make Elspeth unmemorable by dulling her pale blond hair to tan. "You look entirely forgettable."

Elspeth smiled. "So do you. I can feel a faint tug on my power from the stone, so I gather it's drawing energy from me, Cynthia?"

"Yes, and you can turn the illusions on and off. All you have to do is think of yourself as normal. To invoke the illusion, imagine yourself in a gown."

Tory mentally imagined herself as a trousered boy. Elspeth did the same and immediately looked like herself in boy's clothing. "This is wonderfully clever, Cynthia!" Tory exclaimed. "Would it be possible to charge the stone with several different appearances? Perhaps add the look of a frail little old lady."

Pleased by the compliment, Cynthia said, "I'm sure it could be done with more time and more magic. I'll experiment later."

"Do you have any more stones like that, Cinders?" Jack asked. "I'd like to be able to look like someone else, too."

"I have two more stones for you and Allarde," Cynthia said. "I'll charge them for you after we're in Wales. It might be useful for you to look like French troops."

"You have a definite talent for war," Jack said admiringly.

"Time we were off," Allarde said. "Since the invasion is taking place right now, minutes are precious."

There was a flurry of good-byes and hugs and promises to send message stones. Then Tory arranged her friends in a line behind her and turned to the mirror. She cleared her mind of worry about going to an unknown portal and visualized a map of Britain with

Wales to the west. *Please take us to Wales near Carmarthen,* she thought. *Take us as close to the French invasion as you can.*

Energy surged in the portal, and the shimmering rectangle of the mirror appeared before her. She reached out her free hand—and was swept into mirror's wild magic. Her hand locked on Allarde's as reality dissolved into chaos.

Tory returned to the normal world abruptly. Off balance, she stumbled to the ground, still holding Allarde's hand. She found herself on soft turf, not hard chalk, and outdoors. A cold wind was blowing, and fitful clouds drifted across the quarter moon. She automatically invoked enough hearth witch power to keep her warm. Then she scanned the area and caught her breath when she saw that they were surrounded by tall, irregularly shaped standing stones.

Allarde's hand tightened on hers as he helped her to her feet. She created a small hearth witch spell so he would also be protected from the cold.

He asked, "Are you all right, Tory?"

"Better than expected." She felt a little dizzy, but nowhere near as pummeled as she usually did after a mirror transit. She created a dim mage light and looked down the line to see her friends sorting themselves out with no signs of problems. "This was the easiest transit yet."

Tory's hat had fallen off when she landed, so she scooped it up and donned it again. "Here's hoping we're in the right time and place."

Allarde handed her a message stone with a piece of paper wrapped around it. "I wrote this before we left, saying we'd arrived safely, though we haven't determined where and when."

Tory took the stone and held it with her eyes closed, visualizing the Labyrinth at the time they'd come from. Opening her eyes, she tossed the pebble through.

Elspeth got to her feet, her gaze on the standing stones. "We've come to an ancient place of power," she said softly. "Feel the magic in this circle! Perhaps Merlin himself built it centuries ago."

"We need all the magic we can get." Cynthia scrambled to her feet. "We also need food. That wasn't as bad as other mirror transits, but it still left me hungry."

"You're always hungry," Jack said with a laugh. He opened his knapsack and pulled out the bag of meat pies his mother had packed for the journey. Mrs. Rainford had become an expert on providing foods that were easy to handle and good for restoring mageling energy. Tory suspected that there was probably another bag of shortbread deeper in Jack's knapsack.

Allarde was studying their surroundings. The stone circle was on a hilltop, and there was a distant glint of water. "Let's hope we're close to the invaders. If we're near Carmarthen, that's the Irish Sea out there."

Elspeth gazed out at the sea. "The French are near. I can feel them on the wind."

The words sent a shiver down Tory's spine. She asked, "Jack, how well recovered is your magic?"

"I couldn't do major weather work yet, but my finder ability seems to be working well." He pointed to the left. "The town of Carmarthen is several miles east. The French landing is much closer, probably just on the other side of that great hill. Between one and two miles."

"My friend who lives in this area is named Blakesley," Allarde said. "Do you know where his family home might be?"

Jack closed his eyes for a moment, then pointed to the left

again. "It's this side of Carmarthen, but on the other side of where the French are landing."

"That makes our plan simple." Allarde scooped up his knapsack and slung it over his shoulder. "We head east along the coast and see what the French are up to. Is everyone feeling fit enough to start hiking?"

The last of the food was consumed, crumbs were brushed away, and hats and knapsacks were adjusted. Jack, who had been prowling around the edge of the circle, said, "There's a path down this hill that runs in the right direction."

"Give me a moment to absorb some of this wonderful energy." Elspeth stepped up to a standing stone and closed her eyes. Then she flattened her hands and rested her forehead on the rough, damp surface.

Thinking that looked like a good idea, Tory did the same, choosing a different stone. When she closed her eyes and stilled her mind, she recognized that the deep power of this sacred place was similar to the power of the mirror. Since this was supposed to be Merlin's home country, maybe he really did create the mirror portals.

She let the power flow into her, restoring the strength depleted by using the mirror. She was smiling when she opened her eyes and stepped away. Everyone had followed Elspeth's example, so she waited quietly until the others were done with their communing.

Jack was last. As he opened his eyes and stepped away from the stone, he slung his bag over his shoulder and said, "That helped restore a good bit of my power. Now it's time to see if five magelings can help stave off a French invasion!"

CHAPTER 10

Wales, 1804

Tory had been vaguely aware that Wales was a wild, rugged land. But she hadn't realized just how rugged. The footpath Jack had found was leading in the right direction and the footing wasn't bad, but the hills were *steep*. There was a stiff wind blowing, too. Lucky that the girls had hearth witch magic to keep everyone warm.

She was panting as they neared the top of a hill near the coast. Then Allarde, who was a few steps ahead on the footpath, came to an abrupt halt and gestured for quiet.

Everyone stopped to listen. Shouting voices could be heard above the wind, and they were shouting in French. They were also using words Tory didn't recognize but suspected were blisteringly profane.

Allarde dropped to a crouch and moved up to the top of the hill, where he flattened himself in the grass so he wouldn't be visible against the skyline if anyone below glanced up. After a moment to study the situation, he beckoned for the others to come forward.

Tory crept up beside him, then smothered a gasp at the sight of the cove below. Four ships flying French colors were anchored in the dark water, and a dozen or more small boats were moving back and forth from the vessels to the shingled beach. The torches on the beach illuminated stacks of ammunition and supplies, and swarms of soldiers were forming into groups and marching inland.

"So many men!" she said, her throat tight. "This truly is an invasion."

"I'm thinking there must be close to two thousand," Jack said as he studied the activity below.

"There are both regular and irregular troops down there," Allarde said, indicating a mass of dark-coated men who were forming into ranks. "Those are La Légion Noire, the Black Legion. They wear captured British uniforms that have been dyed black."

"Now that's just *vulgar*!" Cynthia exclaimed.

"Perhaps, but they move like well-trained soldiers." Tory watched a company form ranks, then march up the hill along a track that was forming in the soft turf. "And they seem to have a destination in mind."

"They would have sent out scouts as soon as they moored in the cove," Elspeth said thoughtfully. "There are any number of old castles and fortresses scattered around Wales. If they found one nearby, it would make an excellent base of operations."

"We need to follow that track to see where they're going." Allarde said. "Then we can head to the Blakesleys and hope that the general is home. He'll be able to raise the militia and yeomanry far faster than we can. Perhaps the French forces can be attacked while they're still getting organized."

"Let's hope their lair isn't far," Cynthia grumbled. "Traveling parallel to the line of march is going to take us over rough ground."

"I could go alone and catch up with you later," Allarde suggested.

"No!" emerged from four throats simultaneously.

Tory added firmly, "We need to stay together until we have a base of our own. This is wild country, easy to get lost in. Even though you and I are connected, that doesn't mean we can find each other in unfamiliar territory."

"I'd rather know exactly where you are," Allarde agreed as he backed down the hill so he wouldn't be visible to the French when he straightened up. "A good thing they're making so much noise that it will be easy for us to shadow them."

The next hour was a tiring scramble through the darkness as they headed inland parallel to the enemy's route. As Allarde had said, it wasn't hard to keep track of the French, but the ground was rough and the Welsh hills were steep.

Occasionally, they came close enough to catch a glimpse of the line of march. Once they saw four small cannon being hauled along between two companies of foot soldiers. The invasion forces were worrisomely well armed.

Tory swore under her breath when they came within sight of the French destination. The devils had found an old hilltop fortress with much of the stonework intact. It looked to be the highest elevation around, so the French force would have a good view over the surrounding countryside.

Jack gave a soft whistle as he surveyed the fortress. "Once the French dig in there, it will be almost impossible to get them out."

"They need to be out and fighting if they want to conquer any ground, but the fortress gives them an excellent base to work from." Allarde studied the rocky crag with narrowed eyes. "Since they're still getting settled and haven't set up perimeter guards yet, this is a good time to scout around the fortress for weaknesses. Ideally, there would be enough flaws in the stone that I could break off a large chunk of the fortress."

"Not likely!" Jack said.

Allarde grinned. "I know. But one can hope."

"I'll go with you," Jack decided. "Maybe there will be places where Cynthia and I can throw some lightning."

Cynthia groaned. "Just what I need, more hiking."

"You girls needn't come," Jack said. "You can rest here till we finish scouting."

Tory wouldn't mind a rest, but she was all too aware of the passing time. She studied the landscape. The French soldiers were traveling from the shore in a narrow valley between two steep hills. At the end of the valley was the crag crowned by the fortress. The Irregulars were on a hill to the west of the track, and they needed to cross to the other side of the valley to continue toward the Blakesleys and Carmarthen.

"Scouting around the fortress will take time," Tory said. "It would be more efficient if we frail females rest a bit, then cut across the valley when there's a gap in the line of march. We can all rendezvous up at that rocky outcropping on the opposite hill." She pointed.

"That makes sense," Allarde agreed. "Jack, let's get going. We have a much longer hike to get there."

Jack lifted his pack again. "Right. Careful, ladies."

"You males are much more likely to get into trouble than we are," Cynthia pointed out.

"And you wouldn't have us any other way," Jack said with a laugh.

Allarde brushed a kiss on Tory's cheek, then the two boys headed off into the darkness. The girls settled to the ground gratefully.

"Why don't we ever have an adventure with horses?" Cynthia asked with a sigh.

"That would be too easy," Tory said, thinking how nice it would be to have a Welsh pony to ride. "But at least since we're in our own time, we don't have to worry about explaining magic to people who don't believe in it."

They rested quietly, watching the French and their supplies being moved up to the fortress. The marchers weren't a continuous stream, but the spaces between groups weren't usually too long. After they'd had a chance to catch their breath, Elspeth got to her feet. "There's a largish gap coming, so it's a good time for us to start down."

Cynthia said, "We all have our Lackland stealth stones, don't we? Between the stealth magic and it being the middle of the night, there's not much risk we'll be seen."

Tory had been studying the route across the narrow valley. She stood and slung her bag over her shoulder. "We probably won't be seen, but the other side of the valley is rather steep. Toward the top, it will be more like rock climbing than hiking, so we'll need to be extra careful."

"You don't need to worry," Cynthia said with a grin. "If you slip, you can just fly the rest of the way."

"I don't fly," Tory said. "I just float."

"It looks like flying to me!"

They set off down the hill, sticking to the shrubs and trees where they could. The distance to the bottom seemed longer than they'd estimated, and by the time they reached the valley floor, the marchers in the second group were unnervingly close. Tory could hear individual voices and see the faces of the torchbearers.

But the Irregulars had their stealth stones, and a cloud drifted across the moon, making the valley floor very dark. Tory wondered if that was Cynthia's work.

The cloud was a mixed blessing. The soldiers couldn't see the girls, but the girls had to move more slowly since they couldn't see their footing. Tory tripped and almost fell more than once. It was a relief to cross the line of march and start climbing the hill on the opposite side of the narrow valley.

The hillside was even steeper than Tory had realized, and scrambling up toward their meeting place took all her concentration. She swore to herself when they reached the final stretch, which was an almost vertical bluff.

She paused to catch her breath and glanced down at the French troops. Then she wished she hadn't looked, because the drop below was dizzyingly long and steep. But they were now so high that it was unlikely any of the enemy would notice them.

She turned back to the hill and cautiously started to climb. The bluff was a mix of vegetation and rock. While there were plenty of hand- and footholds, the surface was unstable. Once she almost fell when a foothold broke away under her weight and she barely managed to find a new hold. Even though she could float, the near accident made her heart race.

Tory resumed climbing. Cynthia was above and to her right, Elspeth lower and to the left. Cynthia reached the top and pulled herself onto level ground. "I did not expect mountain climbing," she muttered in a voice that carried to the girls below.

Tory grinned. What would they do without Cynthia, who spoke aloud what Tory and Elspeth were too polite, or too inhibited, to say?

Tory reached the top and hauled herself over, gratefully accepting the hand Cynthia offered. "I'm really, really glad I'm wearing trousers," she gasped as she folded onto the grass at the top of the bluff.

"At least we get a rest now." Cynthia leaned over the edge to offer a hand to Elspeth, who was nearing the top.

"The things I do for England," Elspeth said wryly as she reached for Cynthia.

Their hands almost met. Then the earth crumbled away under Elspeth. She gasped and scrambled for better footing, but without success. She lost her grip and pitched down into darkness with a bone-chilling cry.

Tory and Cynthia watched with horror as their friend fell, slid, banged, and rolled down the bluff and most of the hill below. Her fall ended when she came to rest in a motionless heap against a tree, almost invisible from their height. It had happened so quickly that Tory had no chance of flying to catch her.

A French voice called to his fellows that there was someone or something just up the hill. Two men broke away from the column and started hiking up to investigate.

"Dear God!" Cynthia cried, pressing her hands to her mouth.

Tory dumped her bag and leaped to her feet. "I'm going after her," she said, uttering a silent prayer that Elspeth hadn't been killed in the fall. Why, oh why hadn't Tory stayed lower than her friends so she could catch anyone who slipped? "Cynthia, conjure some mist around where Elspeth is lying!"

Not waiting for a response, Tory dived off the bluff into the darkness to rescue her friend.

CHAPTER II

As she fell with terrifying speed, Tory reached for her magic and the inner "click" that triggered her floating ability. It was taking too long, too long, *too long* . . .

Click! She stopped falling just in time, gliding into a hover no more than a yard above the ground. Heart hammering, she moved the dozen feet to where Elspeth was lying crumpled against a tree. The two French soldiers were stamping toward them, complaining about how the squadron hadn't been able to land in Bristol because of the dangerous currents around the city, so they were stuck in this wilderness.

Not even checking if Elspeth was alive, Tory slid her arms under her friend, then swore when she realized she wasn't strong enough to lift a weight equal to her own. She reached for magic again and managed to get to her feet with Elspeth in her arms.

Glancing up, she wondered if she had the strength to carry Elspeth up the whole height of the hill. The last time she'd rescued someone, they'd been going down, not up.

One of the soldiers exclaimed, "*Sacre bleu,* Pierre, it's two little girls!"

She'd run out of time. Tory reached out to Allarde to draw some of his power to her. He was startled but instantly sent magic through the bond that connected them.

As Tory gathered herself for the flight upward, mist began rising from the ground. Thick mist, so dense that Tory couldn't even see Elspeth's face. Mist so sudden that the French soldiers swore in surprise.

Giving thanks, Tory rose smoothly upward, Elspeth a limp weight in her arms. For the whole time they were in the air, her shoulders were tensed as she half expected musket balls to slam into her spine.

She almost wept with relief when they were safely over the edge of the bluff. There were no shots or shouts to suggest that they'd been seen.

Tory stumbled with fatigue and folded to her knees when she landed. She barely managed to lower Elspeth to the grass without dropping her.

"How badly is she hurt?" Cynthia said as she knelt on Elspeth's other side.

"I don't know. But before I forget, that was a good job on the mist. Otherwise they would have had us."

Cynthia gave an awkward nod. She wasn't good at accepting compliments, so Tory made a point of giving them when earned.

Almost afraid to learn the truth, Tory lifted Elspeth's limp wrist and searched for a pulse. Nothing, *nothing* . . .

She shifted her hold, then exhaled with relief when she found a steady beat. "Thank God! She's alive and her pulse is strong. Can you give me a mage light and remove her illusion spell? I need to examine her and the illusion is confusing."

With a snap of Cynthia's fingers, Elspeth's illusion of dull hair and gown vanished, leaving her pale, dressed as a boy, and looking very young. After removing the illusion, Cynthia tugged off Elspeth's carrier bag, which had been slung around her torso so it survived the fall. Then she formed a mage light in the palm of her left hand.

The light revealed masses of bruises and abrasions on Elspeth's face and hands. Her hat was long gone and blood stained her pale blond hair.

Praying that common sense would compensate for the fact that Tory had only modest healing ability, she began her examination with Elspeth's skull. "She's going to have the devil of a headache, but the cut on her head is shallow and there doesn't seem to be a major injury. I'll see if I can stop the bleeding of her scalp."

She managed to halt the blood but didn't try to close the wound, which needed to be cleaned first. With the bleeding stopped, Tory gently skimmed her hands over Elspeth's limbs and torso. A broken bone might be noticeable, but she would be no use diagnosing internal injuries unless pressure caused enough pain for Elspeth to react.

Elspeth shifted a little under Tory's exploring hands, but there were no signs of pain until Tory touched her left ankle. Elspeth whimpered and pulled her leg away.

Not touching the ankle again, Tory asked, "Elspeth, can you understand me?"

Her friend's pale green eyes opened. She seemed disoriented, but after blinking several times, she whispered, "What happened?"

"You fell off a cliff," Tory answered. "You were almost at the top when the soil crumbled away."

"Glad it wasn't my own clumsiness." Elspeth touched the wound on her head and winced again. "How did I get up here?"

"I brought you." Since Elspeth was their best healer, Tory continued, "Can you tell how badly you're hurt?"

Frowning, the other girl moved her limbs and fingers, smothering a cry when she moved her left foot. "I'm in better shape than I deserve to be except for my ankle," she gasped. "I think it's broken."

"Can you fix a broken bone with your healing power?"

"Healers aren't usually very good at fixing themselves." Elspeth tried moving her ankle again and bit her lip to smother a cry of pain. "I need a bonesetter. If the bones aren't straight when they're healed, they'll never be right again."

Cynthia dug out her canteen of water and wet a folded handkerchief. As she gently cleaned the scraped skin and grass stains on Elspeth's face, she asked, "Can you reduce the pain, or should Tory and I do that?"

"Please." Elspeth closed her eyes, her face white. "I'm having trouble focusing to do anything for myself."

Tory laid one hand on Elspeth's knee above the injury and used the other to take Cynthia's hand. As she sent white light to block the pain, Elspeth's expression eased.

When they finished, Tory said, "Now that your ankle isn't hurting, I'll bind it so it won't get worse."

Elspeth nodded, so Tory dug into her bag and pulled out her only spare shift. Oh, well, Elspeth's need was greater. After tearing the muslin garment into wide strips, she wrapped the fabric around the injured ankle.

Just as she finished, Allarde and Jack arrived, looking worried. "What happened?" Allarde demanded. "You drew a lot of power fast, and that's never good."

"Elspeth fell down the mountain. She isn't too badly hurt, but her left ankle might be broken," Tory replied. "She can't walk."

Allarde looked over the edge of the bluff, his expression appalled when he saw how far a fall would be. "Thank heaven she's alive! Jack and I can carry her since she's just a little bit of a thing."

Elspeth's eyes opened. "I am no one's little bit," she said tartly.

Allarde squeezed her hand. "You've just proved that you're not badly hurt, little cousin. Are we ready to head on and hope to find the Blakesleys at home?"

Tory got to her feet, brushing off her trousers. "The sooner we tell the local authorities about the invasion, the better. Did you discover any weak spots during your scouting expedition?"

Jack shook his head. "Nothing obvious. The other side of that crag is really steep. No one is getting in that way. Except possibly you, Tory."

"Let's come up with a better plan than me floating into the middle of a French army encampment," Tory said dryly. "The fact that I can get inside doesn't mean I can do anything useful when I get there."

Jack said, "Allarde, I'll take Elspeth for the first shift if you take my knapsack."

Allarde added Jack's knapsack to his own. "How far is the Blakesley house?"

Jack closed his eyes as he thought. "Maybe two miles. We should be able to reach there before dawn." He bent and gently lifted Elspeth. As she put her arms around his neck, he asked, "Are you comfortable this way, Elspeth?"

She gave a lopsided smile. "I'm rather enjoying it."

Cynthia said caustically, "Just don't either of you enjoy it too much!"

Jack laughed. "I wouldn't dare, Cinders. Now onward!"

After another stiff hike up and down rugged hills, Jack led the Irregulars to a substantial stone manor house. The grounds were well kept, but no lights showed inside, not surprising given that it was well after midnight. "I hope someone is home," Allarde muttered. He'd been carrying Elspeth, but he transferred her back to Jack. "And I hope I can convince whoever is here that Blakesley Major and I were schoolmates at Eton."

"What's his first name?" Tory asked.

Allarde shrugged. "I have no idea. He was Blakesley Major, his younger brother was Blakesley Minor. If there were more brothers, they'd be Maximus and Minimus."

"Boys are just weird," Cynthia said flatly.

"And girls aren't?" Jack asked as he adjusted a sleeping Elspeth in his arms.

Cynthia didn't deign to reply, though she touched Elspeth's shoulder to send a little more painkilling magic. They'd taken turns treating Elspeth so that the broken ankle wouldn't hurt too much from all the jostling.

Tory thought ruefully how much they relied on Elspeth for their healing. Now that she was the one injured, they couldn't do much for her.

They reached the front of the house, so Allarde led the way up the front steps of the portico, Tory beside him. He wielded the door knocker.

No answer. Not surprising at a time when all sensible people were asleep.

Allarde knocked again. The sound boomed hollowly inside the house, but again there was no response. "Do you think I should shout, 'The French have invaded'?"

"That will probably work better if it's shouted inside." Tory put her hands over the lock and used her magic to unlock the mechanism of the door. It was a trick she'd learned from Allarde.

"Let's hope no one inside is armed with a shotgun," Allarde muttered as he opened the door. "Stay behind me, Tory."

She obeyed, not only because he was large enough to be an effective shield, but because he had the ability to deflect bullets by magic. Very useful in a war zone.

Allarde stepped inside and created a mage light that revealed a paneled entry hall with a carved wooden staircase descending on the right side. "General Blakesley?" he called. "General Blakesley, raise the local militia! The French have landed!"

A voice snarled, "Who the devil are you, and what are you doing in my house? Hands up or we'll blow you to hell!"

Despite Allarde's protective magic, Tory's heart jumped into her throat as she saw two men descending the staircase with shotguns in their hands. Both were half-dressed, but their expressions were deadly serious. She raised her hands and tried not to look terrified.

Allarde also raised his hands, but his voice was calm. "It's an old schoolmate. Assuming you're still willing to acknowledge a mageling, Blakesley Major?"

The young man in the lead lowered his weapon, his expression shocked. He was brown-haired, with a tough, wiry build, and he looked to be about twenty. "Allarde? What brings you to Wales? I thought you'd still be at Lackland Abbey."

"Usually I am." Allarde lowered his hands, so Tory did the same. "I'm here with four other Lackland students because we learned the French were invading. Can my friends come in? We've had a hard trek tonight."

"Of course, of course." Blakesley descended, his companion at his heels. They both had a military look, Tory decided.

Jack entered the hall carrying Elspeth, with Cynthia bringing up the rear. Blakesley's jaw dropped when he saw Cynthia. She no longer used illusion magic to cover the thin scar on her cheek, but even so, she was a diamond of the first water who could have brought London society to its knees if she'd made her debut. In her tight trousers, she was a sight to behold.

"I'm Bran Blakesley," he said. "And you are . . ."

Cynthia and Jack might be bonded like magnets, but she was enough of a flirt to bat her eyelashes and give Blakesley a fetching smile. "I'm Lady Cynthia Stanton, and I'm so very pleased to meet you."

Jack rolled his eyes. "Do you have a sofa where I can lay Lady Elspeth down?" he asked. "Even a sprite starts feeling heavy after a mile or two. She needs a bonesetter."

"This way to the drawing room." Blakesley opened the door on the right. "My batman here, Sergeant Williams, can send for the bonesetter." The man behind him nodded and left the hall. Blakesley glanced around at his guests. "And you all are . . . ?"

Allarde performed swift introductions as they moved into the drawing room, using the girls' titles and introducing Jack as the most powerful weather mage in Britain. Blakesley looked impressed, which was the point. Allarde ended by asking, "How is your younger brother doing?"

"He left Eton and is now at Rugby," Blakesley said tersely. "It suits him better."

As Jack laid Elspeth down on a sofa, Tory found a knee robe to cover her friend. Then she created several more mage lights and tossed them up to hover. A portrait above the fireplace showed an older man in military uniform who looked very much the way Blakesley would in a few years. The general, presumably.

When the introductions were complete, Blakesley asked, "What was all that about a French invasion? They've been arming themselves to the teeth in Boulogne, but they haven't a prayer of getting across the Channel. Not with the Royal Navy on patrol."

"Perhaps not, though it would be foolish to underestimate Bonaparte," Allarde responded. "But the invasion that brought us here is happening right now, tonight, only two or three miles to the west. Four French ships are moored in a cove there. We're guessing between fifteen hundred and two thousand well-armed men have disembarked."

"Here?" Blakesley asked incredulously. "In Carmarthenshire? Why on earth would Napoleon want to invade us? We have more sheep than people!"

"Their original target was Bristol, I think. A larger fleet planned to attack Ireland, but Jack and Cynthia wreaked major damage with their weather magic. This small squadron managed to survive, though they were blown off course and landed here."

Allarde gave a succinct description of how foretelling and scrying had helped the Irregulars anticipate the invasion, though he didn't mention the mirror. Like the other Irregulars, Tory kept quiet and let him do the talking. Not only did he know Blakesley, but he always sounded the most convincing.

Allarde ended by saying, "Is your father here? As a general, I assume he can call up the local militia."

"My father is drilling troops in Lincolnshire. I'm staying here alone with my batman and a few servants who come in for the day." Blakesley made a face. "I came to Wales because I wanted a few weeks of peace and quiet before returning to duty."

"Do you have any idea how many men are in the militia?"

"I'm not sure. Between the militia and the yeomanry, perhaps five hundred or so. Nowhere near two thousand men. The militia commander is an idiot called Dawson who bought a lieutenant colonel's commission and hasn't a shred of actual military experience. He just wanted to wear a uniform and wave a sword."

"What about the commander of the yeomanry?"

"I'm not sure who that is." Blakesley ran agitated fingers through his hair. "I could do a better job of commanding troops than Dawson, but I'm barely a lieutenant."

"I gather you followed your father into the army?" Allarde asked.

Blakesley flashed a quick smile. "Much worse. I'm in the Royal Marines. We're the navy's infantry, and we've been doing most of the fighting. Whenever there's a naval battle, we're there. But my father may never forgive me for joining the navy."

"Colonel Dawson needs to be notified even if he's an idiot," Allarde said. "Is there someone in the area who has authority and is respected? The lord lieutenant of Carmarthenshire, perhaps? There's no time to waste."

As Blakesley and Allarde talked, Tory covered a yawn. Cynthia was in Jack's lap as they both slept under another knee robe, and Elspeth was dozing peacefully on the sofa. Tory had no idea what would happen, but she needed all the rest she could get, so she found another knee robe and a love seat that fit her rather well.

From what Blakesley had said, the local defenses wouldn't have a chance against more than a thousand trained French troops. If this battle was to be won, it would take magic. And that meant the Irregulars.

Tory woke when she felt a hand on her shoulder. She knew it was Allarde even before she opened her eyes.

He knelt beside her sofa. Keeping his voice low so as not to disturb the others, he said, "Bran and his batman and I are going to ride into Carmarthen to notify the authorities. Then we'll come back with a bonesetter for Elspeth."

She smiled sleepily. "You're on a first-name basis now?"

He grinned. "I call him Bran, he calls me Allarde. He's a good fellow. I'll tell you about the last time I saw him when we have time." He leaned forward for a kiss, his lips deliciously warm.

Waking up fast, she slipped her hand around his neck and kissed him back. That ended when someone nearby cleared his throat meaningfully. She opened her eyes and saw Bran suppressing a grin.

Allarde smiled ruefully and stood. "We'll be back by dawn, I think. If anyone is hungry, there's food in the pantry. Try to rest as much as you can."

"Then what?" she asked.

"I have no idea, but I imagine it will be interesting."

Tory rolled her eyes, then pulled the knee robe over her head. She was rather tired of "interesting"!

CHAPTER 12

Lackland, 1940

"Rebecca, I'm driving to school this morning." Mrs. Rainford checked her briefcase to make sure she had her lesson plans for the day. "Would you like a ride?"

Rebecca looked up from her bowl of porridge. "No, thank you. Andy and I are going to walk down with some of the little girls from the junior school."

Polly finished off the last bite of her porridge. "By next week I'll be strong enough to walk, too, Mum."

"I hope so," her mother said briskly. "Petrol for the motorcar is hard to come by. No more lazing about for you, Miss Polly." She brushed her daughter's blond hair affectionately.

"I have decided I will never be sick again," Polly said, wrinkling her nose. "Blood poisoning is such a bore!"

Rebecca smiled, enjoying the morning routine of breakfast and chat. Nick's school started earlier, so he'd already left. Polly had returned to classes two days before, so the kitchen was busy in the morning, but the household ran smoothly. Everyone, including Rebecca, had assigned chores. Her job was keeping the kitchen and bathroom clean. She liked the work because it made her feel like a member of the household, not just a guest. It was all wonderfully normal and civilized.

As Polly carried her bowl and tea mug to the sink, she said, "Rebecca, Nick and I wondered if we could do Friday night Shabbat dinners. Could you show us?"

Rebecca halted in her washing up as a vivid memory of life before the war flared in her mind. The songs, the silver candlesticks inherited from her grandmother, the warm sense of belonging and family . . . "Why do you want to do that?"

"To learn, of course. I want to know more of Jewish customs. That is, if you don't mind?"

Rebecca suspected that Nick might have put his sister up to asking for this, but it was a nice thought. "Mrs. R., would you be willing to hold a Shabbat here?"

"Of course." Mrs. Rainford smiled. "I'm as interested as Polly and Nick. Having you here is a wonderful window into French and Jewish culture. If you're willing, we'll talk later about what is required, but for now, it's time for you to be off!"

Rebecca rinsed her dishes, put on her coat, and slung her book bag over her shoulder. "I'll see you in school."

After a scratch on the head for Horace, the Rainford family dog, she headed out. She loved this walk along the cliff path. This morning a light mist lay over the sea, but pale sunshine was struggling to get through. She mentally recited a Hebrew prayer of thanks for having been led to this wonderful place.

When thoughts of Nick and his teasing smile crept in, she firmly dismissed them. He made it a habit to meet her after school so they could walk home together. It was the high point of her day, but that was because they were friends. Nothing more.

She smiled ruefully because she wasn't good at lying to herself. Nick wasn't like anyone else she'd ever met. His energy and appetite for life and learning affected her the way catnip entranced a cat. The day before, Rebecca had received two books on Jewish history and customs from her mother, and Nick had immediately grabbed one and allowed Polly to read the other. Which was probably why a Rainford version of the Shabbat dinner was in the works.

It was impossible not to appreciate Nick's effort and interest. Which made the whole situation more complicated.

As she came in sight of the road down to the village, she saw Andy and three little girls. Andy waved a greeting. "Morning, Rebecca!"

Andy's family also lived on the bluff above the village, on the other side of the road, so they met here each morning to walk down. The three smaller girls had mothers doing war work. Since the mothers weren't able to walk the girls to school, Andy did. The junior school was just a block beyond Lackland Girls Grammar.

"Good morning, Rebecca!" The little girls, Gillie, Margery, and Lizbet, greeted her in a chorus. They were adorable little English blondes.

Rebecca greeted them with a smile, and the group turned into the path beside the road. There was little traffic at this hour except for a couple of people on bicycles. With petrol rationed, no one drove a motorcar without a good reason.

As the little girls chatted, Andy fell into step beside Rebecca. "I heard on the wireless that there were several dogfights over Kent early this morning and fighter planes were shot down near here." She shook her head vehemently. "I hate this!"

Rebecca sighed. "So do I. Were there parachutes?"

Andy nodded. "So the wireless said. God willing, the pilots survived."

Rebecca was glad that the wireless hadn't been on in the kitchen this morning. With Joe Rainford an RAF fighter pilot, news of planes being shot down would upset everyone in the family. It would upset Rebecca, even though she'd met him only briefly.

Such news wasn't uncommon, though. This coastal county, Kent, was right on the major route for Luftwaffe airplanes heading toward London, so the Luftwaffe and the defending RAF aircraft fought regularly in the skies above. Wanting to change the subject, Rebecca asked a question about their upcoming mathematics class, which was always an effective distraction for Andy.

They were nearing the village when a wild-eyed man burst out of the shrubbery, wearing the gray uniform of a Luftwaffe pilot and the life vest worn by pilots who flew over the English Channel. He was dirty and bruised, and blood oozed from a head wound.

"Halt!" he shouted as he clenched the pistol in both shaking hands, aiming at the girls. He looked frightened enough for any kind of stupid behavior. In German, he continued, "Raise your hands! Don't move!"

Rebecca stopped, her pulse hammering. One of the little girls shrieked, and that set off the other two as Andy tried to hush them. Rebecca knew German, so she raised her voice and translated,

"Hold still and raise your hands, and no screaming! He's frightened, he doesn't want to hurt us."

The shrieking subsided to tears as the little girls clung to one another. Rebecca hoped she was right that he wasn't dangerous. She raised her hands and said in German, "We're just schoolgirls. You have nothing to fear from us."

He swallowed hard, his Adam's apple bobbing. "You speak *Deutsche. Sehr gut.* Tell the children I will not hurt them if they behave. I need hostages to get me to a boat so I can sail home across the Channel. Boats are in the village, *ja*?"

He seriously thought he could steal a boat and sail to France? The odds of that were only slightly better than if he flapped his arms and tried to fly under his own power! The man was out of his mind with fear. No, not a man, a boy, surely not much more than twenty. Despite his youth, he was a captain, a *Hauptmann.*

"Yes, *Herr Hauptmann,* there are a number of boats in the harbor," she said respectfully as she tried to inject soothing magic into her voice. Switching to English, she said, "Andy, the captain wants to use us as hostages to get down to the harbor where he can steal a boat. We need to go with him quietly, and then he'll let us go."

Gillie, the most timid of the girls, wailed and tried to run away. As the pistol swung toward her, Andy grabbed Gillie by the arm and pulled her back. "Don't run, Gillie!" Face pale, she lifted the little girl in her arms. "It's safer to stay here."

Gillie buried her face in Andy's shoulder and sobbed. The pilot looked so unnerved that Rebecca was afraid he might shoot just to silence the little girl.

Rebecca decided that it was time to discover just what her magic would do. Soothing again, she said, "*Herr Hauptmann,* walking through the village with five hostages will attract too much attention. The police might be called. One of the little girls might panic and run away and you don't want to shoot anyone, do you?"

He shook his head numbly. "I do not want to hurt anyone. I don't want to hurt anyone ever again."

He was suffering from some form of shell shock, Rebecca realized. After the 1914–1918 war, many soldiers had been stressed to the breaking point. This young fellow had been fighting nonstop for months, and being shot down was the last straw. On top of that, his head injury might mean a concussion. The man was as unpredictable as dynamite. If she could touch him as she had Sylvia, could she heal some of his pain and make him less dangerous?

It was worth a try. "You only need one hostage. Me," she said in German. "Let the other girls walk away up the hill. You can see there are no houses, nowhere they can call the police. I will take your arm like a girlfriend and you can hold your weapon concealed against me so you know that I will not scream or run away. I will walk you down to the harbor. There is a quiet lane parallel to the High Street where we're not so likely to be seen. Then you can sail away home."

It took his befuddled mind time to process that. Finally he nodded. "That is a good plan. Tell the other girls to start walking back up the hill. When they are halfway up, you will take me to the harbor."

She glanced at Andy. "He's agreed to release you and the little girls and just take me as a hostage. Start walking up the hill with the girls. When you're halfway up, he'll take me down to the harbor."

Andy gasped, "No!"

"Do it!" Rebecca snapped. "I should be all right. And if worse comes to worst . . . well, the damage will be limited."

Andy bit her lip. "You are the bravest person I've ever known. Now *be careful*!" She set Gillie down and instructed the little girls to join hands with her and they'd walk home. Confused but obedient, the little girls did as they were told, though Lizbet cast worried glances over her shoulder.

When the retreating girls were well up the hill, Rebecca said, "Now I will take your arm and we will walk quietly down to the harbor."

The pilot awkwardly offered his left arm while keeping the pistol in his right hand under his jacket. It was aimed right at her. Rebecca hoped to God that he wouldn't stumble and shoot her accidentally.

Telling herself that this time she must control the magic rather than let it rush, she took his arm. As when she and Sylvia touched, she experienced a flood of thoughts and emotions, but this time she was less overwhelmed. More controlled.

The pilot blinked uncertainly as energy blazed between them. Though different from the energy of attraction between Rebecca and Nick, it was strong enough that she wasn't surprised that he felt something.

When he frowned down at her, she smiled. "Shall we proceed, *Herr Hauptmann*?"

"*Herr Hauptmann Schmidt*. Your name, *Fräulein*?"

"Rebecca Weiss." She thought it a good sign that he'd introduced himself and asked her name.

As they headed down the street, she sorted through the turmoil of his emotions. As she expected, Schmidt was terrified, but he was also despairing. He'd been raised in a religious home and taught compassion and peace, but he'd rebelled against that. The

Luftwaffe had offered excitement. Glamour. Adoring and cooperative girls. He loved flying, until the war started and he had to start shooting at other men.

His eyes and hands and brain were designed for combat flying, but his soul wasn't. He'd reached the point of half hoping he'd die in a blaze of redemptive fire, but the basic desire to survive had kept him alive. Now he was in England, and on some deep level he expected a horrible punishment and humiliating death for all he'd done.

The deeper she went into his spirit, the more intense his emotions. It was a struggle not to drown in them. Drawing back a little, she wondered what she could do for the poor man that would help him and everyone around him.

With a vague idea in mind, she said, "This war is a terrible thing for all of us."

"Indeed it is," he said bleakly.

"You have been a pilot for a long time?"

"Too long." Changing the subject, he said, "Your German is very good, but your accent is not that of an Englishwoman."

"I am French," she explained. "My family had to flee France. I've only been in England for a fortnight."

He looked at her more closely. "You are Jewish," he said, suspicion in his voice. "Your people rule the world from behind closed doors."

She was both angry and amused. "Not my family. My parents are doctors and I wish to become one, too. We are healers, not rulers of the world." She slid into his mind and sought the anti-Semitism that had been planted by vicious anti-Jewish propaganda. Using her anger, she flooded the ugly prejudice with white light.

He frowned, confused, as if he didn't know what to think now that the bigotry had been removed. "I've heard so many bad things about Jews, but I've not seen such evil myself." He glanced down at her again, his brow furrowed. "You are not evil."

"I should hope not!" Later she might feel guilty about altering his mind and attitudes. But not guilty enough to regret doing it.

Since his attitude was softening, she said earnestly, "*Herr Hauptmann Schmidt,* you will never make it across the Channel alive. Why not surrender? You have served your nation well. It will not benefit the Fatherland for you to die in an attempt to escape England."

"I deserve death!" he said with despair.

"For being a soldier?" she said in a matter-of-fact voice. "Nonsense! Fighting for your country makes you a patriot, not a criminal."

"My father was a Lutheran minister and he taught me a higher law." The pilot swallowed hard. "Under that law, I'm a villain."

"Isn't Christianity a religion of repentance and redemption?"

"Oh, I repent," he said softly. "Every hour of every day. But I have my doubts about redemption."

"If penance will make you feel better, surrender to the authorities," she said with a touch of dryness. "This will be a long war, I think. As a prisoner, you won't be starved or tortured, but you will have to suffer years of mind-numbing boredom as penance." She had a swift mental image of him plowing a field behind a team of horses. "Or perhaps they will make prisoners of war become farmhands since so many men are in the armed forces. That would be another kind of penance."

He liked that idea, she sensed. He'd worked on his grandparents' farm as a boy, and being on the land again would soothe the jagged edges of his spirit. In a flash of what must be foretelling magic, Rebecca felt sure that if he chose this path, he'd meet a girl who could make all the difference in his life.

She poured that image into his mind. *Peace. Redemption. No more killing.* All those elements were blended in the torrent of pure white light that illuminated the darkest corners of his spirit, dissolving the worst of the guilt and leaving hope.

Softly she said, "You have done your duty, *Herr Hauptmann Schmidt*. You can surrender now with all honor."

Lowering the hand that held the pistol to his side, he stopped walking and closed his eyes. Uncertainty and confusion were written on his tormented face. "Can there be honor for a man who doesn't want to fight?"

"Honor and redemption," she said firmly. "I read a story once about one of the Native American Indian chiefs. They were the fiercest of warriors, you know. Yet this Chief Joseph said, 'I will fight no more forever.' All warriors must someday come to an end of war." She held out her hand. "Give me your pistol, *Herr Hauptmann Schmidt*. You need fight no more forever."

She could feel how torn he was between the light she was sending and the darkness that had poisoned his soul for so long. As she waited, scarcely able to breathe, she heard running steps behind her and a soft, anguished gasp.

She glanced to her left and saw Nick approaching. His eyes were wide and he looked as if he'd run all the way from his school. Had he sensed her danger?

Guessing that he might tackle the Nazi pilot, she made a quick gesture with her left hand. *Wait!*

He bit his lip but skidded to a halt a dozen steps away, trusting her judgment.

"I will fight no more forever." The pilot opened his eyes, his expression at peace. Then he handed her the weapon butt first. "I surrender to you, *Fräulein Weiss*."

She pointed the pistol toward the ground, dizzy with relief.

She was wondering what happened next when the front door of the nearest house swung open and a white-haired man burst out, a rifle in his hands. "Get away from that devil, miss!" he shouted. "I'll take care of him!"

Aghast, she realized that he was as likely to shoot as the pilot had been. "No!" She stepped between Schmidt and the white-haired man. "He has surrendered and will go quietly. Do you have a telephone so you can ring up the authorities?" In German, she said, "Best raise your hands, *Herr Hauptmann*."

The pilot raised his hands and the white-haired man lowered his rifle, though he watched Schmidt suspiciously. His wife appeared behind him. Without turning, he said, "Edna, call the police while I keep watch on this damned Nazi pilot."

Schmidt was eyeing his growing audience warily. Rebecca said, "Since I speak German, I'll stay with you until you're safe in custody."

He glanced at the man with the rifle. "Can I lower my hands now?"

Rebecca nodded and said in English, "He's lowering his hands, but truly, he is no threat. He has accepted that his war is over."

Nick appeared beside her. "Want me to take that pistol?"

"Please!" She handed it over, and he expertly opened it and removed the ammunition, dropping the bullets in the pocket of his school uniform jacket. The colors were the same as LGG, with a navy jacket, gray trousers, and a red tie. He looked grown up and authoritative in it.

Nick tucked the empty pistol into his belt and let the jacket fall over it. Then he wrapped a warm arm around her shoulders. Trying desperately not to cry now that the danger was over, she embraced him, shaking.

"I was so terrified," she whispered. "How did you know to come?"

"I felt that something had happened to you." He held her close with a mixture of tenderness and strength. "I bolted out of the middle of my Latin class. A good thing I have finder talent, but I'm going to have some explaining to do!"

She laughed a little and stepped from his arms with reluctance. "Then you'd better go back to school."

Eyes warm, he said, "I'll stop by LGG and tell the principal and Mum what happened and why you're not in class."

"I'll come in when I'm not needed here." She gave him a crooked smile. "I do hope you're planning on walking home with me today!"

"I'll be there," he promised.

He left, cutting his way back through the growing crowd. She wondered if he'd be allowed to keep the pistol. She hated the very feel of guns, but in these times, she understood why he wanted a weapon.

In the distance, she heard police sirens. Turning to Schmidt, she said, "Do you want me to send a letter to your family? I think the Red Cross can deliver it."

He nodded and reached into a pocket inside his leather flying jacket. He pulled out a slip of paper with the name of his parents and his address in a small town she'd never heard of. "I have carried this in case my body needed identification."

Wincing at his bleak practicality, she accepted the paper. "I shall write and tell them you are well and safe."

He clicked his heels together and gave a stiff little bow from the hips. "Because of you, *Fräulein Rebecca Weiss*. I shall never forget your kindness and wisdom."

She smiled and offered her hand. "Your future is brighter than you now imagine, *Herr Hauptmann Schmidt*. Go with God."

"I shall try." As they shook hands, he said, "My Christian name is Hans." Then he turned and faced the two policemen who were cutting their way through the crowd.

His face was composed, though she felt his inner tension as he faced an unknown future. She waited quietly beside him in case her translation services would be required. She also thought of how much more she would have to report when Nick sent her message stone through the mirror.

CHAPTER 13

Near Carmarthen, Wales, 1804

Gunfire. Cynthia was sleeping draped across Jack's lap, her head on his shoulder and her arm around his waist. Then the boom of guns jarred her out of the peace that she found only with him.

Jack also jerked awake and instinctively leaped to his feet. Cynthia slid off his lap and landed on her backside on the carpet. "Owww!"

While she was still sputtering, Jack said, "Oh, my God, I'm so sorry! Are you all right, Cynthia?"

A window of the drawing room exploded inward in a shower of shattering glass. Deciding she'd be outraged later, Cynthia scrambled to her feet. "The French must be attacking! Elspeth? Tory? Allarde?"

Elspeth woke and automatically tried to get up, then collapsed with a cry of pain as she put weight on her injured ankle. As Jack went to help her, Tory rolled from the sofa and crossed the room to peer out the broken window. "It's the Black Legion all right. There's at least a company marching up the driveway. It doesn't look like they expect opposition. They probably want to capture or loot the house and are shooting out windows for amusement."

"We need to get out of here!" Cynthia flinched as another window shattered, spraying broken glass across the carpet. "Where are Allarde and his friend?"

"They and Blakesley's batman rode into Carmarthen to notify the authorities so troops can be raised." Tory turned from the window and waved her hand to douse the mage lights that had been illuminating the room. "As you say, we need to leave. Elspeth, how are you doing?"

"Better, now that Jack has dulled the pain again," Elspeth said in a strained voice. "I can't walk, though."

"I'll carry you." Jack scooped her up in his arms. "Cynthia, can you take my bag? We need to *leave*!"

Cynthia grabbed Jack's bag while Tory snatched up Elspeth's. The front hall led to a corridor that cut through the center of the house. Moving at a fast walk, they headed to the back of the building. Cynthia and Tory lit dim mage lights once they were out of sight of the French. They heard loud French voices speculating on the state of the wine cellar as the soldiers marched up the driveway.

Feeling sorry for the Blakesley family, Cynthia led the way to the morning room in back of the house. French doors led out to a stone terrace. The door was locked, so Tory used her magic to swiftly open it.

Cynthia held the door open for Tory, Jack, and Elspeth before following them into the cold night. As soon as she closed the door, Elspeth raised her head. "Merciful heavens, the French have a mage with them!" she said in a hushed voice.

"Damnation!" Jack swore. "Do you know what kind?"

"Presumably someone with talents useful in war," she said grimly.

Cynthia wondered what those abilities were as she raced down the stone steps and across the lawn. Finder ability? Weather magic? The ability to sense the presence of others? A tangle field to prevent the enemy from moving? There were far too many possibilities, and later they'd have an interesting discussion about it. But right now, all that mattered was bolting into the woods behind the house before the enemy saw them.

They were halfway to the woods when a huge ball of mage light flared above the lawn and hovered over their heads, illuminating the Irregulars with lethal clarity. Cynthia's heart jumped into her throat. She pushed herself to run faster, but the light tracked the running Irregulars.

From the terrace behind the house, a voice boomed in French-accented English, "Halt! If you surrender, you will not be hurt in captivity!"

Cynthia risked a glance over her shoulder and saw a tall, gaunt man in black stalking toward them, armed soldiers in his wake. This had to be the French war mage, for he radiated power.

The mage raised both hands and she guessed that he was about to throw a tangle field to slow them long enough to be captured. From Jack's arms, Elspeth gasped, "Leave me here and make a run for the trees!"

"Don't be an idiot!" Cynthia snapped as she swung around, reaching for the sky to see if there was any lightning she could summon to blast the war mage. But there was no bad weather close enough to help. Nothing!

The mage light above vanished and Tory yelled, "Use your hearth witchery!"

Of course! Cynthia was a powerful hearth witch, and that included the ability to control fire. She visualized a line of flames between her and the French, then created the reality with a furious sweep of her arm. Instantly a curtain of flames blazed across the lawn. Flames and *smoke*!

Gleefully she summoned wind to blow the smoke into the faces of the French. She heard coughing and curses and could barely see the mage or the soldiers.

Then Tory grabbed her arm, sharing her special ability to make other mages stronger. Immediately the fire roared twice as high, completely blocking their pursuers. "Now we run!" Tory ordered.

As the girls raced after the others, horrible laughter followed them. "Magelings!" the war mage shouted. "What a delight! I look forward to consuming you!"

"Not today, you warped beast!" Cynthia hissed as she and Tory entered the shelter of the trees. It was a woodland garden rather than a natural wood, and it had been designed with thick shrubbery and twisting paths. They had to slow and create mage lights, but for the moment they were safe.

A few minutes into the woods, they found Jack sprawled under a tree and panting for breath. Elspeth was beside him, her injured leg stretched out in front of her. "Elspeth, if I didn't know better," he said wryly, "I'd say you weigh more than an elephant!"

"I'm sorry," Elspeth said in a small voice. "You should have left me behind. Better one person be caught than all of us."

"We leave no one behind," Tory said firmly as she dropped to the ground. "Not when we can make Jack do the heavy work."

"You frail girls need a man around to take care of you," he said with deliberate provocation.

Cynthia threw a handful of dried leaves at him. He batted them away with a grin. "Elspeth, you saved me from losing an eye. Do you seriously think I'd abandon you to an invading army?"

"I'm glad you didn't," Elspeth admitted. "Tory, were you the one who doused his giant mage light?"

Tory nodded. "But we'd have been in trouble if Cynthia hadn't been able to call so much fire."

"I didn't know I could do that." Cynthia leaned against a tree trunk, wishing she could curl up here and go back to sleep. Calling the fire had exhausted her. "Mrs. Rainford would not be pleased that I used her hearth witch teachings as a weapon."

"Well, Mrs. Rainford's only son is glad you did!" Jack made a face. "When we were in 1940, the weapons were a lot scarier, but at least we didn't have to worry about the enemy having magic."

"That war mage is scary," Tory agreed. "Let me do some enhancing on our stealth stones. I don't want him finding us."

Cynthia pulled out the pouch that held the smooth, water-polished pebble she'd been given when she joined the Irregulars. Tory held it between her palms and closed her eyes as she recharged the magic. The stone pulsed with energy when she handed it back.

When all the stealth stones had been enhanced, Cynthia said, "Now that we've caught our breath, I guess we head toward Carmarthen."

With a sigh, Jack got to his feet. "Tory, can you let Allarde know that we're on our way and he and Blakesley mustn't return to his home manor?"

"I'll try to pass on the gist of it." Tory closed her eyes, reaching out to Allarde. "He understands that we're all right, but there was trouble and we left the manor. He'll look for us. I gather there is one main road to Carmarthen, so we should meet up." Wearily she got to her feet. "This has been a very, very long night."

"Time to mount up, Elspeth," Jack said. "If I carry you on my back, it will be less tiring." She nodded and he knelt so she could climb aboard, wincing as she did so.

"Time for another shot of pain blocking?" Cynthia placed a hand on Elspeth's shoulder and sent a dose of healing magic.

Elspeth's face smoothed out. "Thank you. If not for the pain blocking, I'd be curled in a ball weeping with pain. It seems unfair that I can help others heal, but when I'm injured, I can't do much for myself."

"We'll find a bonesetter in the morning. A good one who can join the bones smoothly and make the break heal quickly." Cynthia patted Jack on the head. "Which way, faithful steed?"

He chuckled and set off in the direction they'd been heading. "The main Carmarthen road runs behind the Blakesley estate, so we should reach it soon."

Cynthia hoped so. As Tory had said, this night was very, very long.

Endless.

CHAPTER 14

The trek east was made easier when Tory saw an elderly, good-natured pony watching from a fenced pasture. This time it was Cynthia's turn to rip up her spare shift so it could be made into a crude lead.

Tory attached the improvised lead to the pony's halter, then led it from the field, and Elspeth had transportation. Jack hadn't complained about carrying her—apart from the elephant remark—but he put Elspeth on the pony's broad back with a sigh of relief.

Numb with fatigue, Tory kept putting one foot in front of the other. The night had to end eventually. As the sky lightened in the east, they entered a village that was large enough to have a church and an inn with a sign proclaiming it as the Royal Oak, Rhys Morgan, proprietor.

"Is this Carmarthen?" Cynthia asked doubtfully. "I thought it would be larger."

"This is probably the village of Tregwelli," Elspeth said. She was white-faced with pain and exhaustion. "If so, Carmarthen is larger and a mile or two farther east and more inland."

"You've passed this way before?" Tory asked.

Elspeth shrugged. "A long time ago."

"Since there are lights on inside," Jack said, "let's see if a hot breakfast might be available. All in favor say aye!"

The decision was unanimous, so Jack helped Elspeth off the pony's back. Tory untied the lead from the halter and crooned to the pony, "What a sweet girl you are. Now it's time for you to go home."

She laid a hand on the pony's forehead and visualized the route back to the pasture where they'd found her. When she removed her hand, the pony gave Tory a friendly butt in the shoulder that almost knocked her over, then ambled back in the direction they'd come from.

Cynthia stared after the pony. "You can talk to horses?"

"I'm not sure, but I thought it was worth a try." Tory handed the ragged lead to Cynthia. "Here's your shift back."

Cynthia made a face as she stuffed the ruined garment in her bag. "My hearth witch lessons haven't covered how to turn rags into clothing again."

Tory opened the door into the inn's taproom, and Jack carried Elspeth through with Cynthia following. The room was warm and welcoming, with a fire burning cheerily. Jack set Elspeth down on a wooden settle by the fire while Cynthia used the bell rope by the bar to summon the landlord.

A balding, broadly built man entered the taproom and surveyed his new customers with a shrewd eye. Elspeth said a few words in Welsh, to Tory's surprise.

The landlord nodded and said in musically accented English, "I thought you looked English. I'm Morgan. Are you here for an early bite to eat?"

"Yes," Jack said. "But also with grave news. The French have landed an invasion force several miles west of here. A couple of our friends have ridden into Carmarthen to raise the alarm."

Morgan's bushy brows shot upward. "Damnation! The French have really landed, and here of all places?" He frowned. "You children aren't playing a prank?"

He thought they were children? "I wish this was a prank," Tory said flatly, "but the French troops are all too real. Maybe they were heading to Bristol and bad weather blew them off course. They landed last night and immediately set up camp in an old hilltop fortress. Then they captured the Blakesley estate, where we were staying."

The landlord whistled softly. "How large a force?"

"More than a thousand troops," Jack replied. "Probably closer to two thousand, and well armed. The word must spread so people can evacuate their homes."

"Some will leave." Morgan's eyes narrowed. "And some of us will be grabbing up pitchforks and fireplace pokers to fight. If the damned Frogs only just landed last night, there should be time to rally the defense forces."

"We hope so," Cynthia said. "For now, we'd appreciate something to eat."

Morgan opened the kitchen door behind the bar and called, "Olwen, fry up some eggs and bacon for four hungry young people who just outran a French invasion."

A rosy-cheeked woman appeared in the doorway to the kitchen, a wooden spoon in her hand and her expression horrified. "The French? Don't be daft, boyo!"

Morgan gave a swift summary of the situation, then sent Olwen back to cook breakfast. Turning to his visitors, he said, "You young folk aren't Welsh. What brings you here?"

Tory realized that in the twentieth century, they'd had to be discreet about their abilities, but there was no reason not to talk now. Most people in her time respected magic. "We're magelings from Lackland Abbey. Our best scryer"—she gestured toward Elspeth—"saw the invasion, so we came to help."

"Lackland Abbey. Then you must have strong magic," he said, his expression approving. "Sounds like we'll need all the help we can get! I'll see if that food is ready."

He disappeared into the kitchen. Tory sank onto a chair opposite the fire while Jack and Cynthia shared another wide settle, locked together.

Tory closed her eyes and tuned her mind to Allarde. Now that there were no other distractions, she sensed that he was near. "Allarde is close, I think."

"I hope so," Jack said. "I don't like when we separate in strange territory."

Tory's prediction was better than she expected. Breakfast had appeared and they were just finishing their meal when Allarde swept into the taproom, his dark cloak swinging from his shoulders.

She had only an instant to admire what a dramatic picture he made when she realized he was white-lipped with anger. She'd never seen him so furious.

"Justin!" Tory was across the room and in his arms before he took three steps into the taproom. He hugged her hard. He was vibrating with fury, but that diminished as he held her.

"What happened?" she asked.

He ended the embrace but kept his arm around her shoulders as they crossed the room to the breakfast table, where the others waited. "The good news is that I've brought a healer who sets bones, and she's said to be the best in southern Wales. She's coming in through the kitchen to say hello to the landlady."

"Obviously there's bad news, too," Jack remarked.

"Bran was right," Allarde growled. "The local militia commander is an inexperienced idiot. He's dithering and saying nothing can be done until reinforcements arrive and talking of a retreat back toward Swansea. If it's left to him, the French will be able to conquer the whole of Wales without any resistance."

Elspeth pushed herself up to a sitting position to join the conversation. "Surely there must be regular troops stationed in Swansea or Cardiff."

"Yes, but it will take time to send word of the invasion, and more time to march here. Bran stayed in Carmarthen to try to mitigate Dawson's incompetence." Allarde dropped tiredly into a chair. "Dawson is not only an inexperienced fool, but an aristocratic snob. He refuses to have anything to do with magic or mages."

Jack swore under his breath. "So there was no point in our coming."

"Wrong," Tory said firmly. "We're mages, not soldiers, and we don't have to obey orders from the dithering Dawson. We can do things that no regular troops can."

Before she could say more, a plump, capable-looking middle-aged woman entered the taproom from the kitchen. She radiated mage power. "I'm Mistress Jones, the healer." Her gaze moved to Elspeth. "You're looking right peaky. You're my patient?"

"Yes, and I'm so glad to see you!"

"I'll have a look at that ankle now." Mistress Jones headed toward Elspeth purposefully. "I see you're all magelings. None of you are healers?"

"I'm the strongest healer, and I'm no good at healing myself," Elspeth said. "Can you set and heal the bone so I can be up and around today?"

Mistress Jones was taken aback. "That would take a vast amount of power. Usually I give several treatments over several days to knit bones."

"If we can channel our magic to you, would that help?" Tory asked. "We're all powerful in different ways, though Elspeth is the only real healer. I'm good at blending magic and channeling it."

"It's worth a try, though even if it works, you'll need to sleep a few hours, lass." Mistress Jones glanced at Allarde. "Help your cousin onto a table so we can make a circle around her for the healing."

Allarde lifted Elspeth and laid her gently on one of the taproom tables. The Irregulars gathered around as Mistress Jones examined her patient by slowly stroking the air a few inches above Elspeth's limbs and torso.

"For a girl who fell down a mountain, you're in good shape," she commented. "The only bone broken is in the ankle. If your friends can give me enough extra power, I might be able to heal it in one session, but I warn you that knitting the bone that quickly will hurt like the very devil."

"Do what you must," Elspeth said in a thin voice. "I need to be able to help with what comes."

"You." Mistress Jones pointed at Tory. "Hold Elspeth's left hand and put your other hand on my shoulder. Allarde, take Elspeth's other hand and the blonde's. Blondie, hold your sweetheart's hand. His other hand goes on my shoulder."

"Blondie?" Cynthia said, aghast. Tory almost laughed out loud at her expression.

But Cynthia and everyone else complied with the healer's orders. When the circle was complete, Tory collected and blended her friends' energies. In spite of all they'd been through, she was able to send a great deal of power to Mistress Jones.

The older woman's healing magic had a very different flavor from what Tory was used to. She rested her hands lightly on Elspeth's ankle, closed her eyes, and poured a river of burning energy into the broken bone. Tory sensed the jagged ends of bone aligning, then welding together like molten metal.

Elspeth gave a strangled cry and squeezed Tory's hand with numbing force. Tory cringed at the pain in her friend's voice, but she kept channeling the combined power until Mistress Jones said with satisfaction, "Done! I've never fixed a broken bone so quickly. You magelings are a powerful lot."

"Thank you," Elspeth whispered. Her face was white and sheened with sweat. "That was . . . interesting. Different from what I do."

"There aren't many healers with the special bonesetting talent, and I usually don't have enough power available to do such a quick, intense healing." Mistress Jones released the circle, then wiped her sweaty face. "Morgan, this young lady will want to sleep like the dead for a few hours. Show Allarde what bedroom to put her in."

Allarde carried Elspeth as the landlord led the way upstairs. Tory sank wearily into a chair. Thank heaven for Mistress Jones!

Now it was time to plan how the Irregulars could counter the French invasion.

CHAPTER 15

Olwen Morgan brought out a huge pot of steaming tea and a plate of griddle cakes with currants. "This might help perk you up after all that work."

Tory started to thank the landlady, then recognized a glow in the older woman's energy field. "You're a mage yourself, aren't you?"

"Aye, though not so strong as you or Gwyneth Jones, the bonesetter," Olwen said. "I'm the village counselor, with a bit of hearth witch magic as well."

"Join us," Tory suggested. "We're going to have a council of war when Allarde returns. You and your husband have local knowledge, and you're a mage as well. Together we can decide the best course of action."

"In that case, we'll need more tea mugs."

Olwen returned with the mugs as Allarde and Morgan came downstairs. Allarde gravitated to Tory's side. She poured him a cup of tea, adding milk the way he liked it. "I've invited the Morgans to join our planning session."

"Good." He sat beside her and took a grateful swallow of tea before glancing around the circle. "We'll have to leave troops and battles to the authorities and hope the dithering Colonel Dawson listens to more experienced men. Our biggest weapon is the weather. Jack and Cynthia, what can be done with that?"

Jack made a face. "Storm work is more effective over water. Since the French have already landed, we can't damage them as we did the fleet that was heading to Ireland. The most we can do is make them wet and uncomfortable."

"Even a giant soaking rainstorm will be difficult," Cynthia said. "I've been studying the weather patterns for hundreds of miles around, and there isn't a lot to work with. In fact, the weather is so calm that I suspect French weather mages cleared the skies. They obviously have other mages working besides the ones we burned out."

"Would it be possible to do a small, localized weather attack rather than a large storm?" Morgan asked. "I think I know the cove where they must have landed. There are some bad rocks there. If a violent squall hit the ships, they'd have to put out to sea or be crushed into the rocks."

"I like that idea," Allarde said thoughtfully. "With no ships, the French troops have lost their means of retreat. That should make them more inclined to surrender if they feel their position is hopeless."

Jack and Cynthia looked at each other, conferring silently. "We could raise a nasty little squall, I think," Cynthia said. "Enough to smash the ships or force them out to sea. What can we do to convince the French their situation is hopeless?"

"I've an idea that might help," Tory said. "Their ammunition is stored in the hill fortress. If it blew up, they'd have very little left to fight with."

Allarde's brows arched. "You're thinking that together we could fly up to the top of the crag and set off their arsenal?"

"Exactly. I wouldn't know what to do with that much ammunition, but I suspect you would. The two of us working together should be able to manage it."

"You can fly?" Olwen said with amazement. "You must be some of the most powerful magelings in Britain!"

"I haven't met enough other mages to know," Tory said. "But I do have floating ability and Allarde has great lifting power. When we work together, we can rise to the top of the crag." At least, she hoped so.

Allarde's eyes narrowed thoughtfully. "We'll have to wait until dark."

"Not necessarily," Tory said. "When Elspeth fell down the cliff, Cynthia created a splendid dense mist around her so the French couldn't see where she lay. If Cynthia can fog the fortress, we won't have to wait for night. Would you have enough power to do that while also creating a squall?"

"I think so," Cynthia replied. "Wales is generally very wet, so there's a good bit of moisture to work with even if the French have diverted the larger storms."

Tory glanced around the circle. "Does anyone have other plans to consider? Mrs. Morgan? Mr. Morgan?"

After a long silence, Cynthia said, "I can do something with hearth witch fire, but I'm too tired to think what. Do we have time to sleep? I'll need rest before I can do weather work."

"We all need rest," Tory agreed. "But the French are so close! I'd rather not wake with them shooting out the windows." And she did *not* want to meet the war mage again.

"I can help with that," Olwen Morgan said. "As a counselor, I'm good at feeling other people's energy even if they're some way off. Since you told me about the French, I've been able to sense them. Rather like a swarm of angry hornets buzzing in the distance."

"Do you feel the energy of a very powerful French war mage?" Tory asked.

Olwen closed her eyes and mentally searched. "I feel an intense, hostile energy that might be the one you're looking for. He's not close, though. Several miles away and thinking of something entirely different, so you're safe for now. I'll sense if he or the troops march this way, so go along and get some rest. We have two more guest bedrooms, one for you lasses, the other for you lads."

Allarde asked, "Do you know someone who can take a message to Bran Blakesley in Carmarthen? I want him to know where we are since we seem to be turning the Royal Oak into our headquarters."

"There's a lad down the street who will be glad to take a note." Mrs. Morgan got to her feet. "Come along upstairs, my girls, and I'll show you your room."

"Lead on, madam." Tory was so tired that she didn't even mind that she'd be sharing a bed with Cynthia.

The sagging mattress of the bed in the girls' room meant that the smaller Tory tended to slide down toward Cynthia, who would then shove her away. That didn't matter. Tory could have slept on a pile of rocks.

She woke to find herself alone in the bed and Cynthia standing at the window and gazing out at the sky. "What time is it?" Tory asked.

"About noon. Since we arrived here so early, we still have half the day ahead of us." Cynthia nodded at the cloudy sky. "I've been pulling in what wind and rain I can find. We'll be ready to blast that cove with a nice squall by the end of the afternoon."

"Allarde and I should go for the arsenal around the same time. Hit the French two different ways at once." Tory rose and poured water into the washbasin, then splashed her face. She was glad her voice was steady, but inside her nerves were knotted. Flying into the French fortress was a good idea, but she didn't expect to enjoy the experience.

Cynthia said from her window, "Bran Blakesley just rode up to the Royal Oak. He's in his Royal Marines uniform and looks *very* handsome. Also furious."

"Let's see if he has news."

As they left their room, Tory tapped on Elspeth's door, then looked in. Her friend sat on the edge of her bed and rotated her injured ankle in wonder. "I wish I could do bone healing!" she exclaimed.

"No matter how good we are, there are always things we can't do," Tory said philosophically. "Come on down. Blakesley has just arrived."

Downstairs they found Blakesley updating Jack and Allarde on what had happened. In his uniform, he looked older and more commanding. Though he nodded a polite greeting to the girls, he was seething with anger, as Cynthia had observed.

"The French have been pillaging farms inland," he said grimly. "No reports of farmers being killed, but there was a skirmish between some French soldiers and local volunteers. Several men were killed and more were wounded."

"How many British troops do we have?" Allarde asked.

"About three hundred militiamen, a little over two hundred of the shire yeomanry, plus I spotted two revenue cutters off the coast and took a boat out to tell them about the French invasion. The cutters contributed about a hundred more men. Still nowhere near enough," Bran said glumly. "It will take days to get reinforcements."

"We might be able to improve the odds for you," Allarde said.

As he outlined their plans, Blakesley began looking more optimistic. "Mr. Gwillim, a substantial farmer just outside Tregwilli, will loan you horses, I'm sure," he said. "If they're hurt or killed, I'll compensate him."

"Or I will. We can argue about that later," Allarde said. "Now it's time to borrow those horses and get to work!"

Mr. Gwillim had a good assortment of riding hacks, and he was glad to lend them to fight the French. Cynthia's chestnut gelding wasn't showy, but it had smooth gaits and an even temper. The other girls had Welsh ponies, while the boys had larger mounts suitable for their height and weight. The ride back to the French landing site would be much quicker than the walk away had been.

They set off in midafternoon, Jack leading the way and Cynthia behind him. The road was eerily silent. As they headed west, they passed farms that had been abandoned. All looked as if they'd been looted, and at one, the barn had been torched. Cynthia's determination to drive out the enemy became stronger with every mile.

When they neared the French position, Cynthia called to Jack, "Time for some mist, don't you think?"

He nodded. "You're in charge of that. Once you've created a heavy fog, it will take most of my concentration to stay on course."

What he really meant was that his magic wasn't strong enough yet to guide and work weather at the same time, but Cynthia didn't say that since he hated being weak. Shocking that she was learning tact.

Cynthia had never deliberately tried to create fog before Tory had asked her to, but she'd found it rather fun. Now she had the chance to see how much more she could create. Though there was no rain in the vicinity, the earth and plants and sea were full of moisture. She drew that moisture up into floating ribbons of mist.

The ribbons twined and thickened, growing ever more dense until Cynthia could barely see the hindquarters of Jack's horse. Sounds were muffled or echoed oddly through the fog. Jack slowed their pace, though he never hesitated over their path.

Cynthia had trouble estimating how far they'd traveled, but finally Jack halted his horse and gestured for the others to gather close. Speaking in a low voice, he said, "The track the French used to carry their supplies inland is just ahead, with the cove to the left and the hill fortress to the right. When we discussed this earlier, we planned on splitting into two teams, but now that we're here, I have a strong feeling we should stay together."

"I agree," Tory replied. "Cynthia's fog is so dense that we'll get lost without your finder talent. Allarde, do you have any intuition about the best course?"

"Jack is right, we should stay together," he said after looking inward to consult his foretelling ability. "There's a grove to the left of the road. I think we should tether our horses there and walk down to the cove." He glanced at his cousin. "Elspeth, it's best you stay with the horses. You shouldn't overstrain that ankle."

She grimaced. "You're right, I'd just slow you down. Don't anyone get injured without me being there to fix you!"

"I have no desire to let myself be damaged." Cynthia swung from her horse and led it into the grove. The fog and trees concealed Elspeth and their horses perfectly.

After the horses were secured, Cynthia took firm hold of Jack's large, warm hand and let him guide her into the thick whiteness. Though she'd created the fog and was maintaining it with her magic, she would not like being lost alone in the mists.

Tory and Allarde followed closely, also holding hands. The four of them had to climb another steep hill, and Cynthia was panting by the time she reached the top. A good thing that maintaining fog took less effort than creating it in the first place.

Jack stopped and said in a barely audible whisper, "The cove is just below. You can hear the water."

Cynthia listened and heard not only waves slapping the shore, but cursing Frenchmen. The soldiers down on the narrow beach had been ordered to carry the last of the supplies to the fort, but they couldn't see a bloody thing in the bloody bedamned fog.

Her mouth tightened as she listened. "Time to blow them back to France," she muttered under her breath.

"We need enough breeze on the water to reveal the position of the ships," Jack said. He raised a hand and a light wind began blowing through the fog that blanketed the cove. The mists thinned and the four ships gradually emerged. They started as dark blobs but soon were clear enough that Cynthia could see sailors on the decks.

She frowned, a bad feeling chilling her nerves as she studied the tiny forms of the sailors. That tall, thin figure . . .

She gasped with shock, feeling as if she'd been kicked in the stomach. "The war mage is on the deck of the largest ship," she said in a strangled voice. "That tall fellow in black. And I think he knows we're here."

CHAPTER 16

Frowning, Jack pulled a spyglass from his bag and raised it to his eye. He whistled softly. "I didn't see the war mage before, but this fellow radiates menace, and he's scanning the hills around the cove. Is he the one you saw at Blakesley's place?" He handed the glass to Cynthia.

The spyglass brought the distant figure so close that Cynthia instinctively stepped back. He was lean and black like a carrion crow. The mage was standing by a man who might be the captain. As she brought him into focus, the mage swung around and stared straight up at her. She felt an energy line twang between them. A painful line.

Heart pounding, she said, "He's looking right at me!"

Jack snatched the spyglass back and muttered an oath as he saw the war mage glaring up at their position on the hill. "Cynthia, you're better at aiming lightning. Can you blast him?"

She reached into the weather they'd been gathering for the squall and concentrated the jittery energy into a bolt of lightning. Then she hurled it at the mage. Faster than the eye could follow, he lifted a hand and deflected the bolt so that it missed the ship altogether, though the accompanying thunder made the timbers shake.

Cynthia was so furious that she wanted to spit. "No point in wasting another bolt on him," she growled. "He might be able to ward off the squall we planned!"

"Let me see." Allarde took the glass and stared down at the mage. "He's smirking at us. Overconfident. Time to try something other than weather magic. . . ."

Cynthia felt the power gathering around Allarde. Then she heard a crack so loud that it carried all the way up on the hilltop and the energy line that connected her to the war mage snapped. Squinting, she saw that a spar had snapped on the ship and crashed down onto the evil creature. "Oh, well done, Allarde! You've flattened him!"

"I don't think he's dead." Allarde frowned into the spyglass, then passed it back to Jack. "I have the feeling we haven't seen the last of him. But since he's unconscious, this is a good time to blow the ships away."

Cynthia drew a deep breath, centering her energy and calming her roiled nerves. When she took Jack's hand, he gave her a comforting squeeze. She wanted to melt into him, but this wasn't the time or place.

She nodded to indicate she was ready, so he said, "This will be quicker if we work together. Allarde, take Cynthia's hand. Tory, take mine."

Tory and Allarde obeyed so that the four of them formed a line with energy flowing freely between them. "And so we begin . . . ," Jack murmured as he began collecting weather energy.

Cynthia joined her energy to his. This time was very different from the wild exultation of shaping the storm that blasted the ships heading to Ireland. Instead of painting a huge canvas, they were creating a tiny portrait to put inside a locket. Or rather, a squall to ravage a cove.

She and Jack gathered modest winds and light rains and concentrated them in the cove. Wind began rising and waves became larger, rolling the four French ships. With wicked delight, Cynthia sent in a blast of wind that almost flipped one ship over and pushed all four toward the jagged rocks at the side of the cove.

Efforts to haul the spar from the war mage were abandoned as the captain began shouting orders to his crew. The ship lifted anchor and raised enough sail so it could use the wind to escape from the dangerous confines of the cove. As it sailed out into open water, the other three French ships followed.

"Bravo!" Tory said gleefully. "I assume you can send your squall chasing after them so they'll not be able to return?"

"That's the intention." Jack breathed a sigh of relief and put an affectionate arm around Cynthia's waist. "The last ship out of the cove was heavy in the water. I don't think it will survive in the open seas."

"They won't be back," Allarde said confidently. "The French invasion troops are on their own."

Cynthia smiled with satisfaction as she cuddled into Jack. Their weather plan had worked well, and they were rid of the war mage, at least for now. She hoped there were no more like him around.

Now it was Allarde and Tory's turn.

The Irregulars collected Elspeth and the horses and rode to a concealed spot near the hill fortress. Tory and Allarde walked the last distance on foot, circling the crag until they were at the base of the cliff on the side opposite the entrance.

Though Tory had known the crag was high, it seemed much higher now that she and Allarde were contemplating flying to the top. A top she couldn't even see because of the thick, suffocating fog.

Allarde murmured, "Are we ready?"

"I suppose." She laughed a little. "At least we start with the one part of this I know I'll enjoy."

He laughed and put his arms around her. "Dance with me, my lady?"

They'd learned that combining her ability to float with his talent for lifting great weights made it possible for them to literally dance on air. Her tension faded as their bodies and magics came together with sweet intensity.

But there was no dancing this time. Theirs was a critical mission, and Tory was not at all sure how high they could fly together.

Only one way to find out. She blended their magics into a powerful oneness, and they soared upward a few feet away from the cliff face. It felt so *right.* "I love doing this," she whispered into Allarde's ear.

"So do I." He nuzzled her hair playfully. "Magic might have cost us our normal lives, but I wouldn't give up this feeling, or you, for anything!"

"Nor would I." Tory provided the flying magic and the steering while Allarde supplied raw power—enough that reaching the fortress was not a strain.

They came even with the broken wall that surrounded the fortress. She glided into a hover and they listened. Voices were speaking in French, some of them using regional dialects so thick that Tory could barely understand what they were saying. Mostly the comments were complaints about the fog.

She was about to suggest they enter the fort when a voice sounded so close that she almost jumped out of her skin. Allarde felt her shock and his embrace tightened.

The man was swearing, "No point in keeping watch when I can't see a bloody yard into this bloody fog. Bloody wet, boring country! A bloody elephant could come over the wall and I wouldn't see it."

Another man laughed. "As long as the bloody elephant isn't armed, we'd be all right." They must have been walking a circuit around the inside of the wall, for their voices faded away.

When she thought they were safe, she squeezed Allarde's arm to signal that they were going in. Then she swooped them over the wall and toward the center of the fort, staying well above head level.

Jack had used his finder talent to locate the arsenal, and he'd drawn them a map. The building where the ammunition and powder were stored was low and stone built and a little west of the center. Finding it had seemed easier when he'd drawn his map. Now that she was here, the fortress was as confusing for her as for the French soldiers below.

"Stop!" Allarde said urgently, tightening his arms around her.

She lurched to a ragged stop and saw they'd almost crashed into a stone wall because she hadn't seen clearly around Allarde's arm. Heart pounding, she glided to the ground. They landed by the wall she'd almost hit and stayed wrapped in each other's arms as she recovered.

Voices sounded above their heads. Tory glanced up and saw an empty window above them. Surprisingly, the voice was speaking English with an Irish accent. "Why aren't these damned Welshmen rising up to join us?" the man barked. "They have every reason to hate the damned English as much as we do!"

"They don't understand yet what's best for them, Colonel O'Brian," another man said patiently. "We've been here less than a day. Once we've conquered more territory, the locals will flock to our side."

If they thought that, they didn't know the British at all. Allarde released his embrace and took Tory's hand as they walked soundlessly around the building. The ground was rough, so she had to watch her footing.

She felt the mental pressure of so many men around her. Not the whole invasion force, she thought, but a large part of it. At least half.

They rounded the corner of the building and got a clear view of the central courtyard of the old fort. Huge numbers of tents were pitched in the area, their light color making them almost invisible in the fog. Small fires were scattered through the encampment and most of the soldiers were sitting around them, huddled for warmth.

No one seemed to be looking in their direction, so Allarde turned to the right and led Tory to a low, sturdy-looking stone building that fit Jack's description of the arsenal. Allarde slid his palm across the stones, then gave a nod. She wondered if he could sense explosives inside.

Hardly daring to breathe, she followed him around the building to the front. They'd wondered if the arsenal would be under guard, and it was. But because of the dangerous gunpowder, the guards had built their fire thirty feet or so in front of the door. Half a dozen men sat around the flames, looking relaxed because of course no Britons could get into this fortress.

Praying that the combination of fog and their stealth stones would make them invisible, she followed Allarde to the building's door. The knob didn't turn, so he put a hand over the lock and opened it.

The click of the mechanism unlocking sounded as loud as a gunshot. A man by the fire raised his head. "Did you hear that?" he asked in French.

"Hear what?" another man asked, his voice slurred. "There are more'n a thousand men on this rock. Of course there's noise."

Another voice, equally slurred, said, "A good thing the scouts found that wine cellar so we have something to warm us. I'll be glad when this bloody fog is gone, though. Not natural, I tell you."

"It will be gone soon. Then we can march out and conquer Wales."

"Hardly worth the effort," the first man said glumly. "Too bad we couldn't land in Bristol like we was supposed to. That's a proper city, they say."

As the idle conversation continued, Allarde opened the door to the building and they both slipped inside. Tory closed the heavy door behind her as silently as possible.

As soon as the door was shut, Allarde created a mage light and held it high above his head. "Eureka," he whispered.

The light illuminated dozens of kegs of gunpowder and musket balls. There were also wooden boxes shaped to hold firearms. A small cannon sat against one wall. This was a temple of death. Tory said, "Time to get to work. The sooner we're done, the better. As long as we don't blow up ourselves and half the countryside!"

They'd planned ahead and brought the right tools. Allarde produced a small crowbar and pried the top off a cask of gunpowder. Tory had brought a tin cup that she used to scoop up the black powder. She then poured it into little piles in different areas of the arsenal. Allarde followed her, setting unlit candles into each pile of powder.

The last part was the most frightening. Very, very carefully, Allarde used his tinderbox to light the last candle. Then he moved around the storeroom and lit each of the candles that had been set into the powder.

Scarcely able to breathe, Tory pressed her back against the door and prayed. If a spark accidentally fell into the gunpowder, they'd be dead before they knew it.

When all the candles were lit, Allarde moved toward the door slowly to avoid stirring the air. When he reached her, Tory opened the door. Panic spiked through her when a draft from the door caused the candle flames to sway dangerously.

Biting her lip, she slipped outside and closed the door after Allarde. When and if she got to safety, she was going to curl in a ball and *howl*!

As they headed toward the back wall of the fortress, a commanding voice bellowed, "Légion Noire, form up! We're going to march out of here. The fog must be lighter lower down."

Amid complaints and thudding boots, the soldiers began forming directly across their path, so close that Tory could almost have touched one. Clutching her stealth stone, she backed away, forcing herself to move slowly so she wouldn't attract attention.

Allarde was beside her, and when they were far enough from the troop formation, they turned and headed for the nearest section of wall. They were almost there when a gruff voice shouted, "Hey! Who are you? Halt or we'll shoot!"

Tory saw a pair of guards to their right, and they were raising their weapons. She threw herself around Allarde and yanked them straight into the air. For an instant it was a struggle. Then his arms came around her and his magic joined hers and they soared over the wall, followed by two gunshots and a string of curses.

The fortress exploded.

CHAPTER 17

The blast of sound and air smashed into Tory and Allarde like a giant's fist. They hurtled toward the ground as she struggled to regain control. She grabbed as much of Allarde's magic as she could, but they were falling too hard and fast.

At the last possible moment, she was able to slow them into a tumbling roll across moist green turf. Allarde wrapped one arm around her waist and the other around her head to protect her from the worst of the impact as they skidded to a stop.

Tory's breath was knocked out and her awareness briefly grayed. When her mind cleared, she found that she was lying on top of Allarde and his beautiful, strong-boned face was still. "Justin!" she gasped. "Are you all right?"

His ridiculously long, dark lashes fluttered open. "Next time we dance"—he drew a labored breath—"please restrict yourself to stepping on my toes rather than throwing me off a mountain."

She gave a choke of laughter. "I'll try to remember that."

He rested his hand on her arm. "Perhaps you could remove your delightful self from my chest so I can breathe?"

"Sorry!" She slid to one side, feeling bruised all over. Sitting back, she gazed up at the fortress. The hilltop was ablaze and she heard shouting. "I wonder how many men died," she said somberly.

"Too many." He pushed himself to a sitting position and draped an arm over her shoulders. "But this is war. If I must choose between us and them, I choose us."

Shivering, Tory burrowed against his side. "I know you're right, but I lack the killer instinct."

"You wouldn't be you if you didn't care about people," he said softly.

They sat in silence for several minutes before she said, "Time we looked for the others and returned to the Royal Oak."

He nodded and stood, offering her a hand up. As they headed to the grove where they'd left their friends and horses, Allarde was limping a little. They were still surrounded by the heavy fog, which made it hard to be sure of their direction.

Luckily, Jack's finder magic located them. He and the girls emerged from the mists leading the horses.

"You survived!" Cynthia gave Tory a swift, hard hug.

"Ouch!" Tory squeaked at the pressure on her bruised ribs.

Cynthia stepped back hastily and pretended she hadn't forgot herself so much as to hug another female, but Tory found the gesture endearing. Her roommate's surface might still be prickly, but she was having trouble hiding her warm heart.

Elspeth said, "Do either of you need any healing? Allarde, you're limping."

"Just a twisted ankle." He helped Tory onto her pony, then mounted his own horse. "Let's get away from here. You must be tired of holding this fog, Cynthia."

"I have to work harder and harder to pull enough moisture for it." Cynthia swung onto her mount. "I *so* want to get back to the inn for a bath and a good rest!"

"I wonder how our actions will affect the French," Tory said thoughtfully as she fell into line with the others, Jack leading the way. "Maybe the idiot militia colonel will be prepared to attack now."

The colonel was still an idiot. Bran Blakesley slammed into the Royal Oak shortly after the Irregulars had arrived and were wolfing down an enormous supper. Cynthia regarded him with critical approval. In his scarlet uniform, he was almost as good-looking as Jack.

Bran crossed to their table. "We heard an explosion all the way in Carmarthen. What happened?"

"Tory and I blew up the French arsenal and Jack and Cynthia drove their ships out to sea." Allarde pulled up a chair for his friend. "You look like you can use some food."

Olwen Morgan appeared and set a plate before the newcomer. Bran stared at it for a moment. "I'd almost forgotten what food looks like. Thank you, Mrs. Morgan. I've spent the day trying to persuade Dawson to at least send out scouts to see what the French are up to, but he's determined to stay put until troops arrive from Cardiff."

"Does the colonel mind that you keep disappearing to meet us?" Allarde asked curiously.

"He's glad when I'm not around to badger him to behave like a real soldier." Bran dug into his sliced beef ravenously. "Dawson would order a retreat except he's afraid the militia and yeomanry would refuse his orders. They would, too."

"Can't you stuff the man into a barrel or something?" Cynthia suggested. "Not only is the French arsenal gone, but with the ships gone, the invasion force has no way to retreat. Even I can tell that this would be an excellent time to attack, while the French are battered and confused."

Bran gave a twisted smile. "You've just proved you have better military judgment than Dawson, but he's the ranking officer. If only my father was here! He could take command and actually do something useful!"

A thought struck Cynthia. She turned it around in her mind. Yes, this could work. She visualized the portrait she'd seen at the Blakesley manor house, then clasped Jack's hand and summoned her illusion magic. "Your wish is my command."

Bran glanced up, then gasped and shoved his chair away violently from the table. "Father? What strange magic is this?"

Jack squeezed Cynthia's hand. "Cinders, have you made me look like General Blakesley?"

"Yes, or at least like the portrait of him in the house. It's just illusion magic," she explained to Bran. "Jack can't see the illusion on himself, but everyone else sees him as your father. A good illusion should convince your idiot colonel to stand down and let your apparent father take command."

She released the illusion, and Jack was Jack again. "I used Jack, but any of us could be made to look like your father.

You'd be the best choice since you look like him and know him best."

"Impersonate an officer?" Bran said, scandalized. He hesitated, clearly torn.

"If we're going to produce a false General Blakesley, it shouldn't be Bran," Allarde said. "For one thing, everyone knows he's here and it would seem strange if he just vanished when his father showed up. Also, it could ruin Bran's military career if he's caught. If Jack or I impersonate the general, Bran can look shocked if the truth becomes known."

"We could stuff Bran in a barrel," Cynthia said helpfully. "Allarde, you can be the general, and Jack, you can be Bran."

Bran started to laugh, his expression easing so he looked young again. "Jack, I no longer envy you. Lady Cynthia is quite a handful, I see."

"Indeed." Jack grinned and draped an arm around Cynthia. "*My* handful."

Cynthia wasn't sure if she should be flattered or resent his possessiveness. Then she laughed at herself. She *loved* that Jack thought they belonged together. She looked into his teasing blue eyes and loved that he loved her.

Reminding herself that serious matters were afoot, Cynthia said to Bran, "Are you willing? I doubt a convincing impersonation of your father can be done without your military experience and knowledge of the local country and people."

Bran paused, then his expression turned to resolve. "By God, I'll do it! After we finish eating, I'll coach you on how to act like my father, Allarde. Are you good at being fearsome? My father is a general and generals need to be fearsome."

Allarde's mouth quirked. "I can manage. Dukes need to be fearsome, too."

"Generals don't travel alone," Tory said firmly. "Cynthia, can you make the rest of us look like staff officers? We can use our magic more effectively if it's needed."

"That's a good idea." Jack grinned at Tory. "At your size, you'll have to be a drummer boy."

Tory sniffed. "Cynthia can change our appearances to whatever is needed. You can be the drummer boy."

"Staff officers will be best," Bran said. "No one here will know what my father's staff members look like. You won't have to do much except follow my father and say, 'Yes, sir!' regularly. The important thing is removing Dawson from command. The head of the yeomanry is a major with good sense, and there are several experienced soldiers scattered through the ranks. Given the chance, they can make what troops we have behave like real soldiers."

"What about voices?" Bran said. "I can demonstrate my father's voice and how he uses words, but I don't see how you can sound exactly like him."

"The illusion magic includes an element of persuasion," Cynthia explained. "Because Allarde will look like your father, people will be inclined to believe that he really is your father. As long as Allarde doesn't do something completely out of character for the general, it will work."

"I hope you're right," Bran said wryly. "The French are no fools. If we give them time to regroup, we'll have a real war on our hands."

"This will work," Cynthia said, not quite as confident as she sounded. "You'll be the general's aide-de-camp in your own right, Bran. I'll make myself a major, and Jack can be a captain." She beamed at her sweetheart. "That way I can give you orders."

He slid an arm around her waist. "As if you needed an excuse to do that!"

She leaned into him, glad they could all laugh together. They needed laughter, because tomorrow would be a dangerous day.

CHAPTER 18

Allarde had been right, Tory saw. Being raised as a future duke made him a very good general. The Irregulars worked late into the night as Bran instructed them in how to be believable soldiers. Besides learning duties and behaviors, they discussed the military possibilities so Allarde wouldn't have to consult Bran at every step. The two of them were still working when Tory and the others headed up to their beds.

They all rose before dawn the next morning. After they breakfasted, Cynthia transformed the appearance of each Irregular. Allarde was so convincing that Tory had to remind herself that he wasn't really General Blakesley. Not only did he have the stern face and confident manner, but he held himself differently. Like a soldier.

Jack required only an illusion uniform and some aging in order to look like a captain. The girls required more work, but Cynthia managed beautifully. Not only did she make Tory and Elspeth look like older, taller, male versions of themselves, but she made the scarlet uniforms look convincingly travel worn.

Elspeth would claim to be a regimental surgeon if asked, while Tory was a captain and a staff courier. Tory didn't care what her rank was as long as she was close to Allarde. He had the most difficult role, and she wanted to be available if needed.

When Cynthia was finished, Bran shook his head with amazement. "You really do look like my father and a group of his staff officers. Do the illusions require a huge amount of magic, Lady Cynthia?"

She shook her head. "It takes a fair amount of power to create them, but now that the illusions are in place, the magic is maintained by the person who wears it. There's very little work involved for me."

"Fascinating business, this magic." Bran got to his feet. "Now let's ride for Carmarthen so you can displace that idiot colonel!"

It was still early when they reached the Carmarthen tavern that Colonel Dawson had chosen as his headquarters. Allarde dismounted and swept into the taproom, confidence in every line of his body. Following behind, Tory watched appreciatively as he barked, "Where's Colonel Dawson?"

Colonel Dawson was a spindly, callow-looking fellow well under thirty. Obviously his officer's commission had been bought by his family with no belief that he'd actually have to act like a soldier.

Dawson had been drinking tea at a table with other officers and a map, but at the general's question, he scrambled to his feet, his gaze fixed on the newcomer's insignia of rank. "I'm Dawson, sir." He saluted clumsily. "And you are General . . . ?"

"Blakesley," Bran said helpfully. "My father was coming home for a short leave. Naturally, as soon as I informed him of the French invasion, he realized that he was the senior officer in the area and it was his duty to take command."

"Naturally." Dawson had overcome his shock and looked resentful about losing his command, but also relieved. "Allow me to introduce you to the other officers of the militia and yeomanry." He rattled off the names of the other men present.

Allarde nodded curtly. "How many troops do we have?"

"About five hundred, sir. Reinforcements are coming from Cardiff. We've been waiting for them to arrive before attacking." He sounded defensive.

"I see the town is filled with volunteers," Allarde said. "Do you count them?"

"Of course not," Dawson said indignantly. "What can a bunch of farmers do?"

"Fight furiously for their homes, for a start. They can also provide intelligence. On my ride here, I was informed that the French ships have sailed for home and most of the enemy ammunitions stores were blown up. There were a fair number of casualties," Allarde snapped. "We must seize the moment to move against the enemy. Now I must inspect my troops."

After that, things happened quickly. With advice from Bran about who was competent, the available troops were mustered and their small army started marching west. Several roughly organized companies of volunteers marched behind, armed with ancient muskets, pitchforks, and grim determination.

Tory had never ridden at the head of an army before. It turned out to be . . . slow. But the pace was steady. By midafternoon, they'd passed Tregwilli and were nearing the French encampment.

They were heading toward a narrow lane when Allarde threw up his hand and shouted, "Halt!"

The marching companies behind raggedly obeyed. Speaking in a low voice to his staff, Allarde said, "There's an ambush ahead, where the lane narrows. The French are using their remaining resources well, but now is the time to end this." Raising his voice, he ordered, "Bring up the cannon!"

The two horse-drawn cannon were dragged up the line and set up in front of the officers. After they were loaded, Allarde commanded, "Aim high and *fire*!"

Boom! BOOM!!! The two cannons fired almost simultaneously with deafening power. As the echoes bounced menacingly among the hills, Allarde said, "Anyone have a white truce flag? It's time to parley."

Bran turned his horse to the flag bearers who marched behind the officers and borrowed a staff. After reversing it so the militia banner wasn't visible, he tied his own handkerchief to the bare end and raised it into the air. "I'm riding up with you."

Allarde nodded. "Let's go."

Tory didn't bother to ask permission. She just kicked her mount into motion and rode on Allarde's other side.

He frowned at her. Since he wore the general's appearance, it was a fearsome sight. She smiled back sunnily, and the "general's" mouth curved into an unwilling smile. "You're never going to be sensible, are you?" he said in a soft, private voice.

"Where you're concerned, never," she agreed.

Seeing Tory advance, the other Irregulars fell in behind Allarde and his companions. After a fast canter forward, Allarde reined in his horse a hundred yards before the lane where the ambush had been set up. In French, he shouted, "We will not be ambushed, so come out and talk!"

Then they waited. Voices could be heard arguing. Finally two men rode out of the lane, one holding a white handkerchief in the air.

Tory wasn't sure about French insignia, but she thought one was a major and one was a captain. The major had a bandage on one arm and his blue uniform was torn and filthy, as if he'd been thrown in an explosion. But his voice was jaunty when he said in French, "I am Major Girard and this is Captain Fournier. Do you wish to offer your surrender? We will be generous in our terms."

"I commend you on your humor, Major, but we both know who holds the winning cards," Allarde replied icily. "I am General Blakesley, commander of the South Wales Army. This is my aide-de-camp, Lieutenant Blakesley"—he gestured toward Bran, then toward Tory—"and my chief mage, Captain Mansfield."

Tory almost gasped aloud to hear of her new rank. Controlling her expression, she tried to look tough and competent and male.

Girard arched his brows as he studied Tory. "Perhaps this lad has talent, but we brought France's most powerful war mage, Colonel Levaux, with us. This invasion is only the first step. For too long Britain has waged war on France, a nation that wants only peace. We will not cease until you surrender!"

"If France wants peace, she should stop trying to impose it on her neighbors with a sword," Allarde said dryly. "Captain Mansfield, tell Major Girard the fate of his war mage, and what your mage corps did next."

Lowering her voice, she said, "Sir, the mage was defeated by our magic and badly injured. He may not have survived the encounter, but I'm not sure since he left on one of the French ships." She cleared her throat and tried to look fierce. "After the ships sailed, wc blew up the French arsenal."

Looking stunned, Girard said, "I had not known Britain has such an . . . effective mage corps."

Allarde continued, "Since you are the one to parley, Major, I wonder if Colonel O'Brian was killed when we blew up your arsenal."

Surprised that the general knew the French commander's name, Girard admitted, "He was gravely injured, but overall casualties were low. We still have crack troops, including French grenadiers, eager to fight."

"No one doubts the courage and skill of your grenadiers," Allarde replied in a deep, resonant voice. "But we have superior forces, superior weapons, and superior magic. You can kill innocent farmers, but you cannot defeat the Army of South Wales."

Girard scowled. "Bold words, General Blakesley, but only words. What matters in battle is fire and steel!"

"Oh?" Allarde glanced at Tory as if giving an order. "Captain Mansfield, give Major Girard a sample of British magic."

Before Tory could figure out what he meant, a dead tree fifty feet away crashed with a force that made the ground shake. Allarde's work.

He continued, "We also have fire."

Catching her cue, Cynthia set the tree into a blaze so fierce that the horses shied and needed calming. Even Allarde looked impressed at the fire, since he hadn't seen her do that at the Blakesley house.

Quickly smoothing his expression, Allarde continued, "We also have the most powerful weather mages in Europe, perhaps anywhere." Lightning flashed so close that the thunderclap was almost instantaneous. As it boomed thunderously through the air, Captain Fournier's horse reared and almost bolted. Tory suppressed a smile. Jack or Cynthia had been lucky to find the raw material for lightning with such perfect timing.

The French officers exchanged a glance, their faces pale. Turning back to Allarde, Girard said, "You make a compelling case, *Monsieur le Général*. We are willing to negotiate conditions for a possible surrender."

"No conditions!" Allarde barked. "I will accept nothing less than unconditional surrender. Lay down your arms and you will be treated as honorable enemies. If you refuse, defeat and death will be your fate!"

"I cannot surrender unconditionally without conferring with my fellow officers," Girard said, his voice almost apologetic.

"You may confer with them, Major Girard. But if you are sensible, you will not throw away the lives of your men pointlessly." Allarde gathered up his reins. "At eleven o'clock tomorrow morning, I will accept your unconditional surrender at Tregwilli Sands, the wide beach below the village. If you do not meet us and lay down your arms, battle will be joined." Allarde pivoted his horse and headed back to his troops, his expression unyielding.

As the British rode away, Bran shook his head in awe. "That was remarkable, Allarde. I would never have guessed you weren't my father."

Allarde exhaled with relief. "I'm glad I was convincing! I was relying on pure bluster. Are you going to tell your father that his identity was borrowed?"

Bran nodded. "This will be talked about for a long time to come, and he needs to know how he became the hero of the hour."

Tory said, "If it's going to become known, can you say that a patriotic mage pretended to be General Blakesley in order to stop the French? Anything that paints mages in a good light is worthwhile."

"I like that idea," Allarde said approvingly. "Bran, is that possible?"

"I'll discuss it with my father." Bran's brow furrowed. "Why didn't you press them to surrender today? They might well have done it."

"Accepting the surrender of a force several times the size of ours would not be easy," Allarde explained. "I'm hoping the reinforcements from Cardiff will arrive tonight. I'd rather put a real colonel or general in charge."

"Ah, good point about taking so many prisoners." Expression brighter, Bran said, "Don't worry, we'll think of something!"

Conversation ended as they joined their troops and were greeted by roars of approval. So far, so good. Tory wondered if the soldiers realized the British had a tiger by the tail. And she was in no mood to be eaten.

CHAPTER 19

The march back to Carmarthen was even slower than the march out, but there was an air of triumph. The troops were singing General Blakesley's praises, though a few complained that they wouldn't have a chance to kill any Frenchies. Tory suspected those comments came from men who'd never been shot at. Having dodged bullets on several occasions, she prayed this invasion would end without bloodshed.

As part of the general's staff, Tory and the other girls had to maintain their false identities until after the expected surrender. Most of the troops were camped outside of Carmarthen, but the officers and various officials were staying in the town, which was packed to bursting.

An efficient former sergeant in the regular army had taken on the job of assigning quarters and rations. He told Tory, Elspeth, and Cynthia they were lucky to have a room at all, sent them to a tavern for supper, and assigned them an attic room in the mayor's house, which the mayor had offered as headquarters for the general and his staff.

The tavern offered a basic meal of bread, cheese, and beer. After, they returned to the mayor's house. Allarde and the other senior officers were conferring in the drawing room but unfortunately weren't talking loudly enough for the girls to be able to eavesdrop.

As Tory followed her friends up the stairs, she wished she could have private time with Allarde, but that wasn't possible. She sensed that he was patiently dealing with an endless string of requests, complaints, and demands. She hoped Bran would be able to fill in any gaps in Allarde's military knowledge.

Ordinarily the attic rooms were for servants, and the last stairway up was narrow and twisty. Cynthia led the way with a candle. She had to duck to get through the door into the tiny attic room. As soon as Tory and Elspeth entered, Cynthia doused the candle and replaced it with a mage light.

The ceiling slanted down so sharply that the only area where Cynthia could stand straight was by the door. A narrow pallet lay against one wall and a wider one on the opposite side. There were no other furnishings except for a chamber pot and several pegs on one wall for hanging clothes.

"I've had closets that were larger," Cynthia said gloomily. "We'll have to take turns breathing."

"Not quite that bad," Tory said. "But it's certainly an advantage to be short!"

"I'm a major and outrank you two, so I'll take the single pallet," Cynthia announced as she hung her bag on one of the pegs.

Tory laughed as she hung her bag on the next hook. "Ah, but I'm the chief mage of the South Wales Army. Surely I deserve the single bed."

"And I'm the army surgeon," Elspeth pointed out. "My job is to heal your wounds if you try to scratch each other's eyes out."

"Will you accept the argument that I need more space because I'm taller, and whoever I'd share a pallet with wouldn't get any sleep?" Cynthia said sweetly.

Elspeth looked at Tory. "I don't want to sleep with her."

"Neither do I," Tory agreed. "And since Jack isn't here . . ."

"You are *bad*!" Cynthia tossed one of her boots at a grinning Tory, who barely had space to dodge.

"Now that you children have had your fun, I'm going to collapse." Elspeth sank onto the pallet, pulled off her sock, and rotated her foot.

Tory asked, "Is your ankle still hurting?"

"No, it's as good as new. But this has been educational." Elspeth pulled the sock back on. "I've used my healing magic on many people, but never had major healing done on me. I hadn't realized how much energy a body uses when it's being healed. I'll need to remember that when I work on patients of my own."

"Do you think you'll be able to fix broken bones the way Mistress Jones does?"

"She has a huge talent for bone mending that I'll never match. But having experienced her work, I think I'll be able to do a better job with bones in the future," Elspeth said thoughtfully. "I also need to work on being able to use my healing abilities even when I'm injured myself. I'm embarrassed at how useless I was!"

"Anyone who has performed as many miracles as you has no need to apologize," Tory said firmly.

Unimpressed, Elspeth crawled onto the larger pallet against

the wall and pulled up the one thin blanket. "A good thing we have hearth witch magic to warm this room, or we'd freeze."

Tory lay down next to her. "I'm exhausted, too. We've been burning masses of magic in the last couple of days."

Cynthia attached her mage light to the door and dimmed it to a faint glow. "But we've used it well. I think the demonstration of our powers may have convinced the French to surrender."

"I hope so," Elspeth said soberly. "I have no desire to burn myself out repairing broken bodies."

"I just hope the French don't find out they outnumber us three or four to one." Cynthia shook out her hair and finger-combed it before braiding it. "If they realize that, they might decide to fight."

Tory frowned into the near darkness. There was still no sign of the reinforcements from Cardiff. The South Wales Army needed a thousand or more men in scarlet uniforms. That would persuade the French.

Scarlet. She asked, "Have you noticed what most women wear here?"

"Rather dull dresses, usually with red shawls and high-crowned black hats like Quakers wear," Cynthia said promptly. "It's practically a uniform for Welshwomen."

"What might those look like at a distance? For example, if they were standing on that bluff above Tregwilli Sands."

Cynthia's eyes narrowed for a moment before understanding dawned. "Soldiers! With the red and the black, they look a bit like British redcoats!"

"Exactly!" Tory bubbled with excitement. "Do you think you could use illusion magic to strengthen that resemblance?"

Cynthia frowned. "A clever idea, but I've only ever done illusions for individuals. I haven't the faintest idea how I could change the appearance of a group of people."

"It may not be possible," Tory admitted, her initial enthusiasm fading as she considered the complexities of such a large magical working. "But think about it. Perhaps inspiration will strike."

Cynthia smothered a yawn and climbed onto her pallet. "Inspiration is in short supply just now. All I want is to *sleep*!"

Taking the hint, Tory closed her eyes and tried to turn off her mind. Despite her fatigue, she could feel the varied energy currents churning through Carmarthen. Fear, excitement, determination. She doubted that many people were sleeping soundly tonight.

She was particularly aware of Allarde's energy since he was quartered in this same house, sharing a ground-floor room with Bran and Jack. Not that Allarde had been allowed to go to bed yet. She could feel his strain.

She sent him energy in a glow of warm affection, ending with a mental kiss. He relaxed and return the invisible kiss. She dozed off with a smile.

Tory came awake abruptly, wondering if the town was under attack. After a moment she recognized that she was sensing Allarde. He was calling her mentally, and from very nearby. Trying not to wake the other girls, she eased from the pallet, padded quietly to the door, and let herself out into the freezing corridor.

Allarde was right outside. He'd let the general's illusion fade, so the dim mage light he held illuminated his own weary, handsome face.

Wordlessly he gathered her into his arms. His whole body pulsed with tension. She raised her face and kissed him with warmth and empathy. His lips softened under her, and tension faded from his long limbs. "You always know what I need," he whispered as he caressed her hair.

"You've had a very hard day," she said. "But you've managed splendidly."

"I don't know about splendidly, but at least I've been good enough." Taking her hand, he led her to the stairs so they could sit side by side with their arms around each other. "Mostly I listen to what more experienced people are saying. Pretending to be a man of few words means I haven't said enough to reveal my ignorance."

"Have you received word about the reinforcements?"

"A courier from the colonel in charge arrived earlier in the evening. The troops should be here by midafternoon."

"So if you can bluff the French just a little longer, it will be over." Tory tucked her head under his chin.

"I don't know if it will be that easy." Allarde's body tensed again. "I have a bad feeling it could go either way. Major Girard understands that his situation is precarious, but he's not yet convinced that he must surrender. If he realizes how much stronger the French forces are . . ."

When Allarde's voice trailed off, Tory prompted, "Did you see a vision?"

He swallowed convulsively. "I had a flash of the French marching down the beach toward us, then falling into firing position and attacking our forces. There would be blood on the sands. If they defeat us there and go on to take Carmarthen, it will be far harder to dislodge them."

"And this area could become a foothold for landing more French troops," Tory said, chilled as she imagined what Allarde had seen. Remembering her earlier idea, she continued, "I thought of something that might strengthen your bluff."

After she explained her idea about summoning the women of the area in their red shawls and black hats, Allarde said with interest, "That will be wonderful if Cynthia can make the local women look like additional soldiers."

"She isn't sure she can, but perhaps sleeping on the idea will help." Tory sighed. "I'm praying that before the day is over, the French will have surrendered and we can quietly hike up to the stone circle and go home." She smiled. "We've been so quick that the school will hardly notice we're gone."

He smiled agreement but shook his head. "I won't be going back through the mirror."

She stiffened. "You're running away from Lackland?"

"No, no!" His arm tightened around her. "Sorry, I'm so tired I'm not being clear. Remember I told you I was writing a letter to my father to inform him that I've made my choice, and he must disinherit me? It . . . hasn't been an easy letter to write. I think it will be better to tell him in person. Not easier, but better. This is my chance to tell him face-to-face. Since the route from South Wales to Lackland runs very near Kemperton, I'll hire a private coach and stop there on my way back to school."

"Then I'm going with you," Tory said calmly.

"No! It's going to be a difficult, painful visit." His mouth twisted. "This would all be easier if my father despised me."

She took his hand. "Easier for you, or for him?"

"For both of us. He doesn't want to disinherit me from the title and Kemperton, but since I'm choosing you and magic, he has no choice."

So Allarde had to face not only the loss of the land he loved, but the knowledge of how much his choice was hurting his parents. Her grip tightened on his hand and she said again, "I'm going with you."

As he opened his mouth to protest again, she hushed him by laying her fingers on his lips. "Justin, you are wonderfully protective and responsible, and I'm certainly not complaining since you've saved my life several times over. But protectiveness runs both ways. I can't let you face such a trial alone."

"You've saved my life, too," he said, his eyes haunted. "But you shouldn't have to suffer my family's distress."

"I may be small, Justin, but I'm not a frail child to be protected from all unpleasantness. We must be there for each other as needed." She caught his gaze, her expression intent. "Will this visit be easier for you if we're together?"

He hesitated, then nodded. "I always feel better when you're near. But I can't help wanting to protect you from misery as well as danger."

"Go right ahead and feel that way," she said cordially. "And I'll continue to ignore you when I think it best. I'm going with you to Kemperton, and that's that."

His eyes lit with laughter and he hugged her close. "Have I mentioned lately how wonderful you are?"

"You haven't, but feel free to do so any time." She tilted her head back and kissed him. "Now for bed. You have a very demanding day tomorrow, General."

Their kiss transformed from affection to tongues and hands and heat as they sprawled back on the icy wooden floor. Tory came to her senses first. "Oh, Lord," she said, panting as she ended the kiss. "My blood is boiling without even a hint of hearth witch magic!"

Justin's long, lean body had been above hers, but now he rolled to the side, ending up against the wall of the narrow corridor. Pulling her against him in a hug, he said raggedly, "You've done a brilliant job of distracting me from the anxiety of pretending I'm a general. But it's fortunate that you're wiser than I am!"

"We take turns being wise." She pulled away from him and sat up, hating every fraction of an inch that she put between them. "Once again, being with you has restored me to the point where I can face another demanding day."

"You've done the same for me." He sat up, his back against the wall, and tenderly stroked her hair, which had fallen loose over her shoulders. "The first moment I saw you, I thought, 'I'm doomed!' I had no idea doom was so wonderful."

Blushing, she got to her feet, keeping a safe distance away from him. "I think I prefer to call it fate. Sleep well, General. I'll see you in the morning."

He stood and straightened, his appearance changing to the stern visage of General Blakesley. "I really hope the reinforcements arrive soon!"

"They will," she said optimistically, and hoped that her words weren't just wishful thinking.

CHAPTER 20

It was just breaking dawn the next morning when Cynthia shook Tory awake. "I think I've worked out how to make Welshwomen look like British soldiers from a distance," she breathed. "Let's go find Bran. He'll know how to get the word out."

Tory rose quietly so as not to disturb Elspeth, but Elspeth's pale green eyes opened. She sat up and stretched like a cat. "This sounds much too interesting to miss!"

Since they'd slept in most of their clothing, it didn't take long to dress and head down the stairs. The mayor's cook had baked piles of currant buns, so they each grabbed one for breakfast and headed out.

The streets of Carmarthen were filling fast with soldiers

mustering to march out to Tregwilli Sands, where the French might, or might not, surrender. Since Bran was aide to his "father," he was at the command post in the town square. Allarde was at the center of a knot of officers and others, and Bran was standing at the edge of the group.

Tory drew Bran aside and explained, "We realized that the Welshwomen's costume of black hats and red shawls looks a bit like British soldiers, and Cynthia can use her illusion magic to enhance that. Is there any way the word can go out to the women of the area to gather along the bluffs above Tregwilli Sands?"

"You can do that? You're amazing!" Bran gazed admiringly at Cynthia, even though she was wearing her officer illusion. If it weren't for Jack, he'd be courting her, Tory suspected.

"I believe so," she replied. "Is there any place around the town where we can find a number of women and see if my magic will work? I've never tried to change a whole group all at the same time."

"If the French think we have hundreds more troops waiting, they'll be far more likely to surrender. And I know just the place where we can find out how effective your illusion magic is." Raising his voice, he called, "General Blakesley, I'll be leaving for a few minutes with several of your staff members."

Allarde nodded but said gruffly, "Make it quick, Lieutenant. We'll march within a quarter of an hour."

Bran snapped a salute. "Yes, sir!"

Then he led Tory and Cynthia away from the town center. "The Methodist minister's wife, Mrs. Llewellyn, is improvising a field hospital in a barn on the west edge of town in case there's a battle rather than a surrender. She'll have a number of volunteer nurses with her making preparations, so you can test your magic."

Tory and Elspeth had to skip to keep up with Bran's long

strides, but it wasn't far to the spacious barn where the hospital was being set up. The wide door was open, and inside a dozen or more briskly busy women were visible as they arranged tables and bandages. Most wore the local garb.

Cynthia said, "Stop and let me try this."

They halted. Cynthia closed her eyes, her face screwing with concentration as she tried her new technique. "Is it working?"

"Yes!" Tory said jubilantly. "Look!"

It now appeared as if a dozen soldiers were moving around inside the bar. The illusion was far from exact. If Tory singled out a particular figure and studied it, she could see that it was a woman. But the general impression was of a group of redcoats.

"Oh, *yes*!" Bran exclaimed. "This will do very well. Let's go talk to them. Mrs. Llewellyn is the tall woman on the left. I'll bring her out here to meet you."

He trotted into the barn, and after a brief conversation he returned with the minister's wife. Tall and middle-aged, she had an air of command. "You are magelings?" she asked, her words rolling with a musical Welsh accent. "And your magic can help us women contribute to stopping the French?"

"We hope so," Cynthia said. "Turn around and look into the barn."

Mrs. Llewellyn obeyed, then caught her breath in wonder. "That's amazing! Our men have gathered what weapons they could find and they're about to march to Tregwilli Sands. We women have wanted to do something more than stand by and roll bandages. If we can help persuade the French to surrender, we won't need these bandages!"

"To do that, a large number of women will have to assemble on the bluffs," Tory said. "So we have to spread the word as quickly as possible. Can you help with that?"

Mrs. Llewellyn grinned. "You've come to the right woman, lass." Raising her voice, she called out, "Angharad!" When a woman inside raised her head inquiringly, the minister's wife said more in Welsh.

Angharad joined them, looking intrigued, and a rapid conversation in Welsh broke out among the two women, Bran, and Elspeth. When the words slowed, Elspeth said, "They'll send offspring and servants in all directions to get the word out."

"Aye, there will be hundreds of us on those bluffs," Mrs. Llewellyn said. "Some will come to watch what happens even if they don't hear about our plan, and they'll all be part of the Women's Army of South Wales." She gave a cackle of laughter. "I suggested everyone bring a broom or rake or something else that will look like a weapon."

"Excellent thought!" Cynthia agreed. "The closer you are to soldiers, the less strain on my magic."

"Mrs. Llewellyn, since I speak Welsh, would it be helpful if I join you and help organize our troops?" Elspeth suggested.

"Aye, and time we got started." Mrs. Llewellyn turned abruptly and entered the barn, calling commands. Smiling, Elspeth followed.

"Now it's time for us to join the main column of march." Bran pivoted and headed back toward the center of the town at a pace just short of running.

Tory and Cynthia followed a little more slowly. Between breaths, Tory said, "If this works, Carmarthen should give you a tall black hat of your own!"

"Have you looked at them?" Cynthia asked incredulously. "I should only get one if this doesn't work and we lose!"

Tory laughed and hoped the South Wales Women's Army would be enough to turn the tide.

By ten thirty, the British troops were drawn up in formation on Tregwilli Sands. They faced west toward the French position. Allarde, in his role of general and commander in chief, was on his horse in front of his troops, flanked by his staff and the subordinate commanders.

Behind the officers, the militia and yeomanry stood in parallel columns with a wide space between them. Behind the official troops, volunteers whose only uniform was a red band tied on their upper arms formed two more columns.

Above on the bluff were ranks of Welshwomen in red shawls and tall black hats with brooms and mops in their hands. Since Cynthia would be using so much magic, Tory kept her horse within touching distance of Cynthia's so she could enhance her friend's power. As the time of the ultimatum approached, Cynthia looked up at the hundreds of women and exercised her illusion magic.

Tory gave a low whistle. "I'm impressed! You've made the local women into convincing British troops."

"It is working well, isn't it?" Cynthia said, pleased. "Lucky the French will be far enough from the bluff that a general impression of redcoats will do."

"Let's hope the French are sufficiently intimidated!" Tory hadn't told the other girls about Allarde's vision of a possible battle. There was no need for all of them to worry. But Tory's nerves were tied in knots.

Then they waited. Eleven o'clock was the hour Allarde had specified in his ultimatum. It came and went. Waves rolled onto the sands, then retreated. Seabirds hopped by, unimpressed by military might as they searched for rations.

By eleven thirty Tory was twitching with restlessness, but Allarde maintained his calm expression. He had the nerves to make a real general.

Then she heard a sound in the distance. "Drums," she breathed. "I hear *drums*."

Boom. Boom! BOOM!!! The drums grew louder and louder, sending ominous vibrations through the noonday air.

The French troops appeared in the misty distance as they approached along the wide sweep of sand toward the British. Major Girard rode at the head of the column with a handful of other officers. They looked as if they were marching to war, heads up, banners flying, and no white flag in sight.

Tory barely breathed, knowing the next moments were crucial. Even now, Girard might shout the order for his men to drop into firing position and pour a fusillade of musket balls into the British formation. She had a brief, horrific vision of broken bodies sprawled across the sands and the incoming tides turning red with blood.

Sensing the catastrophic possibilities, Allarde stood up in his stirrups to his full, impressive height. Cupping one hand around his mouth, he called out in a thundering voice, *"Surrender, Major Girard!"* He swept his hand toward the bluffs on his left. "You cannot hope to defeat a force of our size on our home ground!"

Tory felt Cynthia's magic surge, and the hundreds of figures at the top of the misty bluff became even more convincing ranks of British troops in scarlet jackets and tall black shako hats with muskets at the ready. Tory would have wondered if the reinforcements really had arrived if she hadn't felt the huge strain in Cynthia.

She unobtrusively nudged her horse closer so that her calf touched her friend's. As she added more magic, Cynthia's tension eased to the point where she should be able to maintain the illusion for hours.

Girard turned his head and lifted a hand to shade his eyes against the sun. His posture stiffened and his face twisted with anguish as he accepted that he must surrender his forces. War and peace had been weighing in the balance, just as Allarde had foretold.

Tory exhaled, dizzy with relief. There would be no blood on the sands today. The French halted two hundred yards away, close enough that Tory could see the expressions of individual soldiers. They looked grimly resigned.

Girard dismounted and walked toward the British, several of his officers accompanying him on foot. Allarde also dismounted and moved forward, Tory and the other staff and senior officers a step behind.

When the commanders met, Major Girard bowed from the waist, then pulled his sword from its sheath. Holding the blade with both hands, he offered the weapon to Allarde. "Sir, my sword. I ask that you allow us the traditional honors of war."

Tory saw Allarde's hesitation and guessed that he didn't know what the traditional honors of war were. Certainly Tory didn't.

Bran said smoothly, "General, I recommend the French be allowed to keep their banners, for they have not been defeated in battle, but they must lay down their weapons."

Allarde nodded gravely as he accepted the sword. "It shall be as my aide says, Major Girard. You surrender because you are a wise officer who will not lead his men to death for no reason. But your troops were not defeated, and they may carry their banners into captivity. It's likely that you will be exchanged for British prisoners before too many months have passed."

"I pray it shall be so." Girard stepped back and saluted. Allarde passed the sword to Jack, who was on his other side, and returned the salute. Tory was intrigued by all the formality. She hadn't known that surrender had its own set of rules.

Allarde glanced at her and for an instant let his enormous

relief show. Then he turned stern again as he began to oversee the laying down of arms. Long lines of French troops marched between the columns of British militia and yeomanry, then laid their muskets on the sand in piles that grew higher and higher.

The surrender was almost complete when marching music was heard in the distance. "'Rhyfelgyrch Gwŷr Harlech'!" Bran exclaimed joyfully. "'The March of the Men of Harlech'! It's the Welsh marching song. The reinforcements are almost here!"

The sound made Tory's heart leap. The Cardiff troops had arrived in time to take over the French prisoners. The Irregulars could go home.

The troops appeared from the east, marching down the wide expanse of sand. They were dusty and showed signs of having pushed themselves to the limit to get here, but they maintained good order. They halted by the growing mass of French prisoners.

"It's time to turn over my temporary command," Allarde said as he remounted and rode to meet the new arrivals. Naturally his staff followed. Tory had come to realize that following the leader was what staff did.

The commander of the reinforcements was a stocky colonel with a muscular build and shrewd eyes. He looked like a real officer, not someone who had bought a commission. Allarde rode up to him. "Sir, I relinquish command of my forces. It's time I returned to my own duties."

As they exchanged salutes, the colonel said, "Good that you were here, General Blakesley. After we've got this lot safely locked up"—he glanced at the French prisoners—"join me for dinner so you can explain how you persuaded a much larger force to surrender."

Tory winced internally. The colonel must know the real General Blakesley. This could prove awkward.

Allarde inclined his head politely. "I thank you for the kind invitation, but I must be off immediately."

The colonel looked puzzled. "Surely you can wait until tomorrow, Blake?"

"I'm afraid not. It's good I happened to be here when the French landed, but I can't neglect my own command." Allarde nodded toward Bran. "My aide-de-camp here will be happy to provide you with the details."

The colonel nodded approvingly. "I see you put your Royal Marine training to good use, lad."

"I've done my best, Colonel Griffith," Bran replied as he snapped a salute.

Griffith chuckled. "You're too junior an officer to invite to dinner, but as my godson, you can come and tell me all about it."

The colonel was Bran's godfather? The sooner the Irregulars got out of here, the better! Allarde obviously agreed as he said farewell to Griffith.

As the colonel rode off to take charge of the surrender, Allarde turned to Bran and offered his hand. "We made a good team, didn't we?"

Bran shook his hand fervently. "I already owed you a debt. Instead of being able to balance the scales, I now owe you even more."

"Since neither of us wanted to see a French invasion succeed and all our skills were needed to make this happen, I'd say we're even," Allarde said with a smile. "We'll be off now. I hope there wasn't too much damage done to your house."

Bran grimaced. "My mother is *not* going to be happy to hear about this, but at least they didn't burn the place down."

He and Allarde exchanged salutes, then Bran headed off to help with the surrender. Allarde collected the Irregulars with a glance. Then he rode away from the crowded beach, still in character as the terse general.

When they were well out of sight and earshot, Allarde halted and they gathered in a circle. "That was close!" Jack exclaimed. "It would have been awkward to explain who we really are, and that you aren't General Blakesley. But we did well."

Elspeth asked gravely, "Did blocking this invasion eliminate the danger of Britain being conquered by the French?"

"No," Allarde said, his voice flat. "There is worse to come."

Some of the exhilaration faded. "If there are more threats, we'll just have to deal with them as they occur." Cynthia shifted restlessly in her saddle. "But for now, I'm ready to head for home. I want to sleep in a comfortable bed tonight!"

"Rather than walk, we can ask the farmer who owns these horses to ride out to the stone circle with us," Elspeth suggested. "Then he can bring our mounts home."

"Tory and I will go with you and return the horses." Allarde released the illusion of General Blakesley and became himself again. "We're returning to Lackland by coach so I can visit my parents at Kemperton."

After a moment of startled surprise, Cynthia said, "You're not taking us back through the mirror, Tory?"

"You don't need me," Tory said. "Elspeth got you safely to France, so I shouldn't think she'd have a problem hopping from here to Lackland."

Elspeth nodded. "But you'll be gone for days more, Tory. Allarde's absence can be excused on the grounds of a summons from his father or some such, but you've claimed to be sick in your room before. The school authorities will surely get suspicious."

Tory shrugged. "I suspect that as long as we don't do anything obvious that requires us to be punished as an example to the other students, we'll be left alone. If I'm questioned, I'll say that I accidentally wandered into mysterious tunnels under the abbey, and it took me days to find my way out."

"Which is certainly plausible," Jack said with a grin.

Tory glanced down at herself. All three of the girls had long since given up using the gown illusions Cynthia had created. Since they were riding astride and pretending to be army officers, it was easier to stay with the trousers they actually wore. "I wish I'd brought some proper clothes with me. Allarde's parents will not be impressed."

"They've met you before, and they both like you," Allarde said with a warm smile. "What you wear this time won't matter."

Wrong. Even if his parents didn't care, Tory did. Confidence mattered, and she needed to look like a girl who was worth the renunciation of a dukedom.

"Perhaps I can buy a simple used gown here, then enhance it with the illusion stone Cynthia gave me." She dug out the stone and imagined herself in the illusion gown. A shiver of magic moved over her.

The stone still worked, because Cynthia remarked, "It looks odd for you to be suddenly sitting astride a horse in a gown, but at least it's proper female attire. Illusion gowns are convenient since they never need washing or ironing. If you use the illusion with a real gown, it won't take much magic at all for you to maintain it."

Tory handed the stone to Cynthia. "Could you add a second illusion to the stone? One that shows me dressed appropriately for a family dinner with a duke."

Cynthia folded the stone in her palm and closed her eyes. After a few moments of concentration, she handed it back. "This should work. I added a fancy blue gown that will go well with your eyes. I also made the existing day dress fashionable enough that you won't look like a housemaid."

"For which I am grateful." Tory mentally thought of herself in an evening dress. Again magic tingled over her skin.

"Oh, very nice," Jack said admiringly. "That really makes Tory's eyes shine like the evening sky. You do such good work, Cinders."

"Indeed," Allarde said with a slow, appreciative smile for Tory.

Tory closed her eyes and thought of herself in the new day dress. When she'd done so, Cynthia commented, "Good. You look like a female of means and taste."

"You could make an excellent living for yourself creating faux gowns," Elspeth said with a laugh. "A woman who aspires to fashion could hire your services to make it appear she has a huge wardrobe."

Cynthia chuckled. "I can have a shop and call it Lady Cynthia's Weather Work and Fashion Consultancy."

"Now that we have everyone sorted out, it's off to the stone circle," Jack said. "I'm ready to go home!"

So was Tory. But she'd be taking the long way round.

CHAPTER 21

Tory and Allarde escorted their friends to the stone circle, watched them go through the mirror, and waited to receive a message confirming that they'd made it safely home. Then they led the borrowed horses back to their owner.

It was almost dark by then, so Mr. Gwillim, the farmer who'd loaned them the mounts, invited them for dinner. He and his son had loaded their fowling pieces and stood with the volunteers while his wife and two daughters had worn their red shawls and black hats in ranks of women on the bluff, so they were in a celebratory mood.

The Gwillims also wanted to hear more about the magelings' adventures. Tory and Allarde described driving off the French ships and invading the French fortress to blow up the arsenal, but Allarde's impersonation of the general was not mentioned. The real General Blakesley could take the credit if he wanted to.

Deciding to take advantage of the goodwill, Tory asked if there was an old gown she could buy. Gaenor, the younger Gwillim daughter, was happy to produce a morning gown she'd outgrown. "I was going to put a ruffle on it to make it longer," she explained, "but it's happy I'll be to give it to one of the heroines of Tregwilli!"

The gown was pale blue linen, simple in style but sturdy and well made. Tory said doubtfully, "Are you sure? If you lengthen this, it will be good for years longer."

"If I give it to you, my mam will have to buy me the fabric to make another," Gaenor explained. "There's the prettiest calico print at the draper's shop in Carmarthen!"

Tory laughed. "In that case, I'll accept it most gratefully."

"I'll give you a shift as well. 'Tis mended but clean."

Tory gave Gaenor a swift hug. "I'll keep both forever in remembrance of the South Wales Women's Army!"

The Gwillims were still celebrating when Tory and Allarde walked back to the Royal Oak. Tory was so tired that she stripped off her male garments, donned the soft muslin shift, and went right to bed. But she couldn't sleep. The bedroom seemed very empty without Cynthia and Elspeth.

She gazed into the darkness and realized that some of her restlessness was Allarde's. Impersonating a commanding general had been hugely stressful, and he was about to return to his beloved home and renounce his inheritance. Of course he was tied in knots.

With Jack gone, Allarde had the boys' room to himself. Tory climbed from the bed and wrapped a blanket around her shoulders against the cold. Sometimes a blanket was just easier than using magic. Then she slipped from the room and walked quietly down the corridor to Allarde's bedroom. The lock was simple and it took her only a moment to unlock the door and step inside.

"Justin?" she said softly.

He sat up in the bed, a shadow among shadows. "Is something wrong, Tory?"

She took a deep breath as she gathered her nerve. "We both agree that we must wait until we can be . . . fully together. But it's dreadfully wasteful to be sleeping in separate beds when we have this opportunity to share one." When he hesitated, she added uncertainly, "We spent a night together in France."

"Fully dressed on the rocky floor of a cave," he said tautly. "Lying in a real bed would be . . . more challenging."

Her face burned in the darkness. "I'm sorry, I shouldn't have suggested this." She turned to leave.

"No!" He leaped from the bed and caught her before she opened the door, pulling her back against him when he wrapped his arms around her waist. He rested his cheek against the top of her head. "It will be worth every shred of challenge to have you with me."

The blanket fell from her shoulders as she turned in his arms. They held each other for long minutes while tension dropped away.

Allarde skimmed his open hand down her spine, her waist, and her backside, his palm warm through the thin fabric of her shift. "I love your curves," he murmured. "Like an hourglass. Petite and perfect."

Because he wore only his drawers and a loose shirt, she was equally aware of his body. Tall, lean, broad-shouldered, and muscular. She pressed herself into him. Yes, tonight would be challenging—but indeed worth it.

With a half-laughing groan, he took her hand and led her to the bed, tucking her against his side so that her head rested on his shoulder. "Thank you for coming, Tory," he whispered. "For helping me make it through the night."

Smiling, she settled into sleep.

Tory woke early the next morning so she could return to her room before the Morgans woke. Allarde caught her hand before she left and kissed it. "Properly speaking, the gentleman should be the one leaving the warm bed for discretion's sake. But since this is my room, I must allow you to return to yours. Fare thee well, my lady."

She tugged her hand away and brushed her fingertips through his tousled dark hair. "Not farewell for very long. Till we break our fast, my lord."

She returned to her room with a smile on her face.

It was the high point of a long day. By dawn, they'd had their breakfast and were heading east toward Swansea in a hired local carriage. In Swansea, Allarde hired a yellow bounder—one of the fast, yellow-bodied post chaises that changed teams of horses every few miles. Though expensive, a post chaise was the fastest way to travel long distances.

Allarde had always had as much money as he needed no matter what happened. Tory wondered if that would be true after he was disinherited. No matter. They'd manage even if his father cut him off without a shilling.

Even in a post chaise, traveling from western Wales to Shropshire was a long day. Tory let her hair fall loose around her shoulders and clung to a handhold by the window as the carriage rocked and rattled its way east.

The weather was dry, courtesy of their weather mage friends. Jack had promised them a smooth trip back to Lackland, which made for swift progress. Even so, night was falling by the time they approached Kemperton.

The landscape outside was a dark blur to Tory until Allarde made a soft sound in the darkness. It was a sigh of—relief, perhaps. Recognition. Welcome. When Tory glanced a question, he said, "We've just entered Kemperton."

In the dimness of the carriage interior, Tory could see the faint glow of magic that bound him to the land. Her heart twisted. She'd tried to end their relationship rather than deprive him of this deep, abiding connection with his family home. It hadn't worked, but she still hated knowing he would lose all this because his chosen mate was another mage rather than a safely mundane girl. Quietly she said, "You can still change your mind."

"No." His hand closed over hers in the darkness. His voice deep, he said, "I'm a stubborn fellow, you know. I've chosen you, and I won't change my mind. Ever."

She'd known he'd say that, but she'd had to try. She raised their joined hands and pressed a kiss on the back of his fingers, but she said no more.

A few hundred yards short of the vast stone house, Allarde signaled for the coach to stop. "I'd like to walk the last distance," he said to Tory. "I'll meet you at the house."

"I'll walk, too. I need to stretch." She hesitated. "Unless you'd rather be alone?"

"I'm always glad to have you near." The carriage stopped and he climbed down, then helped her to the ground. Since they had almost no luggage, he'd consolidated their possessions into one bag, which he slung over his shoulder.

After he paid off the postilion for the carriage rental, the post chaise turned and rumbled away. Rather than starting to walk immediately, he gazed at the house where he'd been born. Faint moonlight sculpted the strong planes of his face, and the magical bond that connected him to the land was palpable.

"The land endures," he said softly. "It doesn't need me. My cousin George, who is next in line to inherit, will surely come under Kemperton's spell."

Perhaps, but she had her doubts that the unknown cousin would connect as deeply as Allarde. She asked, "Is there any part of the estate that isn't entailed? Perhaps you could build a home of your own here."

"Every square foot is entailed to the current Duke of Westover." He shrugged. "I doubt I could be happy living in a corner while knowing that Kemperton belongs to another. It's better I move away and get on with my life as a commoner."

She studied the dramatic stone turrets and central tower of Kemperton Hall. The structure had been built over centuries, but the warm gray stone gave the different styles a sense of unity. In the moonlight, it was mysterious and rather haunting.

"The land here is almost like a living being, isn't it?" Tory said. "It has an awareness that's deep and very inhuman, but real."

"You feel that?" he asked with surprise.

"Yes. The mirror has a similar quality of being alive but utterly different."

"I knew you'd understand," he murmured.

When he reached for her hand, she said, "Give me a moment to create the illusion that this modest farmer's daughter's gown is elegant enough for a proper young lady."

He smiled. "You always look like a lady."

"If so, sometimes a tattered one!" She cradled the illusion stone in her palm and imagined herself dressed appropriately for a family dinner with a duke. Thinking that Allarde needed some distraction, she visualized the décolletage as shockingly low.

Allarde's eyes widened. "You'd best raise the neckline, or I'll be so distracted that I'll forget what I came to say!"

She drew a finger higher across her chest and visualized. "Did the neckline become more modest?"

He swallowed hard. "Yes, though watching you rearrange yourself is distracting in its own right."

Smiling to herself, she raised her hem to her knee and visualized her half-boots into dainty kid slippers. "Cynthia did a marvelous job charging the illusion stone. I can make any adjustments I want to her original image." She glanced at him sideways and saw that he was staring at her bare leg.

"You give the illusion magic much to work with." Suddenly he laughed. "You're trying to take my mind off the upcoming interview, aren't you, my little witch? And being most successful!" He offered his arm. "Shall we walk to Kemperton Hall?"

"Indeed we shall." She dipped a laughing curtsy before taking his arm. The sounds of the retreating carriage faded and they were alone in the cool, silent night.

Both of them became sober as they walked the driveway to the great house. This wouldn't be Allarde's last visit to Kemperton, for he'd surely return when his parents died. But it was his last walk across the land as heir to the ancient title and property.

Though the night was cold, a touch of hearth witchery kept them warm. There was no hurry since they were not expected. Allarde could take as long as he needed.

They reached the steps and ascended to the portico. Allarde wielded the heavy, lion-headed knocker. It boomed menacingly.

The footman who opened the door was startled to see the young master, but he recovered quickly. Bowing, he said, "Lord

Allarde. Lady Victoria." He must have seen Tory when she'd visited at Christmas. "The duke and duchess are dining."

Allarde handed the servant his travel bag. "The family dining room?" When the footman nodded, Allarde continued, "Then we shall join them there."

Tory took his arm again and they headed into the depths of the great house. A tall antique mirror hung on the wall of the corridor. The mirror was old and discolored, but reflective enough for Tory to see the two of them as they walked past.

Oddly, the mirror showed the illusion of Tory, not how she looked in her plain gown. She liked seeing the deep blue garment Cynthia had imagined for her. She looked cool and elegant, and Allarde was handsome beyond belief.

The footman preceded them and announced, "Lord Allarde and Lady Victoria Mansfield," when they reached the dining room.

There was a suspended moment as the Duke and Duchess of Westover looked up and saw their son with the mageling girl whose existence meant that Allarde would be seen as too much of a mage to be worthy of a dukedom. The duke inhaled sharply and the duchess made a small, anguished sound as she covered her mouth with one hand.

Allarde bowed. "Sir. Madam."

Tory curtsied gracefully, wishing she didn't have to see the mingled shock and grief on his parents' faces. Allarde had been a late, only child. His father was easily old enough to be his grandfather, and his mother was not much younger. They both doted on him, and justly so, for they could not have had a more admirable son. Until his magic appeared and their love collided with the harsh realities of society.

Despite his height and erect posture, the Duke of Westover looked frail and every bit his age when he rose to his feet. "I see your choice has been made, Allarde." A muscle jerked in his cheek. "I shall inform my London solicitor to draw up the disinheritance papers."

"I'm sorry, sir," Allarde said softly. "After visiting here at Christmas, Tory tried to end the relationship because she did not want me to be estranged from you. But . . . we couldn't stay apart."

His father's smile was deeply sad, but not angry. "I can see that."

Tory realized that she and Allarde were holding hands. Tightly. Allarde glanced down, his warm gaze meeting hers. "Tory and I are connected on every imaginable level. That's a bond too rare and precious to be severed."

The duke sighed. "There is no more to be said. Morton, set the table with two more places. I imagine you are tired and hungry after your journey from Lackland."

Tory said, "We came not from Lackland, but from near Carmarthen. Your son was instrumental in bluffing a much larger French invasion force into surrendering to the local volunteer troops."

His father's bushy white brows rose. "Well done! I'd heard of the invasion, and this afternoon a courier brought word that it had been foiled, but no details. You used magic to do that?"

"Yes, but I was only one person," Allarde said uncomfortably. "Five of us magelings came from Lackland, and we all contributed to the British victory. Even without us, I'm sure the Welsh would have triumphed, though it might have taken them longer and they would have suffered more casualties."

"I look forward to hearing more." The duchess had regained her composure, only her eyes showing her sadness. "But first, Allarde, come and give your mother a kiss."

"I'm grateful that you aren't throwing both of us from the house," Allarde said with a choke in his voice as he obeyed his mother's order. Tory saw the tenderness of their embrace and ached for them and his father.

"Though you cannot become the next duke, your father and I will insure that you're left comfortably off," his mother said. "I'll not see my son suffer because of your magical talents." She cocked an elegant silver brow at Tory. "You needn't fear starving, though you may not be able to afford many gowns as elegant as the one you wear."

It was a nice compliment for an imaginary gown. "What is a wardrobe compared to Justin?" Tory said. "Even if neither of us inherits anything, we are capable of supporting our own household."

His mother nodded approval for the sentiments. While they talked, two footmen had brought in place settings and were swiftly arranging the heavy silverware and splendid porcelain and glassware. Even here in the family dining room, spaces between settings were wide.

As the butler poured wine, the duchess gestured to Tory. "Please sit by me."

As Tory obeyed, the duchess said with a twisted smile, "I believe you'll be a true and devoted wife to my son. I just wish you weren't also cursed with magical power."

"If I were normal, we would never have met," Tory said as she took her chair. "And without our magic, we would be different people."

Allarde nodded agreement as he sat by his father. "We are what we are. I can't imagine forswearing my power, nor can I imagine Tory other than as magically lovely and honorable as she is."

After that, no more was said about disinheritance. Magic was discussed only in respect to their adventures in Wales. Tory could see in the faces of Allarde's parents how proud they were of their son, and how saddened by the choices he had made.

It was all wonderfully civilized—except for the deep pain she felt from everyone at the table.

CHAPTER 22

Lackland, 1940

Nick entered the kitchen in a gust of raw autumn air. As he dropped his book bag on the floor, he asked, "What is the source of all these wonderful smells?"

Rebecca glanced up from the broad kitchen table, resigned to the fact that she must have matzo meal on her face. "Tonight is the Shabbat, so I'm making matzo ball soup and Polly is preparing a jam tart."

Nick discovered the two loaves of braided bread on a side table. "Is this Shabbat bread? I like the way it's braided."

"It's challah," Polly explained. "We made it yesterday after school when you were playing rugby." She grinned. "And we hid it so you wouldn't eat it."

He tapped the shiny brown surface of a loaf with his knuckles. It made a hollow sound. "I am wounded by your lack of trust."

"Oh, we trust you," Rebecca said with a laugh. "It's your appetite we don't trust."

"Are there always special foods for the Shabbat dinner?"

"Shabbat, the Sabbath, is a holy day," Rebecca explained. "'Holiday' means 'holy day,' you know. A joyous day for celebrating family and for prayer. Your Sabbath, Sunday, is similar, though Christians are often busier on Sundays."

"Especially with a war on." All three of them unconsciously stopped and listened for the sound of airplanes. Somewhere in their sky, there were always airplanes.

"My parents often work at their research laboratory on Shabbat," Rebecca said soberly. "Their research is too important to take much time off."

Nick nodded, understanding. "The book your mother sent said that Shabbat runs from sunset Friday to just after sunset on Saturday. To the time where it's dark enough to see three stars in the sky?"

"Yes, but one must often guess at sunsets and stars in cloudy Britain!" Rebecca stepped into the cool pantry to retrieve a bowl of matzo dough that had been chilling.

"Is there anything I can do?" Nick glanced around the kitchen. "Ah, the candlesticks need polishing. That's part of the Shabbat ritual, isn't it?"

She nodded. "We give thanks for the candles, for the wine, and for the bread."

"Wine?" Polly asked hopefully.

"It may be symbolic wine," Rebecca said. "I'm not sure what your mother intends. She was considering cider, which is easier and less alcoholic."

Nick dug some metal polish from a drawer and started cleaning the silver candlesticks. "Can you teach us the Shabbat prayers? They're like songs in Hebrew, aren't they?"

"Yes, and they'll take time to learn," Rebecca warned. She scooped a spoonful of matzo dough from its bowl, dipped her hands in a pot of water, and quickly rolled the dough into a sphere about the size of a golf ball.

As she dipped her hands in water and rolled another, Nick said, "I presume those are matzo balls. Are they like little biscuits?"

"More like Jewish dumplings. They're made from matzo meal, which is not something that can be bought in Lackland, so my mother sent a box from Oxford. The matzo balls have to be poached in simmering water before they're added to the chicken soup we made earlier." Rebecca wetted her hands and formed another. "The trick is to make them light, but substantial enough that you know you're eating something."

"I can see there's an art to making them," Nick observed.

Rebecca thought wistfully of the many times she'd helped her mother make matzo balls. "Mothers teach daughters and down through the generations. Matzo ball soup is lovely. You'll see."

Polly, who was spreading raspberry preserves on the crust of the tart, said, "Mum was so clever to start keeping chickens before the war started. Not to mention the tons of fruit preserves we put up." She gave an exaggerated shudder. "I resented making the preserves and I do not love taking care of chickens, but the results are worth it."

"Where did the chicken stock come from?" Nick asked. "I don't recall our having chicken lately."

"One of the old hens wasn't laying and she met her fate," Mrs. Rainford said as she breezed into the kitchen with a heavy book bag over her shoulder. "Yesterday we boiled up the old girl and made stock for the soup with enough left to make stewed chicken with gravy and potatoes and vegetables."

Nick lifted the lid on the stewpot on the back of the stove and sighed blissfully. "Are Shabbat dinners always so fine?"

"Sometimes even better. You should taste my mother's brisket!" With food rationing, there would be no beef brisket anytime soon. Rebecca continued, "Always we try to make the meal a little special with whatever is available." There had been no way they could make the prison food special, but at least all the prisoners had sung the Shabbat prayers together, which helped keep their spirits up.

She laughed suddenly, remembering better times. "My mother said that all Jewish holidays boil down to, 'They tried to kill us, we survived, let's eat!' "

Everyone burst into laughter and preparations for dinner came to a dead halt. When Nick finally sobered, he caught Rebecca's gaze. "That's a history lesson as well as a joke, isn't it?"

She nodded. "The history of my people."

The moment of connection between them ended when Mrs. Rainford said, "That history is definitely worth a chicken for our first Shabbat." She set the book bag on the floor and hung her raincoat, hat, and scarf on a hook by the door. "Sorry I'm so late. The faculty meeting ran longer than I expected. It must be almost time to light the candles, Rebecca?"

Rebecca glanced out the kitchen window at the nearly dark sky. The day had been rainy and overcast, which made it hard to judge sunset. "Soon," she said. "It's certainly time to draw the blackout curtains."

As Mrs. Rainford closed the curtains, Rebecca asked, "Will you light the candles when we're ready, Mrs. Rainford?"

"Shouldn't you be the one? You're the only person who understands the ritual and knows the prayers."

"I can sing the prayer anywhere at the table." Rebecca used a slotted spoon to gently place her matzo balls into the simmering water one at a time. "The candles are usually lit by the mother because she is the heart of the household. As you are."

Mrs. Rainford smiled. "In that case, I shall be most honored."

Rebecca adjusted the heat so the matzo balls wouldn't boil too vigorously and fall apart. "By the time we've changed, the soup will be ready. Everything else is done, except for Polly's tart."

"And this will be baked by the time dinner is finished." Polly slid the sheet holding the jam tart into the oven. She was back in school again and looking so healthy that it was hard to remember she'd recently been at death's door.

Nick opened the kitchen door that led to the dining room. "Dressing up and eating in the dining room as well! This really is a special occasion."

"It's the first Shabbat dinner I've had in over a year." Rebecca looked down, ashamed of the catch in her throat. When they'd escaped from France, her parents and brother had gone almost immediately to Oxford to join Dr. Florey's research project. There had been no opportunity to celebrate a Shabbat together.

She missed her family. In particular, she missed her father, who had been separated from the rest of the family while he was forced to do research for the Nazis.

Seeing her expression, Mrs. Rainford put an arm around her shoulders and gave her a gentle squeeze. "Then we'll do our best to make this a good one."

Having Shabbat with the Rainfords was a mixed blessing. Rebecca enjoyed the familiar ritual, but she missed her family the whole time. She wanted to weep when Mrs. Rainford lit the candles because the silver candlesticks were very similar to the ones her mother used to light.

Those candlesticks, which had been in her mother's family for three generations, were now gone forever. When the Weisses had been arrested and dragged from their home, they'd had only the clothes on their backs. Rebecca had sometimes wondered what had happened to their house and all their possessions.

She tried not to think about it. She was amazingly lucky that she and her family escaped safely to England. That had been entirely because of Nick, who'd led the mission to find her father.

In the candlelight, his face was intent and interested. He'd even learned the first two lines of the Hebrew prayer of thanks for the candles, though his accent was terrible. The chasm between Jew and gentile didn't seem as wide tonight.

After Rebecca sang the prayers for the wine and the bread, Nick took his first cautious bite of a matzo ball. "This is good!" He immediately took a larger bite.

"I said you'd like it," she said smugly.

"You did," he agreed. "But it takes an act of faith to bite into something that looks like a poached cricket ball!"

Their shared laughter set the tone for the Shabbat, and the peacefulness and joy were familiar even though the faces around the table weren't her family. No one was in a hurry to finish and do homework or read, and the wireless was turned off.

As Polly cut and served the jam tart, Mrs. Rainford said, "We haven't really discussed this, Rebecca, but I've assumed that during the Christmas school break you'd like to go up to Oxford and stay with your family?"

Rebecca almost dropped her dessert. "I can do that? It's possible?"

"Of course," Mrs. Rainford said, surprised. "You just take the train from Dover to London, then another train to Oxford. Half a day's travel at most. Your English is so fluent now that I'm sure you'd have no problem."

Rebecca locked her shaking hands together under the table. "I didn't know traveling on the railroad could be so easy and safe." Such travel wouldn't have been easy in France, and it certainly wouldn't have been safe. Not for a Jewish girl in wartime.

"I could escort you up there," Nick suggested. "My friend Hal is a student at Magdalen College. He's invited me to stay with him and look around a bit. I'd like to go to Magdalen, if I ever get to university."

With the war, he'd probably go into the military as soon as he finished school, but they didn't talk about war tonight. "That would be lovely. If you permit, Mrs. Rainford?"

"Having company for your first venture on the British railroads would be good," Mrs. Rainford said. "Nick will come home for Christmas, of course. But if you're not confident traveling alone, one of us can come up and accompany you back here at the end of your holiday."

"You are all so kind!" Blinking back tears, she started on her jam tart. The raspberry preserves had the scent and the flavor of summer.

A week in Oxford with her family would be a great gift. She needed them to be a family again. She could also test her parents' feelings about her keeping company with a gentile boy.

As they finished off Polly's jam tart with their tea, Nick said, "I understand the Shabbat better now. A whole day of peace, of special meals, of being with one's family—it's very spiritual."

"It really is," Polly said. "And I definitely like the matzo ball soup!"

"With all the demands on our time, I don't think it's practical to treat all of Saturday as a proper Shabbat," Nick said. "But I'd like to do this every Friday evening. If that's all right with you, Rebecca?"

She nodded vigorously. "This makes me feel more myself. More Jewish, even though I am the only Jew here."

Polly grinned. "And I like the special food."

"Same time next week, then." Nick pinched out one of the candles.

"No!" Rebecca exclaimed. "The candles must be allowed to burn out naturally."

"Sorry," he said hastily. "I didn't know."

"I forgot to tell you." She leaned forward and lifted the candlestick that he'd pinched out and touched the blackened wick to the candle that still burned.

The wick flared and joined the flame of the other candle, and in the heart of the fire she saw images. Soldiers sailing across the English Channel, disembarking in England with their evil weapons, shooting and burning and killing. She cried out and almost dropped the candlestick.

"What's wrong?" Mrs. Rainford placed a worried hand on Rebecca's arm.

When she did, the image clarified. Rebecca swallowed hard. "You haven't given me the lesson in scrying yet, but it's possible to see images in flames, isn't it?"

"Oh, yes," Mrs. Rainford said. "You've seen something?"

Rebecca nodded. "I saw soldiers invading England. Sailing over the Channel and wreaking death and destruction. At first I thought it was the Germans, but it wasn't." She took a deep breath to steady her nerves. "When you touched my arm, the vision became clearer. It was French troops. Napoleon's Grande Armée."

"Allarde's vision," Polly said in a hushed voice. "Is the invasion he saw taking place now?"

"Not yet, I think." Rebecca closed her eyes and analyzed what she'd seen and felt. Opening them, she looked across the table at Nick, her gaze stark. "You and I are going to 1804."

CHAPTER 23

Lackland, 1804

Tory and Allarde had held hands for most of the width of England. He wasn't talkative during the two days of travel, but she knew he was glad for her company.

They were nearing Lackland when he said, "Not long after my magic appeared, my father told me how difficult it would be if I were a lord who was known to be a mage. I would be ignored by my peers, given the cut direct, insulted to my face and behind my back. There was a mage baron from Yorkshire who took his own life because he could no longer bear the persecution."

Tory shuddered. "I've never really understood why so many aristocrats despise those of us with magic. Except for the power, we are exactly the same as them."

"That's the reason right there," he said quietly. "We are exactly like them, but we can do things they can't do. No amount of money and no aristocratic title can create a weather mage. When average people have power, a nobleman can still feel superior because of his birth. But we have the birth and the power. So small souls despise us."

"I hadn't thought of it that way," Tory said. "But it makes sense. The irony is that there are aristocrats who have magic, but keep quiet about it. My mother and sister both have some power, but were better at concealing it than I was."

"You have too much power to conceal. Most of us who end up at Lackland are the same way." He smiled. "My situation is the best possible. I'll have a comfortable income so I never need to starve, and I won't have the problems I'd face as a peer of the realm with magical abilities."

Her return smile was wry. "What will we call you? Everyone uses your title, but once the disinheritance is official, you won't be the Marquess of Allarde anymore."

He shrugged. "My family name can't be taken away from me, so I'll be Falkirk. Except to you."

"Justin," she murmured. "I love the intimacy of being one of the only people permitted to use your Christian name."

His eyes sparked with unexpected humor. "That's effective since I'm usually so serious and boring. I've been told I was born middle-aged."

"Never boring!" she protested. "Mysterious. Enigmatic. Wise beyond your years." She leaned forward and brushed her lips against his. "Madly attractive."

His arm circled her shoulders. "I am so very glad you see me that way."

They stayed silent as the carriage drove up to the Lackland

Abbey gate. The school wall was designed to keep students in, not out, so returning was easy. Particularly when one was riding in an expensive carriage with a duke's crest painted on the doors.

As the gates swung open, Tory sank in her seat so the gatekeeper couldn't see her. He waved the vehicle through without looking inside.

As soon as they passed through the gate, Tory was hit by the suffocating magical suppression spell that blanketed the abbey grounds. As Allarde offered her a hand to sit up, he remarked, "It would have been easier for you to enter the school through one of the outside tunnels."

"I've never been on the boys' side and I was curious to see it," she explained.

"The two schools are mirror images," he pointed out.

"Yes, that's what the school officials say, but I don't know if I can trust them," she said darkly.

"What will you tell the headmistress if she noticed you've been gone for several days?" he asked. "When I show up after this absence, I can say loftily that I was summoned by my father, and no one will question how I left the school in the first place. What will you say? That you were sick and stayed in your room?"

"I've used that excuse in the past and I'm not sure I can get away with it again. I plan to say that I got lost in the tunnels below the school." She tried on her best expression of innocence. "It wouldn't be at all hard to get lost there, you know."

"I wish I could see that!" As the carriage started to slow, he said quickly, "We need to have a meeting tonight in the Labyrinth to discuss what comes next."

"But we stopped the invasion. Is there more to come?"

"More, and worse," he said grimly. He caught her in a swift, intense kiss. "Time for you to slip away if you don't want to be seen."

She ended the kiss reluctantly and said, "Until this evening." Then she quietly opened the carriage door on the side opposite the school and climbed out while the carriage driver and the school porter were welcoming Allarde back. She slipped behind the boxwood hedges that edged the driveway, then worked her way around the administration building.

As it turned out, the school officials hadn't lied. The two schools really were mirror images of each other. Lackland Abbey had been built centuries earlier with monks on one side and nuns on the other.

The modern school claimed that the abbey had been built to suppress magic. In fact, the opposite was true. Magical power was intensified under the abbey, and that made the Labyrinth a wonderful location for learning magic. There, monks and nuns had worked together as the students did now.

Allarde had explained exactly how to find a tunnel down to the Labyrinth behind the school. It was just where he'd said, and the entry opened easily to her touch. She followed the color coding on the tunnel to the center hall where the Irregulars met. It was empty at this hour, so she entered one of the tunnels that led to the girls' school.

She surfaced in a ruined outbuilding on the girls' side and headed back to her room. Since she still wore her boys' trousers, she used her magic to activate Cynthia's illusion stone. The suppression spell made working the stone like swimming through treacle, but she managed to look properly dressed.

Life at Lackland was easiest when one wasn't noticed.

The last class of the afternoon had just let out, so there were girls crisscrossing the cloister garden as they moved between the classroom building and the girls' dormitory. Tory quietly moved toward the dormitory room along with several taller girls.

Then the group ahead of her turned to the left, and Tory found herself face-to-face with Mrs. Grice, the headmistress, and Miss Macklin, the mean-spirited language teacher. The last two people Tory wanted to meet.

She bobbed her head politely and stood aside to let them by, but to no avail. The teacher and the headmistress both halted and glared at her. Mrs. Grice said in a freezing voice, "And where have you been, Miss Mansfield? I'm told you've missed several days of chapel and classes."

Tory opened her eyes wide and imagined herself small and hapless. "Mrs. Grice, it was the strangest thing! Did you know there are tunnels below the school? I've heard they have tunnels under Dover Castle, but I didn't know there were any *here*."

"The tunnels are well-known to the school governors," the headmistress said tartly. "Since you didn't break your leg falling into one, what has that to do with you?"

"I was taking a walk on the school grounds. You know how we're encouraged to walk to keep us fit." Tory's eyes widened even more. "Then I saw an odd door in one of the ruined outbuildings. The door swung open when I touched it, and there was a stairway going down! Since I was curious, I took a few steps inside. And then the door closed behind me! I was left in the dark!"

"For over three days?" Miss Macklin asked skeptically.

Tory nodded and summoned tears by thinking of Allarde's sadness at losing Kemperton. "It was *horrible*! There are a maze of tunnels and stairs, and not a *shred* of light! Black, black, black. And *cold*! I bumped into walls and fell and got bruised all over. It was pure luck that I found a way out. I thought I was going to *die* down there!" Her voice turned into a wail. As the youngest child in her family, she wailed well. "I was down there for days, and now I'm *so hungry*!"

Mrs. Grice and Miss Macklin recoiled as if Tory were a ticking bomb. Then a quiet voice said, "It must have been terribly upsetting, Miss Mansfield."

It was Miss Wheaton. As she patted Tory's arm, she said to the headmistress, "I'll make sure she's taken care of, Mrs. Grice. It was foolish of her to enter an unknown tunnel, but I think she's been punished enough."

Miss Macklin hissed, "Make sure you don't do it again, you fool girl!"

Dabbing at her eyes, Tory let Miss Wheaton lead her away and inside to the teacher's office. As Miss Wheaton closed the door, she said with humor, "You can end the tears now. You did an excellent job of terrorizing the teachers."

Tory grinned as she wiped her eyes. "I thought it would work, though probably only once. What's been going on here? Allarde thought we should have a crisis meeting in the Labyrinth this evening."

"He's right," Miss Wheaton said soberly. "I'm so glad you're both back. The situation is . . . not good."

Tory's amusement died as she recognized the exhaustion and anxiety in the teacher's eyes. "Then I'll see you later in the Labyrinth. Do Elspeth and Cynthia know there will be a meeting?"

Miss Wheaton shook her head. "You'll see them sooner than I will, so please let them know."

Tory started to ask for more information but refrained. Miss Wheaton needed some rest before the meeting, and Tory wanted a few hours without the burden of Britain's safety weighing on her shoulders.

It was a somber group that gathered in the Labyrinth that evening. Because it wasn't a regular study night for the Irregulars, the central hall was private. Jack was there with his mother, along with Allarde, the teachers, Tory, Elspeth, and Cynthia.

After they pulled the more comfortable chairs into a circle, Tory asked bluntly, "What's gone wrong?"

"There have been constant magical assaults on our wards," Mr. Stephens said with equal bluntness. "If not for Mrs. Rainford and the other mages who have joined the network, the wards might have crumbled. We're strained to near breaking point."

"And it isn't only the wards under attack," Jack said, his lips tight. "Two more small squadrons have sailed from Brest and attempted to land in Britain. One was headed to Yorkshire and the other to Devon, I think. It looked as if its destination was near your home, Tory."

Tory felt as if she'd been punched in her stomach. She'd guessed things were bad, but not this bad. "You were able to head them off with weather magic?"

"Yes, but we can't keep it up forever," Jack said, his face tired. "Cynthia and I are the strongest weather mages around and we've had to do most of the work. I still haven't fully recovered from when we fought with the French mage circle. At this rate, I might never have a chance to recuperate."

"The French seem to be far ahead of us in using magic for military purposes," Cynthia added.

"There are more war mages like the one we encountered in Wales?" Tory asked with alarm.

Elspeth nodded. "I've done a lot of scrying since we returned. I think the fellow we tangled with, Colonel Levaux, is chief of the

French military mages. He survived the spar Allarde dropped on him. I saw him wearing a cast on his arm."

Allarde frowned. "I should have tried harder to drop it on his head."

"We're fighting a magical battle with the French," Mr. Stephens said. "And we're losing. We have stronger mages, I think, but fewer of them, and we're not as well organized. So far we've been able to counter all of the French assault. But we can't keep this up indefinitely. If we fail even once, the French may acquire an unbreakable foothold in Britain."

Tory glanced at Allarde and saw that he looked as tense as she. They'd been proud of what they'd done in Wales, but that had been just one battle in a much larger war. "Does anyone have any suggestions of what we might do to turn the tables?"

"I think there's only one possible solution," Miss Wheaton said starkly. "We must go after Napoleon himself."

CHAPTER 24

"Assassination?" Tory said, aghast. "We've caused deaths under battle conditions, but the idea of seeking out and murdering a particular man is repellent."

"Worse than repellent," Elspeth said vehemently. "*Wrong*. Evil! I can't believe you're suggesting that, Miss Wheaton!"

"She isn't," Mr. Stephens said sharply. "We like the idea of assassination no more than you do, though if I thought that it would end this war, I would shoot Napoleon myself even if it meant I was damning myself to hell. But I don't think that killing him will improve our situation."

"Why not?" Cynthia demanded. "I have fewer qualms than you. If I had a chance to shoot Bonaparte in the heart, I'd take it." She considered. "Though maybe it would be easier to push him off a cliff."

"Mr. Stephens is right," Allarde said slowly. "Napoleon is first consul of France, and it's just a matter of time before he declares himself emperor. But he is surrounded by other skilled, ruthless generals. If Napoleon died, his successor might be even worse. Especially if it looked like Bonaparte had been murdered by the British. There would be a fury of vengeance by the French."

"Exactly," Mr. Stephens said. "Best for us will be if Napoleon stays in power, but he's freed of his obsession with invading England."

"It's a good theory," Jack said. "But how are we to change the mind of a tyrant?"

"We may have a way." Miss Wheaton produced a folded piece of paper. "Two days ago, this message came through the mirror from Rebecca Weiss. As you know, she has powers that involve the mind."

"Yes, she reads emotions really well, and sometimes thoughts," Tory said. "Even without training and not realizing that magic existed, she knew what the Nazi commandant had planned for her family."

"It's an unusual kind of magic," Miss Wheaton said thoughtfully. "Most mages have some ability to read feelings, but her talent goes far beyond that. She has discovered that she can literally change minds and emotions."

The teacher opened the paper and read Rebecca's terse account of how she had dissolved the enmity of an angry, bigoted classmate and how she had persuaded a desperate Nazi pilot to surrender without injuring himself or others.

When Miss Wheaton finished reading, Jack gave a low whistle. "That's quite a talent. She's developing fast. But it sounds as if she must be touching the person to make the change. How do we get that close to Napoleon? Are there any mirror portals near Paris?"

"There are several in France," Tory replied. "I don't know exactly where, but I should be able to find out."

"Napoleon isn't in Paris now," Elspeth said unexpectedly. "Yesterday in my scrying, I saw that he's visiting the Army of Boulogne. He travels to Boulogne regularly to review the troops and observe their drills and keep up their morale."

Tory involuntarily glanced in the direction of France. "So he's just there across the Channel, like a spider in his web! Even now he might be planning on invading with his whole fleet and army."

Mr. Stephens frowned. "That would explain the way his mages have been pounding our wards. We've already been weakened. A concerted attack by French mages could bring down the wards and make an invasion much easier for them."

"There may be some advantage to having Bonaparte relatively close, but that doesn't make it any easier for Rebecca to get within touching distance," Tory said.

"She could disguise herself as a maid," Jack said rather dubiously.

"Perhaps, but parlor maids don't come anywhere near lords and first consuls," Miss Wheaton said. "If he's staying in a military camp, the servants might all be male."

"Maybe Tory could fly Rebecca in?" Jack sounded even more dubious.

Tory shook her head. "Trying to fly someone larger than me across a sprawling military camp without knowing exactly where to land has a great potential for disaster."

"It might be possible to enter the camp with stealth stones," Elspeth suggested. "You're the best at stealth magic, Mr. Stephens.

Could you create stealth stones strong enough to allow a couple of us to enter the French camp unnoticed?"

The teacher shook his head. "I don't think it's possible to create true invisibility. Illusion magic to make Irregulars look like French soldiers would be more effective."

"You're all overlooking the most obvious solution," Cynthia said. "These are soldiers. *Men.* And men like touching attractive women. It wouldn't take much illusion magic to make Rebecca and me look like ladies of the night who have been sent to entertain the first consul."

Everyone stared at Cynthia. She smiled wickedly and leaned back in her chair as she used illusion magic to make herself look wild and wanton.

Jack swallowed hard. "Cinders, sometimes you terrify me."

"Good," she purred. "If we look like very expensive dolly mops, we should be able to get admitted to Napoleon's private pavilion. The real question is whether Rebecca can get him to change his mind if we get her there."

"We'll have to ask Rebecca about that," Tory said. "And she might not know since she's still so new to magic. I agree that your plan could get us into Napoleon's camp, Cynthia. But it might be much more difficult to get out. If we present ourselves as ladies of the night, he might want to bed at least one of us." She shivered. "I find the thought of dying for my country more acceptable than seducing for it."

Cynthia looked uncomfortable. "That part of my plan needs work."

"I might be able to help with that," Elspeth said. "A healing spell could be modified to put a person to sleep. If Rebecca could also plant a false memory in his mind, he'd wake up thinking he had an amazing night and not be suspicious."

"Could you provide a demonstration?" Mr. Stephens asked.

Elspeth glanced around the circle. "Does anyone want to volunteer? I'm not entirely sure this will work, but I don't think I'll damage my victim."

"So comforting," Allarde said with an amused gleam in his eye. "Practice away, cousin. This is unlikely to be any worse than some of the tricks you played in the nursery when our families visited together."

"I never did you any real harm then, either." Elspeth rose and crossed the circle to where Allarde was sitting. Placing a hand on his shoulder, she caught his gaze and said throatily, *"Monsieur! Milord!"*

Tory sensed a tingle of magic, and Allarde's eyes widened. Then he slumped unconscious. Anticipating that, Elspeth caught him and tilted his torso back so he didn't fall from the chair.

Tory blinked. "Should I be jealous?"

Elspeth laughed. "Not at all. Allarde, wake up now."

He blinked, then straightened as awareness returned. "That was . . . interesting."

"This could be very effective if a false memory or dream can be planted," Elspeth said thoughtfully. "But so much rests on Rebecca, who has so little experience."

"We don't even know exactly what her powers are," Miss Wheaton agreed. "Will she be willing to travel back in time? And does she have the temperament to do something this dangerous?"

"She promised she'd come if needed," Tory said. "As for temperament, Rebecca let me jump her off a cliff. I didn't learn till later that she's afraid of heights, so I think she'll have the nerve to enter an enemy camp. I don't know if she can rearrange Bonaparte's mind, but we need to find out if it's possible."

"Time to send a message and ask her to come back here," Jack said. "Then we can find out what she can do."

Tory frowned. "If I go forward, I can explain what we need and bring her back if she thinks she can help."

Allarde shook his head. "You shouldn't tire yourself out by making two trips close together when we're on the verge of a dangerous mission. Nick can escort her here. He's good with mirror travel, and he'd never allow her to travel here without him."

That was true. Nick was the responsible sort, and he'd also seemed rather smitten by Rebecca. "I'll write a note and send it through." Tory glanced around at the faces of her friends. "Does anyone have any other suggestions we need to discuss? What will we do if this doesn't work?"

"We'll keep doing what we've been doing," Mr. Stephens said with a sigh. "For as long as we're able to keep doing it."

And when the British mages failed—Napoleon and his army would come.

CHAPTER 25

Lackland, 1940

"You've been studying magic, math, and biology all weekend," Nick said with a grin as he stuck his head into Rebecca's room. "You need a walk and some fresh air before it gets dark."

Rebecca leaned back in her chair and stretched her arms. Nick had been so busy that she hadn't seen much of him since the Shabbat Friday night. "You're right. I'm knotted up like a pretzel and my brain is becoming numb."

She stood and brushed back her dark hair, thinking it was probably snarled since she ran her fingers through it when she was solving difficult math problems. "Maybe your mother or Polly would like to join us?"

"Polly is off doing something with one of her friends, and Mum is correcting papers for school. It's just you and me, kid."

"You've watched too many American movies," she said with a laugh. "I'll be down in a couple of minutes."

After he left her room, she combed her hair and tied it back with a ribbon. It was cold and sunny out, so she added a red scarf and knit hat to the dark gray coat she'd been given by Mrs. Rainford. They were of similar height, which was convenient since Rebecca had needed a whole new wardrobe.

Nick was waiting downstairs, bundled up as warmly as she was. "That coat really brings out your gray eyes," he observed.

"Gray eyes aren't very interesting," she said, surprised. "Blue eyes are much prettier and come in lots of different shades."

"I'm glad you think so." Nick's blue eyes sparked teasingly. When she blushed and looked away, he said, "I thought we could walk out to Lackland Abbey to check if there are any message stones."

She nodded agreeably. "I like that walk along the cliffs. The wind is bracing."

He laughed as he opened the door for her. "When we walked out to send the message about your developing talents, 'bracing' meant 'be careful or you'll be blown into the next county.' "

She laughed also. As she brushed by him on her way out, she was very aware of his lean strength. Nick played several sports, and it showed.

She found the contrast between Nick and Jack Rainford interesting. Despite the many decades between them, they were clearly related, with similar blond hair and blue eyes and regular features, but there were differences. Jack had broader shoulders, a teasing smile, and a more relaxed personality. By contrast,

Nick was leaner and a bit taller, and he had a quick, intense energy.

She liked them both—but Nick intrigued her more.

As they turned onto the cliff path, Nick asked, "How is the magical training coming along?"

"Your mother is a good teacher and she's giving me a solid grounding in the basics, but neither of us knows what to do with my particular talents," Rebecca said. "The most useful lessons have been in blocking the emotions of people around me. I keep my mental shields up so usually I don't feel others unless I want to."

"That has to be essential for a talent like yours," Nick observed. "What about reading thoughts? Do you hear them more clearly now when you try?"

"Thoughts are a lot harder. I can usually catch the gist of what someone is thinking, and occasionally I hear words or phrases. Most people's minds are a jumble. Like trying to read alphabet soup." She made a face. "I avoid listening for thoughts because I hate invading the privacy of others. I won't even try unless it's a situation where they're not likely to be thinking of anything very personal."

"Does that spare you from too much knowledge?"

"It works better with females than males. Males always seem to be thinking about sex," she said with exasperation.

He stared at her, startled. "I do hope that you don't try to read my thoughts!"

She blushed, wishing she hadn't said that. Though it was true. "I never try to read you or anyone else in your family. That would be really wrong."

"I'm glad to hear that," he said. "It's an alarming power that you have, but it will be amazing when you become a psychiatrist. Have you had occasion to adjust anyone else's emotions?"

"There's a girl at school whose father was killed in the merchant marine," Rebecca admitted. "She was so horribly upset that she couldn't function."

"I know who you mean. Did you take her pain away?" Nick asked with interest.

"I haven't the right to do that. Pain is needful when you've just lost someone you love." Rebecca hesitated, wondering how to describe what she'd done. "Instead, I . . . I put some distance between her and the pain. It's hard to explain. She still mourns, as she should. But she's no longer crippled by her loss. She's in better shape to support her mother and younger brothers."

"That was well done, Rebecca," Nick said warmly. "How are you and Sylvia Crandall getting along?"

Rebecca laughed. "Would you believe that we've become friends? She and Andy and I have lunch together every day. Sylvia is very clever, and she has a droll sense of humor now that she isn't miserable all the time."

"Well done indeed!" Nick said, impressed. "You should start keeping case notes like a proper physician."

"I do," she said shyly. "With initials, not names, of course. With both my parents doctors, I know the importance of observation and records."

"You are going to make a phenomenal doctor."

"I hope so." Rebecca stopped to say hello to a cow in the field they were passing. A dark brown creature, the cow had broad white stripes painted on her sides so cars wouldn't hit her if she escaped during blackout hours. It was a strange world where painting cows made sense.

They reached the abbey grounds and had to pick their way through stones that had been thrown about when a Nazi bomber released part of its load overhead. The entrance to the Labyrinth was concealed behind a ruined wall.

When they reached it, Nick touched a faint bluish patch on the edge, and the stone slab silently moved aside, revealing steps leading down into darkness. Rebecca felt a shiver of awe for the ancient magic that moved those stones. She'd been raised to believe in science, and sometimes it was still hard to believe in magic. But not when the evidence was right in front of her eyes.

Nick cupped his left hand and a glow of light appeared on his palm. "How are you coming with your mage lights?"

She mimicked his cupping gesture and imagined a glow of light in her hand. An unsteady spark appeared, flickering unevenly. She concentrated and it stabilized but was much smaller than Nick's. "I don't think I have much talent in this area."

"You're still new with it all," he said as he led the way into the passage. When he closed the door by touching another blue patch, the mage lights looked much brighter. "But it's true that every mage has a different collection of abilities. Strong in some areas, weak in others."

"Your strongest ability is as a finder, isn't it?"

"Yes, and sometimes it's handy. Not as impressive as flying or weather work, though." He started down the stairs. "I wish it was possible to go to Lackland Abbey in the past and study seriously with the Irregulars. Any one of them knows more than I do about magic."

They followed the winding route that led to the chamber that held Merlin's Mirror. Each time Rebecca came here, she was more aware of the great, ancient power of the portal. She suspected it was a gauge of how her magic awareness was growing.

"A message stone." Nick tossed his mage light in the air to hover above them, then scooped up the paper-wrapped rock.

"What does it say?"

Nick unwrapped the paper and scanned the message. His face became very still. "You were right about going to 1804."

He handed the message to Rebecca and she scanned it eagerly. Written in a lovely clear script, it read:

Rebecca—

Please come. Your developing talent may be exactly what we need. Let me know if you want me to travel to your time and escort you back.

Tory

She swallowed hard. She hadn't truly expected this to happen. "I guess I'd better send a message and ask Tory to come for me. Do you have a pencil?"

"Don't be ridiculous," he said gruffly. "I'll take you. Tory has to know that, but she's such a bloody lady that she doesn't want to make assumptions."

"Are you angry with her?" Rebecca asked with surprise. Nick almost never swore. "I thought you were friends."

"We are. But I hate that they're dragging you into their problems." His mouth tightened. "Their bloody missions are always dangerous."

Her jaw dropped. "Correct me if I'm wrong, but aren't you the one who dragged Tory and the others into Nazi-occupied France? And in the process, saved me and my family, not to mention your sister? I hardly think you're in a position to complain when they ask for help!"

"Of course I'm not!" He began pacing tensely around the chamber. "But this time, you're the one endangered. I don't mind risking my life, but not yours."

She didn't know whether to laugh, sigh at his romantic protectiveness, or just roll her eyes. She settled for saying, "Nicholas, I truly appreciate your caring. But I have faced danger before. All of us do just by living in a war zone. I owe your Irregulars a debt so vast that my life would not be too high a payment."

"You are too damned rational!" he said tightly.

She intercepted his pacing and laid a hand on his wrist. "Nick . . ."

He spun to face her, his eyes burning. Then he locked his arms around her and kissed her with all his repressed emotions. A neighborhood boy had kissed her in the garden once. She hadn't been impressed.

This was blazingly different. She'd done her best to block Nick's emotions, but now the floodgates burst. He wanted her in ways beyond words, and as her arms went around him, she realized she wanted him just as much. The surging emotions were both his and hers, and their power overwhelmed sense and reason.

But sex was definitely part of the torrent, and his desperate urgency and tenderness and passion terrified her. Gasping, she broke away and retreated until her back was against the wall. "This is a really bad idea," she said, her blood hammering through her veins. "We should be thinking about traveling to the past. What should I wear? What do I take? And what can a novice mage like me do to help?"

Rather than follow her across the chamber, he stood still, his hands clenching and unclenching. "My head knows you're right, but my heart is doing backflips at the realization you care for me as I care for you."

She briefly thought of denying that but decided not to try. He wouldn't believe her when she couldn't believe herself. "I do care for you, but we are in very different places about this."

"I know, which is why I've done my best to keep my distance, but it's been hard. From the first time I met you, I've felt that you're 'the One.' "

She stared at him. "I'm not sure if that's romantic or alarming. You didn't even know me."

"Not in the usual way. But I felt that in some deep way, we were connected. I've felt that all along, and I knew it was only a matter of time until those feelings came roaring out. The knowledge that you'll be going into great danger set me off." He shook his head. "I wish you weren't so intrepid."

"No, you don't," she said. "I'd be someone else if I was a coward, and probably it would be a girl you didn't much like."

"There you go, being rational again." His engaging smile lit his eyes.

"That's part of me also," she said wryly. "A part you don't much like."

"Not true!" He caught her hand, though he didn't try to draw her closer. "I like everything about you. Like and admire both. Even your extreme rationality."

She gently disengaged her hand. "Which says it's time to think about time travel."

"Yes. But what about us?"

She gave a very French shrug. "I have no idea. I'm not even sixteen for another month. I've never had a boyfriend. I've barely been kissed. I'm a French refugee in a foreign country, and the fact that you like matzo ball soup doesn't mean there are no religious issues. I just . . . don't know where to go from here."

He took her hand again and pressed a kiss on the back before letting go. "Where we go from here is 1804. And we stop trying to pretend there is nothing special between us, because that pretense was fraying fast." He shrugged. "As for the rest, we take it as it comes, and I'll try not to be too intense and romantic. If I am, just tell me to slow down."

But how would Rebecca slow down when Nick dazzled her mind and senses? He was right. They would have to take this amazing, alarming relationship day by day. Since they were living under the same roof, it would be hard to keep their hands off each other. They wouldn't want to. She must hope that her common sense and, yes, rationality, would keep her from doing anything really stupid.

"Day by day," she said. "Moment by moment. And the question of the moment is whether you have a pencil so I can write a return message for Tory."

"Indeed I do." He pulled a dull pencil from an inside pocket.

Rebecca wrote, "Nick will bring me through the mirror as soon as we inform Mrs. Rainford. See you soon. Should we bring anything special?"

Nick saw the message as he tied it to the stone again. "Tory has an unnatural passion for fish and chips, but I don't think they'd travel well."

"What's unnatural about a passion for fish and chips?" she asked indignantly. "One of the first things you did was take me to the Codfather to try them!"

He laughed, and the tension between them eased. "Fish and chips are good for the soul, and I hope they're never rationed. As for the trip to the past, it would probably be best to wear trousers in case it's necessary to climb cliffs or crawl through tunnels or something else unladylike. Your dresses would look out of place there anyway."

"I don't have any trousers."

"We'll find you something." He held the message stone between his palms and closed his eyes as he visualized when and where he wanted it to go. As he did, the mirror shimmered to silvery life on the other side of the chamber.

Rebecca shrank back against the wall, intimidated by the sheer raging power of the portal. Nick tossed the stone. When it hit the mirror, silver turned night black, then both mirror and stone vanished.

"Time to go home." He waggled his brows at her. "You said that you've never had a boyfriend before, thereby implying that you have one now. Therefore, as your boyfriend, may I hold your hand as we walk home?"

By way of reply, she extended her hand and his warm fingers closed around it as they navigated their way back to the surface. Burning passion and intense emotion were too much for her now.

But holding Nick's hand felt exactly right.

CHAPTER 26

Mrs. Rainford was in the kitchen putting together supper when they returned from the walk to Lackland Abbey. As soon as she saw Rebecca and Nick, she wiped her hands and turned to face them. "What has happened?"

"Tory has asked Rebecca to go back in time to help," Nick said. "I'll take her. She'll need to borrow a pair of trousers."

Mrs. Rainford's face tightened. "I was afraid of this. Your luck had better not run out, Nicholas Rainford! I expect you and Rebecca to return safe and sound because I do not want to explain to her parents or your father that you've run into catastrophe."

"You are a mum in a million," he said affectionately.

Mrs. Rainford studied Rebecca. "You look worried. You don't have to go."

"Yes. I do." Rebecca swallowed. "If I look concerned, it is partly because Nick and I have admitted to a . . . a romantic interest in each other."

"It's about time! To anyone who has taught as many years as I have, the mutual interest was obvious."

"You don't mind?" Nick said, his expression pleased.

"I don't think I get a vote on how you feel about each other." Mrs. Rainford's gaze was sober. "That doesn't mean I'm not concerned. You're living in the same house. You're traveling back in time on a dangerous, exhilarating mission that will draw the two of you even closer. Perhaps when you return, Rebecca should go to her family."

"No, Mum!" Nick said, horrified. "Quite apart from our feelings for each other, Rebecca needs more training for her magical abilities, and she won't get that in Oxford."

"She has learned quickly and can continue growing on her own if necessary." Mrs. Rainford shook her head. "During a war, it's easy to forget tomorrow and live for today, and young passions burn with special fierceness. Please, promise me you'll both use your excellent minds and behave with good sense. The future may be uncertain, but you'll probably have one, so don't throw it away in the heat of the moment now."

"I promise," Rebecca said, her voice almost inaudible.

"Nick?" Mrs. Rainford prompted.

"I promise." He gave his mother a wry smile. "Even if I forget a gentleman's honor, I know darned well that you'll skin me alive and feed me to the Channel fishes if I hurt Rebecca."

"You are so right!" his mother said feelingly. Turning back to the stove, she said, "You need a decent meal before you race into the past, so time to put food on the table."

No wonder Nick liked her, Rebecca thought. His mother was also a very rational woman.

It didn't take Rebecca long to prepare for—whatever lay ahead. Polly lent her a pair of trousers and a warm knitted jumper to go over her shirt. With the addition of her jacket, hat, and sturdy shoes, she felt ready to scramble around on cliffs and woods if that was required.

She also wrote a letter to her family that she hoped would never be sent.

Dearest Maman, Papa, Joel—

Don't blame Mrs. Rainford for letting me go on what could be a dangerous journey. You know why I must answer this call. If I do not return, know also that I love you with all my heart.

Shalom,
Rebecca

She also scribbled short notes to Andy, Dr. Gordon, and Sylvia Crandall. Sylvia in particular needed to know that Rebecca had valued their brief friendship. The notes apologized for not saying good-bye in person, but family duty called her away. It was a kind of truth.

All three Rainfords were waiting for her downstairs. It was dark by now, and they spoke little as they hiked out to the abbey again. All four of them created mage lights when they entered the Labyrinth. Rebecca's was the weakest. She wondered wryly if she could really be a vital element in saving Britain from a French invasion.

Even if she wasn't much help, she'd try. At the least, she'd be glad to see Tory and the others again.

They reached the mirror chamber, and the lights revealed two large, irregularly shaped packages lying in the middle of the floor. "These are too large for message stones," Polly said as she scooped one up and unwrapped part of the fabric covering.

Inside was something hard and white. Polly touched it gingerly, then dug in a nail and licked her finger to taste it. "Sugar loaves!" she said with delight. "We'll be able to make a splended birthday cake for you next month, Rebecca." She looked warily at her mother. "You aren't going to consider this black market, are you?"

Her mother laughed. "I consider it a generous gift from friends. I have a sweet tooth, too, you know."

Polly set both loaves by the exit, and the mood turned serious. Nick faced the end of the chamber where the mirror burned invisibly. He raised his right hand and concentrated. The energy of the portal coalesced and the mirror shimmered into sight, as alluring as it was menacing.

Time to say good-bye. "Mrs. Rainford. Polly." Rebecca gave each of them a swift hug. "Thank you for making me part of your family."

"Thank you for becoming another daughter so quickly," the older woman whispered.

Polly's embrace was intense. "When do I get to go on exciting adventures through time?"

"I think you have to be at least fifteen," Rebecca said with a lopsided smile. "That's what it says in the Adventurers Code Book."

"And you'd have to go off without your brother," Mrs. Rainford said. "I still haven't recovered from the terror of both of you sailing off to Dunkirk."

"But we returned in triumph, Mum!" Nick hugged his mother. "We will again."

"See that you do." Mrs. Rainford's voice was stern, but there were tears in her eyes as she released Nick. "Rebecca, look after him. Young men forget they're mortal."

"I'll try my best."

"Off we go, Rebecca." Nick's smile was cheerful, but his eyes were serious. Traveling through time could not be taken lightly. "This will be more uncomfortable than traveling through the mirror from France to here. You'll feel like you're being torn into small pieces, but don't worry. You'll be reassembled."

"You are *so* comforting, Mr. Rainford!" Rebecca took his left hand, holding on hard. She didn't even want to think about the chance that she might be lost in time.

He smiled encouragingly. "Don't worry, I'm almost as good at this as Tory."

"Still more comfort!" Rebecca's smile was strained, and she was starkly aware that she might never return to her own time and place. But Nick had made this trip before, and she trusted his power and protectiveness to take her to their friends. "Lead on, Mr. Rainford!"

Through their clasped hands, she felt Nick's power and concentration intensify. The air in the chamber thickened with magic and dangerous possibilities.

Nick reached out his free hand toward the shimmering mirror—and suddenly they were being dragged into hell. Rebecca wanted to scream, but she had no voice, no strength, nothing but dissolution and despair. . . .

Normal awareness returned with a jolt. She realized that she was on her knees on cold stone, her body folded into a trembling knot. Darkness was absolute until a mage light appeared to illuminate the empty stone chamber.

"Rebecca, are you all right?" Nick's voice was urgent in her ear, and his arm wrapped around her with warmth and strength.

"You said it would be bad, but this was even worse than I imagined," she said unsteadily. "No wonder no one makes the trip without a really good reason!"

His other arm came around her and he cradled her head against his shoulder. "It gets a little easier with time."

"Easier, or you just know better what to expect?"

He chuckled. "You are ever the scientist, Mademoiselle Weiss. Maybe I've just become experienced. I do know that the farther the jump in time, the harder the passage. We land at the end of the journey exhausted and ravenously hungry, so it is wise to always have food available." His embrace tightened. "You may be affected more badly because you're still too thin from being imprisoned. I've brought bread and cheese. Would you like some?"

"Oh, please!"

Nick created another mage light and tossed the pair of them in the air so his hands were free to open the book bag he'd brought. He pulled out a paper-wrapped package. "Good English Cheddar and some of the challah from the Shabbat."

He used his pocketknife to slice thick slabs of cheese and bread and make open-faced sandwiches. When he handed the first to Rebecca, she almost swallowed it whole. Nick gave her a second piece before preparing one for himself.

By the third sandwich, her eating had slowed to normal speed and she was no longer shivering from shock. She studied her surroundings and saw that she was in a familiar stone chamber. "Have we come to the right time?"

"I think so. I've developed a sort of internal clock and it says we're where we want to be." He gestured at the white chalk walls. "It's hard to say, though. This chamber doesn't change much."

He swallowed the last of his third sandwich. "Are you up to walking? We need to head toward the central hall. If there's no one there now, we wait. Some of the Irregulars will eventually show up."

Rebecca lurched to her feet, still drained by the mirror passage. "If no one is there, can I sleep for a few hours? A bed on cold chalk would be perfectly fine."

Nick put an arm around her waist to steady her. "No need. The hall is furnished with old sofas and chairs so you can nap in comfort. The upholstery in this time isn't as soft and comfortable as what we're used to, though."

Her curiosity flickered to life. "What was it like to come to a different time? Did you find it very confusing?"

"Actually, I've never been out of the Labyrinth." He grinned as they walked from the chamber. "I'm hoping to remedy that this trip."

"Having been shot at by the Nazis, do you now want to be shot at by the French?" she asked dryly.

"I don't mind as long as their aim is bad."

Footsteps sounded in the tunnel in front of them, and a moment later the petite and swift-footed Lady Victoria Mansfield tore around the curve ahead. Despite her ankle-length gown, her speed was impressive.

"You're here!" Tory exclaimed. "I felt the mirror energy surge when you arrived. I'm so glad to see you!"

Nick released Rebecca and gave Tory a hug. "It's good to be back! Are you going to let me out of the Labyrinth this time?"

"Absolutely!" Tory turned and caught Rebecca's hands, her gaze searching. "How are you? The first trip through time is particularly difficult."

Rebecca made a face. "An understatement! But Nick got me here safely."

"You're looking well. Less thin than you were." Tory frowned. "But you feel cold. Let me give you some hearth witch magic."

Rebecca hadn't realized how cold she was until warmth flowed through her limbs, bringing comfort to every cell of her tired body. "I wish I could do that! Hearth witch magic, you say?"

"Yes, hearth witchery is several related abilities to control temperatures and keep a household running well," Tory explained as she released Rebecca's hands. "Most women have a touch of this kind of magic. It's not common in men. Cynthia is very strong in hearth witchery. We can give you some training in it while you're here."

"I'd love that."

As they started walking back the way Tory had come, Tory asked, "How do you like life in England?"

"I hate living apart from my family, but the Rainfords have been wonderful, and I love being back in school again." Rebecca frowned. "But I don't know how a novice like me can help you."

"Perhaps you can't," Tory said soberly. "But we're desperate because time is running out."

CHAPTER 27

Lackland, 1804

When Tory had last seen Rebecca, the other girl had been gaunt and strained by the months of imprisonment and their dangerous escape. Now Rebecca was slim and composed, her dark hair sleek and her large gray eyes wise beyond her years.

Tory could also feel that Rebecca's magic was much stronger and more focused now that she was receiving training. That didn't necessarily mean she had the power to change a dictator's mind . . . but it was grounds for hope.

They entered the central hall, where dozens of Irregulars were working in groups of half a dozen or so. Tory explained, "As you can see, it's a class night, but the usual subjects have been suspended. We're all working to maintain the magical wards that have been helping to hold off the French."

Rebecca's brows furrowed. "I can feel a great pressure. A . . . a kind of tug-of-war between invisible opposing forces."

"That's it exactly." Tory scanned the room, catching the eyes of Allarde and Elspeth and the other time-traveling Irregulars. "Before we have our briefing session, do either of you need something to eat or drink?"

"We had bread and cheese as soon as we landed, but I could use a mug of hot tea," Nick said. "And if there are any of Mrs. Rainford's cakes, that would be even better. Rebecca, would you like the same?"

Rebecca nodded. "Yes, please."

Tory led the new arrivals across the room. With almost everyone working on the wards, the hall was unusually silent. Most of the Irregulars would have to return to the school soon, but their aid now gave the regular ward mages a break for several hours. The best hearth witches in the group were taking turns in the kitchen area to provide warm drinks and food for tired magelings. Alice, one of the strongest hearth witches, produced a steaming pot of tea in minutes.

The teachers and the time-traveling Irregulars converged on Tory and her guests, and there was a flurry of greetings and welcomes. After Tory made the introductions, Miss Wheaton said, "I'm so glad to meet you. Let's move to the conference room so our talk won't disturb those working the wards."

After everyone who wanted tea and cakes had acquired them, the group moved to the small side room that was used for special projects and discussions. Inside was a round table, a dozen or so chairs, and an old sofa. Rebecca sat next to Tory, with Nick on her other side. She looked resigned.

Once everyone was settled, Tory said, "Nick and Rebecca, I'll summarize what we're facing." She explained about the buildup of French troops and ships and the way the French had been testing British defenses with small-scale attempts at invasion. Then Mr. Stephens explained the wards, which were deteriorating under the constant assault of the French mage corps and might be close to failing.

Rebecca and Nick listened attentively. After the situation was explained, Rebecca said, "This sounds grave, but what do you think I can do to make a difference?"

"We're hoping you can change Napoleon's mind about invading England," Tory said flatly.

Rebecca gasped. "You're mad! How could I possibly do anything like that? Especially to a man on the other side of the English Channel!"

"When you described how you were able to alter the minds of your schoolmate and the Nazi pilot, you mentioned that you were touching your subject," Elspeth said. "We'll get you into the French camp so you can touch Napoleon and rearrange his ambitions."

Face white, Rebecca asked, "Are you going to fly me in, Tory?"

Cynthia answered instead. "We're going to dress as trollops and flounce into the camp and announce that we're there to entertain Bonaparte. I'll provide the illusion magic to make us look like doxies, Elspeth will knock out the first consul afterward, Tory will enhance everyone's magic so we can accomplish all we need, and you'll persuade Bonaparte that he'd really rather invade Russia."

"Russia?" Rebecca asked feebly.

"Or Austria or India or China for all I care," Cynthia said with a shrug. "Anywhere, as long as it's far from here."

"You're beautiful, so I'm sure you can make yourself look

glamorous and seductive," Rebecca said, her brow furrowed. "But I'm a schoolgirl and look it. I doubt I can make a convincing trollop."

"Don't underestimate my illusion magic," Cynthia said with a mischievous smile. "Look at Elspeth."

Everyone shifted their gaze to Elspeth, whose petite size and silver blond hair meant she usually looked like a spun-sugar angel. Under the influence of Cynthia's magic, she became a sultry blond temptress.

Rebecca and Nick gasped. "I retract my statement," Rebecca said, staring. "If you can make Elspeth look wanton, you can certainly do the same for me. But still—change Napoleon's mind?"

A sudden thought struck Tory. "I hadn't considered this because everyone here hates Napoleon for what he's doing, but you're French. You lived your whole life in France until a few weeks ago. Does it bother you that we're asking you to fight against your native country?"

"It does feel odd," Rebecca admitted. "In French schools, we're taught that Napoleon Bonaparte is our greatest national hero. That he was a man of incredible strength and ability who shaped French law and government and changed the face of Europe before other countries ganged together to bring him down, like jackals. His tomb is a magnificent monument in Paris."

"I hear a 'but' in your voice," Tory said.

"It's true that he helped pull France out of the Middle Ages and did many good things, but he was also a tyrant. Like Hitler." Rebecca's lips tightened. "And I despise tyrants. England has given me and my family sanctuary, and I will defend England in my own time or the past."

"Good lass," Nick said warmly.

From the way Rebecca gazed up at him, the mutual attraction

Tory had noticed from the beginning was developing fast. Smiling to herself, she said, "The biggest question is whether your magic is strong enough to reshape the mind of a man as forceful as Bonaparte. We must test your abilities before we put all our necks on the chopping block by taking on the Army of Boulogne."

Rebecca winced. "In this era, the chopping block is not just a saying, is it? It's only been about ten years since France was guillotining too many of her citizens."

Mr. Stephens nodded. "The revolution had some fine goals and ideals, but it veered into horror, and now into the hands of a tyrant who wants to conquer the world."

"He won't if we have anything to say about it!" Jack said.

"We have work to do before we go into France," Allarde said. "We need to find the nearest mirror portal and get maps of the Boulogne area. And Elspeth, you need to scry as much information as you can so we can find Napoleon in his camp."

"My finder ability will be useful," Nick said. "Once we're near the camp, I think I should be able to find Bonaparte without a problem."

"Useful indeed." Miss Wheaton covered a yawn. "That's enough for tonight, I think. None of us will be very effective if we exhaust ourselves."

"Rebecca and Nick, you'll be staying with us while you're here," Jack said. "That way you can see what the world is like outside the school. Rebecca, you can work with my mother. She's powerful and a good teacher."

"She's also a very skilled hearth witch, Rebecca," Tory said. "While you're there, you can pick up some of the basics."

"Since coming through the mirror is like being stomped on by a bull, I'll go home and bring back a carriage so the two of you don't have to walk to our house," Jack said.

"That would be lovely," Rebecca said with a tired smile. "Though I could fall asleep on the sofa against that wall."

"You'll be a lot more comfortable at our house." Jack got to his feet. "We seem to be done here, so I'll head for home to get that carriage. Tell my sister I'll be back soon so she can ride back in comfort, too."

As Jack left the room, Rebecca covered a yawn with her hand. "I'll just rest here until Jack returns."

"Lie down on the sofa," Tory suggested. "There's a knee rug to keep you warm. Nick, do you want to rest here also?"

He shook his head. "The trip wasn't as hard on me, so I'll use the time to talk to you and the others."

As he left the room, Rebecca curled up on her side on the sofa. Tory spread the knee robe over her. "Thank you for coming," she said softly.

Rebecca's eyes opened, her clear gray eyes direct. "You knew I would."

"Yes, but that doesn't mean I'm not grateful. Rest well." Tory headed toward the door. For the first time in days, she was hopeful.

CHAPTER 28

Rebecca barely remembered the drive to the Rainford farm. When Jack returned, she met his sister, Rachel, who was a year or two younger than Rebecca but close to the same size. Rachel promised to lend what garments their guest would require.

After a lengthy walk through another chalk tunnel, they emerged in a small grove of trees where a plain closed carriage with a patient pony waited. Once they were all inside, Nick put his arm around Rebecca and she promptly fell asleep on him despite the novelty of a carriage ride. She loved sleeping with his arms around her.

The farm was large and impressive from what Rebecca could

see. Jack's mother, Lily, was petite and unflappable. She loaned Rebecca a flannel nightgown and put her guest to bed in a wonderfully comfortable featherbed. Rainfords were as hospitable in this century as in Rebecca's time.

Firmly shutting off the part of her mind that was shrieking over the fact that she was expected to march up to Napoleon and persuade him not to invade England, Rebecca burrowed into her borrowed bed and slept like a stone.

When she awoke the next morning, it was too gray to guess the time, but she suspected it wasn't early. She pushed herself up in bed. The night before, she'd been too tired to pay much attention, but today she examined the nightgown Lily Rainford had loaned her. The fabric was a pale natural color, and it was well-worn but very clean.

She flipped up the hem and studied the tiny stitches. Amazing to think that every single stitch in the nightgown had been sewn by hand. She'd never worn a hand-sewn garment in her life.

How long did it take to make a nightgown by hand? She couldn't even guess.

She slid from the high bed and found that the floor was icy cold. Nick had said that if they arrived when they intended, which they had, it would be early spring. Cold.

A mirror was mounted on the wardrobe, so she studied her image. Her shoulder-length dark hair was shorter than girls wore it now, but there was nothing else to mark her as a girl from the future.

The yoke of the nightgown was beautifully embroidered with blue flowers and green leaves. She touched one of the flowers, impressed again at the quality of the hand sewing. But the amount of time required for even simple clothing meant that most people would own only a handful of garments. In the days before the Nazis came, Rebecca had had a full closet of shoes and clothing. In this time, only the rich could own so much.

A knock sounded on the door and a voice called softly, "Rebecca, it's Rachel. Are you awake?"

Rebecca replied by opening the door. "Good morning, Rachel. I assume it still is morning?"

"It is," Rachel said with a laugh. "The fog should burn off and we'll have a sunny day, I think."

Jack's sister was fully dressed in a gown made of a sturdy blue fabric that looked as though it would wear well, and her blond hair was coiled neatly at the nape of her neck. She had a patterned blue-and-gray shawl draped around her shoulders, and several garments were draped over her left arm. "May I offer you some clothing? I rather envy you the men's wear you traveled in, but you'll never pass for a local in trousers."

"Thank you. Please, come in." Rebecca stepped back so Rachel could enter. "I understand that Jack is the best weather mage around. Do you have the same ability?"

Rachel entered and laid the clothing on the bed. "No, except for Lady Cynthia, most strong weather mages are male. Though Jack said Nick's sister, Polly, has weather talent. I can predict weather, but that's much less useful than making it! My strongest ability is as a hearth witch, which is very useful, but not at all glamorous."

"I'm hoping to learn something about hearth witchery while I'm here," Rebecca said. "None of the twentieth-century Rainfords have it."

"My mother is the one to learn from. She keeps this house warm all winter."

"What a wonderful ability," Rachel said, thinking of how cold the crowded cell in France had been.

"I didn't realize how wonderful until I stayed with a friend who didn't have it!" Rachel shook out the gown she'd brought. It was long-sleeved and made of a soft blue gray fabric. "This should fit you. Do you understand the underwear that goes with it?"

"I'm beginning to realize the depths of my ignorance," Rebecca admitted. "You'll have to start at the beginning."

"This is everyday wear, not at all complicated," Rachel said as she displayed each garment. "The morning gown fastens in front so you won't need help to put it on. I've brought a shift and light stays, an extra petticoat since the weather is cold, stockings and garters, and a shawl."

Rebecca examined the stays, a quilted garment with bones and lacing up the front. It started at the waist, covered the torso and supported the breasts, and had shoulder straps. "Does this go over or under the shift, and how tightly do I draw the lacing?"

"The stays go over the shift, and tighten them enough for support, but not so much as to make you uncomfortable. Most stays lace in the back, but I like to be able to lace myself." Rachel held up a pair of tan ankle-high shoes. "I've outgrown these half-boots, but I think your feet are a bit smaller than mine, so with luck they'll fit."

Rebecca examined the shoes, puzzled. They were made of a heavy woven fabric and laced up the ankles. "Which is for the right foot and which is for the left?"

Rachel looked surprised. "There's no difference in how they're made, though I usually wore this one on the right foot and the other on the left because they start to take the shape of the feet."

How long would it be until shoemakers started making shoes shaped specifically for right and left feet? There was so much Rebecca didn't know!

Rachel said, "If you have no questions, I'll meet you downstairs in the kitchen. Go left out this door to the steps, down the stairs, then right into the kitchen."

"The adventure begins," Rebecca said with a smile. "I hope to be down soon."

"By the way, my mother thought it would be best to introduce you as Rebecca White, since that's the English version of your name," Rachel said. "Do you mind?"

"Not at all. I want to attract as little attention as possible," Rebecca said. "I know that magic is accepted here, but I don't want to have to explain time travel!"

"I don't know if anyone can explain it," Rachel said. "It just *is*."

"Does it bother you that your brother and the others are the ones who have the adventures?" Rebecca asked.

"Dangerous adventures!" Rachel said. "If I was needed, I'd go. It's very satisfying to work on the wards since the work is vital. But I have nothing like the power that the time travelers do. They also work really well together. A lot of that is Tory, I think. Her ability to blend different energies together has made a team with tremendous combined power. I envy them their closeness. But not their danger!"

"I'm not enthralled by the danger part myself," Rebecca said wryly.

"They're not only powerful," Rachel said as she left the room. "They're *lucky*."

Rebecca managed the clothing without much difficulty. No zippers, but lots of things that needed to be tied. She kept her twentieth-century knickers because it felt odd not to wear them. The other garments went on easily, and the stays were surprisingly comfortable as well as adding a layer of warmth.

The gown was in the flattering Empire style that everyone wore in this time period. The waist was just below the breasts, and the skirt fell straight to her ankles from that point. The unshaped half-boots felt a little strange, but at least they didn't pinch.

Hoping her garters wouldn't come undone and fall around her ankles, Rebecca made her way downstairs. The house was attractive and well furnished, with beautiful views of the sea on one side and lush farmland on the other. The Rainfords might not be aristocrats like the students of Lackland Abbey, but they were obviously prosperous.

She found Rachel and Mrs. Rainford sharing cups of tea with a comfortably round woman who wore an apron. Mrs. Rainford said, "Good morning, Rebecca. Nick and Jack are studying maps in the library. This is Mrs. Brewster, our cook. Be very, very polite to her, since she is much too good a cook to lose! Mrs. Brewster, this is Rebecca White, who will be staying with us for a few days."

"You need feeding up, child." Mrs. Brewster finished her tea and stood. "I've some nice bacon and potatoes I fried earlier, and I'll cook a pair of eggs to go with them."

This was a complication Rebecca hadn't thought about. "I'm sorry," she said apologetically. "I can't eat any kind of pork or shellfish."

"They don't agree with you?" the cook asked, surprised.

"No, I'm Jewish and they are forbidden to my religion," Rebecca explained. "So sadly, I can't eat any of that delicious-smelling bacon."

Mrs. Brewster clucked sympathetically. "Poor girl! I'll scramble your eggs with some cheese and make extra toast."

"You can't eat bacon?" Rachel grinned. "I'd say that was unfortunate except that now I can ask Mrs. Brewster for the pieces she was saving for you."

"While we're waiting for your breakfast, tell me more about

your mental magic," Mrs. Rainford said. "From what I've heard, it's rare and different."

Rebecca liked that her religion didn't seem to matter to anyone here. "I don't really understand it myself," she admitted. "But this is what I've done."

She outlined what had happened with Sylvia Crandall and the German pilot and finished just as Mrs. Brewster set a plate containing a fluffy herb-and-cheese omelet, fried potatoes, and toast in front of her. Realizing she was ravenous again, she said, "If you'll excuse me . . . ," and attacked the food.

"We need to find you a person who needs his attitudes adjusted," Mrs. Rainford said thoughtfully.

"How about the vicar?" Rachel suggested. "He's been rather difficult lately."

"Ah, a perfect choice. When you've finished your breakfast, Rebecca, we shall pay Mr. Andrews a call."

Rebecca swallowed another bite of eggs and potatoes. "What is Mr. Andrews' problem?"

"I have my suspicions, but I'll let you draw your own conclusions."

Rebecca suddenly felt less hungry. "What if I can't affect his mind? I won't be of any use to you."

"Then we'll think of something else." Mrs. Rainford patted Rebecca's hand. "There's no point in worrying. Concentrate on the fact that you'll be walking in the past! I'm sure you'll find it interesting."

Rebecca knew she would. She just hoped she didn't do anything really stupid by mistake.

CHAPTER 29

"The village is so much smaller now!" Rebecca exclaimed as she and the Rainfords walked down into Lackland. Her gaze on the parish church, St. Peter's by the Sea, she said, "I suppose that's not surprising, but it's odd to see familiar features like the church tower and the harbor when so much else hasn't been built yet."

Rachel looked wistful. "So far, mirror travel has only been done for urgent reasons. It would be lovely if one could go through just to see another time."

"Time tourism?" Rebecca shuddered. "You do *not* want to go through the mirror without a good reason!"

"So says everyone who has done it," Mrs. Rainford observed. "I am content to learn from the experience of others and stay in my own time. Let's stop by the church." She paused. "Are you allowed to enter a Christian church, Rebecca?"

"Oh, yes, that's not a problem." Rebecca followed the Rainfords into the building. Beautiful stained-glass windows admitted jewel-toned shafts of light. In 1940, those windows had been taken down and removed to a place where they would be safe from Nazi bombs. But the church still radiated the peace of centuries of worship. Rebecca's family synagogue in France had had a similar sense of peace.

"Mr. Andrews is probably in the vicarage unless he's paying calls on parishioners," Mrs. Rainford said as she led the girls out through a side door. A line of trees divided the churchyard from the sizable stone house next door.

As they took the irregular footpath that connected church to vicarage, Rebecca saw a young woman with a child in her arms sitting on a bench in the vicarage garden, her bleak gaze on the sea below.

Mrs. Rainford said, "That's the vicar's wife. Let's say hello." Raising her voice, she called, "Hello, Mary! Enjoying the sunshine?"

The young woman looked up. She was quite lovely, with a pale oval face, golden hair pulled back into a sober knot at her nape, and blue eyes reddened by tears. She did her best to smile. "Lily, Rachel, it's good to see you."

Tactfully ignoring the evidence of tears, Mrs. Rainford said, "Mary, this is Rebecca White, daughter of an old school friend of mine. She's recovering from a bout of fever, so she's visiting us to benefit by the fresh sea air."

As Mary and Rebecca exchanged greetings, Mrs. Rainford bent over the child, who was perhaps eighteen months old and had golden curls, rosy cheeks, and a cherubic smile. "And how is my goddaughter today?" she cooed as she tickled the girl's throat as if she were a kitten. "How is Miss Felicity?"

The girl giggled happily. "Aunt Lily! Ray-shell!" Her pronunciation left something to be desired, but she seemed like a happy baby.

"She's so beautiful!" Rebecca exclaimed. "May I hold her?"

"If you wish. She's getting heavy."

Rebecca scooped up Felicity, making sure that her hand brushed that of Mary. *Sadness, confusion, love, and longing for the kind husband she'd married who had now turned disdainfully from her.*

Thinking the wife's misery was surely related to the husband's, Rebecca exchanged baby talk with Felicity for a bit before handing the child back. Then she and the Rainfords said farewell and headed into the house.

A young maid directed them to the vicar's study. Mr. Andrews was at least fifteen years older than his wife, with a spare build and haunted eyes. As he stood and politely greeted his visitors, Rebecca thought, This man is in hell.

She could feel pain radiating from him, though she wasn't sure of the cause. Needing to know more, Rebecca offered her hand when Mrs. Rainford introduced her. "It's a pleasure to meet you, Mr. Andrews. What a lovely church you have!"

He looked surprised that a young girl wanted to shake hands, but he cooperated. "I am but the steward of it," he said, his face tightening. "It belongs to God."

When their hands touched, she felt a rush of desperation that almost knocked her over. *The church belongs to God and Lackland, and I am unworthy of either of them.*

His faith was broken, she realized. But why?

She slid deeper into his mind and found herself in a dark

morass of doubt and misery. And at the center was his wife. His beautiful wife, whom he loved desperately, and didn't trust. The daughter he adored, but who wasn't his.

The bones of the story revealed themselves in a jangle of pain. Mary had been abandoned after her young lover seduced her and ran off to join the army. Terrified, fearing she was pregnant and that her family would throw her out of the house, she'd gone to her vicar to ask for help and consolation.

Mr. Andrews had always admired Mary's beauty and sweetness, but with the gentle distance of a pastor. As she cried in his arms, he saw her as a woman who was young and desperate. She needed a man to care for her, and he yearned for a loving companion to banish his loneliness.

Impulsively, he had offered marriage. Not only did he want to help her, but his given name was Joseph. Without being quite aware of it, he considered himself to be like the biblical Joseph, who had compassionately married the very young Mary to save her from condemnation and possible death when she discovered she was with child.

But while the Bible said that God was the father of Mary's baby, Joseph Andrews was all too human. Not sure if she was with child, they married quickly so it wouldn't be too obvious if the baby arrived early. For a handful of happy months, they shyly fell in love with each other.

But after Felicity was born, the vicar found himself studying the baby's face, looking for features of the other man. Gradually he became consumed by jealousy and horrible visions of his wife with her lover. He no longer trusted Mary and was tormented by nightmares of her leaving him for another man.

Losing faith in her led to a loss of faith in himself and his God. All because human jealousy had warped his basic goodness.

The torrent of agonized emotions made Rebecca sway on her feet. The vicar frowned. "Are you all right, Miss White?"

She clung to his hand both for his support and because she needed time to try to reach into his damaged spirit. "I'm . . . just a little dizzy."

Where should she begin to heal such deep pain? Working from instinct, she said, "Mrs. Rainford, Rachel, please leave the room. I must speak with Mr. Andrews."

Surprised but obedient, they left the study while the vicar stared at Rebecca as if she were mad and possibly dangerous. "Do you have a problem you wish to discuss?"

Rebecca shook her head. "I have been brought here today to say that your wife loves you, and only you." She poured healing light into him, trying to scour away his jealousy and doubts. "There is no other man in her heart. Give her the love she craves and deserves and there never will be."

He yanked away from her, his face twisted with anguish. "How dare you say such things! Has my wife been complaining about me?"

"She said nothing to me, Mr. Andrews. I perceived the pain at the center of your marriage because I'm a mage and a healer of the mind." She had not fully believed that until now. "You are a good man who has let baseless jealousy destroy what is best in your life. Forgive yourself, and your wife and your God will forgive you."

He folded into his chair and buried his face in his hands as he began shaking with sobs. "I am no longer capable of forgiveness!" he said with despair. "I drown each day in darkness."

She touched his shoulder so lightly that he was unaware of it and channeled more healing and hope. "Isn't Jesus called the light of the world? Wasn't he sent to earth to dispel darkness? As a vicar, surely you have helped others see that light. Be still, and allow the divine light to illuminate your soul."

As she continued to send her healing, she recognized that this power she had been granted surely came from the divine. Though her faith was not the same as the vicar's, both came from the same source and she was blessed to be able to transmit this healing to those in need. Silently she prayed that Mr. Andrews would find the peace that would allow love to be reborn in his spirit.

He became very still, and she sensed a shift in his energy. The darkness began to fade, taking his despair and self-hatred. She stepped back from him.

He raised his head and asked unevenly, "Are you an angel?"

She smiled and shook her head. "Only a mageling, Mr. Andrews, and a rather young and inexperienced one. But I am doing my best to learn how to channel healing from a higher power."

"You have learned your lessons well, Miss White." He pulled out a handkerchief and wiped his eyes. "With your help, I have found my way back to my God and myself."

"I am so very glad to hear that," she said softly.

The vicar got to his feet. "Felicity," he said hesitantly. "Is she my child? Or that other man's?"

"Does it matter?" she asked quietly.

His face changed, the doubts smoothed away. "No. She is my beloved daughter no matter who sired her." He smiled, and his face was transformed from what it was when she'd arrived. "Thank you, my dear child, for teaching me the true meaning of Christian acceptance and compassion."

She didn't bother to explain the irony of that.

"Will . . . will Mary forgive me?" he asked.

A touch of sternness entered Rebecca's voice. "I believe so, but don't ever give her a reason to regret that she has."

"I won't. Now if you'll excuse me, I must go to my wife." Face serene, he bowed, then left the room.

Rebecca followed him out of the study. Mrs. Rainford and Rachel stared at the vicar in amazement as he passed them with a brief nod and left the drawing room at a near run.

A few moments later, they saw him through the window as he emerged into the garden. He went to his wife and took her hands, talking earnestly. The words couldn't be heard, but she swiftly rose and moved into his arms, tears of happiness on her face.

Mrs. Rainford drew a shaken breath. "I think this is too private for us to see. Come along, girls, it's time to resume our walk into town."

Rebecca and Rachel followed her from the house. When they were on the street and no one was in earshot, Rachel asked, "What was the problem?"

Rebecca shook her head. "That's private, too."

"Wise girl," Mrs. Rainford said. "But it's fair to conclude that you were able to sense and adjust the vicar's mind and emotions?"

Shivering from burning so much healing magic, Rebecca drew her shawl around her. "So it seems."

"Well done!" Mrs. Rainford took her arm and hearth witchery warmth flowed through Rebecca. "So your next case will be Napoleon Bonaparte, first consul of France and aspiring ruler of the world."

CHAPTER 30

Merlin's Mirror seethed invisibly, the energy waiting hungrily for the Irregulars to travel through it. "This is madness, you know," Tory murmured to Allarde as they waited in the chamber for everyone to gather for the journey to France.

His smile quirked. "Indeed it is, but no one came up with a better plan."

Allarde's arm was around her, which calmed her nerves as she studied her troops. Rebecca, their novice, was pale but determined as she stayed close to Nick. This mission rested on her abilities, which was a huge burden for a girl who hadn't even known that magic existed a month before.

Cynthia's illusion magic was also vital. Her usual brash confidence strained, she was leaning back against Jack, who had his arms linked loosely around her waist. Even Elspeth, generally an island of calm, looked tense.

Seven people was a large party, but every one of them was essential. Allarde was the only one of the boys who spoke fluent French. Jack was an experienced driver, so he'd handle the carriage, and Nick was their finder. Tory was the best at mirror travel, as well as blending and enhancing magic. And they certainly didn't want to go into danger without their healer, Elspeth.

"If this doesn't work, at least we'll go down in good company," Tory said, trying to sound jaunty.

"We've gone into danger before and come out unscathed," Jack said. When Elspeth arched her brows, he grinned. "Well, a little scathed, but we all made it home and our missions were a success."

"Somehow it's worse this time." Tory's nails were biting into her palms. "Hitler wasn't quite real to me. Not the way Napoleon is."

"Napoleon is the monster of our own age," Jack agreed. "Which is why he bloody well needs to stay on his own side of the Channel!"

Miss Wheaton, Mr. Stephens, and Lily Rainford entered the mirror chamber, their faces serious. The three adults had been working the wards, but they were taking a brief break to see the Irregular raiding party off.

Besides the regular ward mages like Mr. Stephens and Miss Wheaton, other British mages were adding what power they could spare to help maintain the magical protections. Many of the Irregulars came to the Labyrinth at night to contribute so that the chief ward mages could rest and avoid burning out.

Nonetheless, Tory could sense the magic fraying. Originally

the wards had felt like an invisible wall of protection stretching from earth to sky. Now the magic shivered like a tattered, gossamer veil that could fail at any time under the fierce hammering of the French mage corps.

If the wards failed, how long would it be before the French launched their main invasion of Britain?

Not long. Not long at all.

Mr. Stephens said, "With Tory's help at enhancement, I've prepared a new set of stealth stones."

He moved among the Irregulars, distributing the smooth, water-polished pebbles. "Instead of keeping you out of physical sight, these should make you less visible to the French war mages. Rebecca, I have one of the regular stones for you as well. They don't make you invisible, but they make it less likely that you'll be noticed. People won't look in your direction."

Tory hoped he was right about the new stones. She did not want a French war mage crashing down on them in the middle of their mission. The thought of Colonel Levaux gave her chills. They'd caught him unaware before. That wasn't likely to happen a second time.

"Thank you," Rebecca said as she examined the stones with interest, testing the magic with her fingertips. "The more stealth, the better."

After a round of hugs, the adults stepped back as Tory said, "Time to form up. Nick, you take the far end with Rebecca next to you."

Knapsacks were slung over shoulders and hands were clasped as Tory positioned her friends. When she took hold of Allarde's hand, she could feel the individual pulses of power coming from each link in the chain.

When they were ready, Tory said reassuringly, "Remember

that this isn't going to be a particularly difficult transit. Is everyone ready to go?"

Nods all around.

"Godspeed," Mrs. Rainford said softly. "You can do this. I know you can."

Wondering whether that was foretelling or motherly hope, Tory raised her free hand to the mirror. "Next stop, France!"

She concentrated on their destination. She and Nick had located a mirror portal that was close to Boulogne, probably only a few miles from the town.

Unfortunately, they knew nothing else about the site, so this was another leap of faith. *Mirror, mirror, take us safely through.*

The mirror shimmered into visibility, the power pounding through her. Then the portal turned to infinite black and once more they tumbled into the heart of chaos.

Tory felt a cool draft on her face and a gritty surface under her knees. Allarde's hand was locked in hers. Whimpers and a muttered, "I will *never* get used to this!" from her friends.

"Is everyone all right?" Tory asked. "Countdown! Allarde?"

"I'm fine," he replied.

"Elspeth here," came next.

"Jack here, with Cynthia growling energetically in my ear," he said with amusement in his voice. "It's rather romantic, actually." His comment produced a chorus of chuckles, even from Cynthia.

"You were right, this wasn't as bad as traveling from 1940," Rebecca said, her voice uneven. "But not fun."

"We're all here," Nick said. "Wherever here is."

"A cave, I think. The French seem to like them for mirror portals." Tory created a mage light. "Merciful heavens, what is that?"

she gasped, scrambling backward as she saw a huge beast looming over her.

More mage lights came on, and the increased illumination showed a rough stone wall with a huge painted image of a creature rather like an elephant. More pictures of different beasts were revealed in a mesmerizing display. The walls of this chamber were covered with the paintings, as if they'd landed in the middle of a herd of wild animals.

"I've never seen anything like this," Tory said in a hushed voice.

"Neither have I," Allarde said. "But I suspect the paintings may be why the portal is here. Feel the earth magic in this cave!"

Elspeth skimmed her fingertips over the image of a strangely shaped giant bull. "These paintings are incredibly ancient. I can't even guess how old they are, or who painted them."

"I wonder if this place was used as a shrine." Allarde flattened his palms on a bare section of wall as he savored the energy.

"We need to rest after the mirror passage," Elspeth said. "Let's spend the rest of the night here so we can absorb more of this lovely power."

Everyone liked that idea, so they found spots to sleep in. All of them carried more clothing than usual, so the knapsacks made good pillows. They'd also brought long cloaks, which substituted for blankets. Cynthia warmed the air in the chamber so it was comfortable enough that no one would spend the night with chattering teeth.

Cynthia and Jack cuddled up in one corner of the cave, while Rebecca stayed close to Elspeth in another corner. Apparently Rebecca and Nick weren't yet a couple, so he stretched out beneath the image of the hairy elephant.

Even though there was no real privacy, Tory was happy to

spend another night with Allarde. She stretched out beside him, drained by the effort of coming through the mirror. "You're more comfortable than the best mattress in England," she murmured as they settled together spoon fashion.

"And I always sleep well when you're close," he whispered back. His hand drifted down her body, moving very discreetly under her cloak since they weren't alone. "Good night, my lady."

His gentle caresses sent pleasant shivers through her. She relaxed back into his firm body. She could almost forget the dangers that lay ahead when she was in his arms.

Almost. Not quite. This time Tory didn't sleep well, even though Allarde cradled her all night. When Jack announced that the sun was rising and so should they, Tory blinked and rolled onto her back. "I had the strangest dreams. As if I was trapped underground, rowing away like a galley slave or something like that."

Jack stood and stretched mightily. "I felt like a canal mule pulling a barge."

"I dreamed I was that Greek fellow being punished in Hades by having to push a rock to the top of a hill, and then it rolls down and he has to do it again and again forever," Nick said as he creakily got to his feet.

"Sisyphus." Elspeth covered a yawn. "I guess it wasn't such a good idea to sleep in a place where there is so much power."

"I'll be glad to get out into fresh air," Allarde agreed as he stood and gave Tory a hand up. "Now we need to find our way out of this cave, find a suitable carriage, and invade the Army of Boulogne."

"You make it sound easy," Tory said.

Allarde grinned. "We can hope!"

In fact, their mission did proceed so smoothly that it made Tory nervous. They had arrived at the portal they wanted, which turned out to be only a short walk from the main road that ran between Paris and Boulogne.

Less than a mile north on the road, they found a busy coaching inn and were able to purchase a hot breakfast. Then, his age increased twenty years by Cynthia's illusion magic, Allarde went in search of the inn's landlord to inquire about hiring a good-sized travel coach.

There were no coaches available for hire, but with lavish amounts of the gold Allarde had brought and his natural air of authority, the landlord was persuaded to sell them outright a team of horses and an old carriage. The vehicle was shabby, but when the time came, Cynthia could make it look newer and more fashionable.

By midmorning, they'd set off for Boulogne. Jack was on the box driving, his appearance that of a middle-aged coachman. Beside him was Allarde, ready to speak French or spell Jack with the driving if necessary. The two of them were the only ones with the skill to handle a team of horses.

The rest of the party rode inside the coach. Tory quietly watched the countryside and wondered if it was possible to stay this lucky through the whole mission and until they returned home.

No. It wasn't possible.

CHAPTER 31

Cynthia was buzzing with nervous energy by the time they found a small, unoccupied barn near the French camp. Getting into the camp and close to Napoleon wouldn't be possible without her illusion energy. She knew she could manage the individual illusions—but could she do everything that was required at once?

As the girls headed into the barn's tack room to change, Tory said soothingly, "You have a huge amount to handle, Cynthia, but we'll be here to help and feed you extra power if you need it."

Cynthia gave her a crooked smile. "I thought Rebecca was the mind reader."

"It doesn't take magic to see that you're ready to jump out of your skin. Remember that we're a team." Tory laid a hand on Cynthia's arm and power flowed between them. "We'll do this together—and on the illusions, you get to give the orders, which you'll love."

Cynthia gave a crack of laughter. "You know me too well." She closed the door behind them. "You and Elspeth are easy since you're going to be our lady's maids. You both have boringly demure gowns?"

"Deeply boring," Elspeth said as she took off her boy's clothing, then dropped a dark blue gown over her head. "Tory, will you lace me up?"

Tory complied. "Our gowns are almost identical. Boring."

As the two maids prepared, Cynthia retrieved her gown from her bag. They'd all brought more clothing than usual to equip them for going into the camp. Wearing their own garments meant Cynthia would need less power to alter their appearances.

Cynthia lovingly removed the strumpet gown from her bag. Made of nearly translucent sky blue silk and with a neckline cut indecently low, it would be perfect for this mission. Of course, she'd never had a chance to wear it at Lackland. Jack would faint when he saw it.

Tory and Elspeth finished changing and Tory bobbed a curtsy. "Your humble maids await, my ladies. Do we look convincing?"

Cynthia studied the pair, then touched Elspeth's silvery blond hair. "I just dulled your hair, Elspeth. The natural color attracts too much attention." After she altered the color to a pale ashy tan, she turned to Tory. "You look too lively and interesting. Can you stop that?"

Tory thought, then shook her head. "Not reliably. Can you make me look demure and obedient?"

"A challenge, definitely." Cynthia had loathed Tory's vibrant personality when Tory first landed on her as a roommate. Now she liked that bounce. It was so . . . Tory.

She placed a hand on Tory's shoulder and imagined her with a drab, unmemorable appearance. When she had a satisfactory result, she transferred the illusion magic to Tory for maintenance. "There. A pair of modest little maids are you. Now it's time for me to transform myself into a wicked woman."

Cynthia swiftly stripped off her travel clothes. In her bare skin, the tack room was chilly, so she warmed it with a dash of hearth witch magic as she dropped the strumpet gown over her head. "Lace this up for me, girl," she ordered.

"I have a feeling I would not like being your maid for real," Tory observed as she smoothed down the folds of fabric, then started on the back laces.

"You'd be terrible at taking orders so I'd never hire you anyhow." The silk shimmered sensually over Cynthia's skin. She loved silk. It made her want to purr like a kitten. She smoothed down the long straight skirt with her hands as Tory tied the golden ribbon that established the waist just below her breasts.

"Now my hair," Cynthia ordered. She never had a problem sounding imperious. "Lush, decadent waves falling over my shoulders, and that feather thing on the left side."

Tory obeyed. They'd practiced the hairstyle at school, so it didn't take long to brush out the waves and pin some of Cynthia's glorious blond locks up on one side.

Cynthia gazed down, wishing they had a proper mirror. "How do I look?"

Tory grinned. "Jack is not going to like the idea of anyone seeing you look like this! Not to mention that you'll risk catching lung fever. A good thing we have Elspeth along to cure you if necessary."

Cynthia perched on a chair and pulled on her stockings, securing them with embroidered garters. "Not needed when there's hearth witch magic to be had." She glanced at Rebecca, who had been watching the banter in silence. "We'll generate some warmth for you as well. Tory, could you bring out Rebecca's gown? It's the red silk."

Tory obeyed. Holding up the dark scarlet garment, she said, "Your turn, Rebecca. This red will be beautiful with your dark hair."

Rebecca stared aghast at the lightweight, translucent silk gown. "I can't wear anything under that but stockings?"

"Don't worry, we'll make sure you don't freeze," Tory said.

Looking embarrassed, Rebecca stripped off her clothing. When almost everything had been removed, Cynthia said, "You're wearing short drawers? What a very odd garment."

"We call them knickers, and they're pretty much universal in my time." Rebecca turned her back and pulled off the knickers. For modesty's sake, Elspeth hastily dropped the scarlet gown over her head and laced it up the back.

Rebecca turned warily. "The color is good," Cynthia said critically, "but you'll need more hair and curves since you're still too thin after months of being half-starved."

"You're right that her hair is too short, but I think she looks very slim and elegant," Tory said.

"Most men prefer lavish to slim and elegant," Cynthia said with authority. She stepped forward and took Rebecca's wrist, focusing her illusion magic.

"Oh, very good!" Tory exclaimed as Rebecca suddenly appeared to have glossy dark hair spilling over her shoulders and a curvier figure. As Tory moved in with combs to sweep up some of Rebecca's hair, she added, "You definitely make a fine strumpet."

"Not as good a one as me," Cynthia stated, "but very good."

"None of us could come close to matching your strumpetry," Tory said solemnly.

"Wait until I redden my lips and darken my lashes." Cynthia had experimented with cosmetics enough to know how they should look, so it was the work of a moment to make her lips look full and inviting and her eyes sultry.

"Heavens!" Elspeth exclaimed. "You look quite thoroughly scandalous."

"Just what is required. Now I'll add the illusion of cosmetics to Rebecca's face." She held Rebecca's wrist again as she added color to lips and cheeks and made her lashes outrageously long and dark. "But magic can't do everything, Rebecca. Imagine yourself beautiful. Head up, shoulders back. Think of yourself as the kind of girl who can enter a room and stop conversations dead. It's all about confidence, you know."

"And to think my goal was always to be respected for my intelligence!" Rebecca raised her head as directed and put her shoulders back. "I am a *strumpet*!"

The other girls laughed. "It's a good start," Cynthia said. "Now put on your stockings and kid slippers, and we'll go out to see how the lads are doing."

When Rebecca was ready, Cynthia opened the tack room door and swayed into the main barn. The boys had been grooming and feeding the horses. When they were done, Cynthia would create the illusion of expensive footman costumes for Allarde and Nick, and coachman's gear for Jack.

When Cynthia and Rebecca entered, the boys stopped dead in their tracks and stared. Jack said in a strangled voice, "I wish you weren't as good at this, Cinders! Can't you at least wear your cloak till we get there?"

"I will," she said naughtily. "But not yet."

Nick's admiring gaze was riveted on Rebecca. "If your parents could see you, they'd beat me for allowing this!"

Rebecca fluttered her very long lashes and said in a dangerous purr, "Whatever made you think that I need your permission?"

"You're getting into the mood very quickly," Allarde said with a laugh. "Elspeth, Nick feels that Bonaparte is in the army camp now. Can you scry more details?"

Elspeth produced a pocket mirror and Tory laid a hand on her shoulder to enhance the magic. Elspeth's gaze became unfocused. "He's in his residence with several men," she said slowly. "Officers, I think, for a meeting. His quarters are in the middle of the camp and guarded, of course."

"At least he's in the right place," Jack said. "With luck, the meeting won't run too late and we can move in on him."

Tory's brow furrowed. "We studied the layout and strength of the encampment when we were in England, but what about the magical defenses?"

Elspeth closed her eyes as she cupped the scrying glass in her hand. "I don't feel there is much magic being used around the camp. They probably think an army is protection enough so they're using their mages in other ways."

Tory frowned, thinking it was time to check the British wards. She did and swore under her breath. "The wards are on the verge of vanishing! Elspeth, can you find if there is a headquarters for the war mage corps near here?"

"I hadn't thought to look. Let me see. . . ." Elspeth studied the mirror again, then sucked in her breath, her expression aghast. "There's a mage camp very close! Colonel Levaux is in charge. A fair number of mages work under him. There don't seem to be any as powerful as he, but they work well together. I think they're completely focused on bringing down the British wards so the invasion can be launched."

"Shall I use finder magic to locate their camp?" Nick asked.

"No!" Tory shivered. "It's probably just worry on my part, but I'm afraid that if you seek them with magic, they'll notice us. I'd much rather we stay unnoticed. I hope the new stealth stones will help us keep our magic hidden."

"This will be quite a test of Mr. Stephens's new stealth stones," Elspeth agreed.

As the conversation about the French mage corps continued, Cynthia noticed that Jack had withdrawn to where the horses were munching on hay. She knew that he loved animals, but she sensed some odd emotion from him. Fear? No, not that, or no more than might be expected when waiting on the edge of danger.

Quietly she followed him to the other side of the barn. "Is something wrong?"

He used a handful of straw to wipe down the neck of a tall bay carriage horse. "Apart from the chance of not living to see the morning, everything is fine."

She stepped closer so that her silk gown was almost brushing his ankles. He moved away immediately, confirming her belief that something wasn't right. "You don't feel fine to me. Is it something I've done?" She gestured at her translucent gown. "You know this masquerade is necessary to get us close to Bonaparte."

"Yes." He stared at the horse's sleek neck. "But you're enjoying it so much that I have to wonder if we have a future together."

"Jack!" she gasped, feeling as if ice water had just poured over her. "How can you think that? I'm a flirt, but it means nothing! You're the only one who matters."

He finally looked at her, his eyes bleak. "You're rich and

beautiful and glamorous. An aristocrat while I'm a commoner. You can have the world at your feet. You don't need me."

"Don't forget that my aristocratic world exiled me because of my magic! I suppose I might be a success as a courtesan if I had no other choice, but that's not the life I want." Seeing that Jack looked unconvinced, she laid a hand on his arm, feeling as if the earth had just opened beneath her feet and a yawning chasm loomed. "You are the center of my life, Jack. My foundation. Without you—"

Her voice choked and she couldn't speak for a moment. She finished in a raw whisper, "Don't ever leave me, Jack. And believe me when I say I will never leave you."

His tautness vanished and his arms came around her. "Ah, Cynthia. Cinders. I can't bear it when you look at me like that." She felt the beating of his heart against hers. "But we come from such different worlds."

"You come from a world where people love and trust each other," she whispered. "I don't. You are honored for your magic. I was despised. Those *are* different worlds, and yours is better. I want to live with you forever in your world." She lifted her face and said haltingly, "I love you, Jack. I'm not very good at showing love, but I swear I'll work hard until I get it right."

He kissed her then, strong and kind and utterly reliable. "As long as you get it right with me, Cinders. I love you, too. There's no one like you. Even if you are a sharp-tongued flirt."

"Thank God you like me the way I am, flaws and all." She burrowed against him, shaking with dry sobs. She was going to need a lot of illusion magic to fix herself up to dazzle Napoleon. But that was unimportant.

What mattered was that she and Jack had repaired a potentially fatal crack in their relationship, and now they were closer than ever.

CHAPTER 32

The closer they came to the French army camp, the deeper Rebecca's nails dug into her palms. She wished Nick were beside her, but he was riding on the back of the carriage on a footman's perch.

As the coach rolled through the night, she asked, "Do we even know if Bonaparte likes strumpets? I've always heard that he and Josephine adored each other."

Cynthia sniffed. "From what I've heard, he doted on her until he found out that she was wildly unfaithful whenever he was away. So he started taking mistresses. No one will be surprised when we show up looking like high-class doxies."

Rebecca thought that was good for their plan, but she was

sorry that the legend of Napoleon and Josephine's great love wasn't true. Apparently she had a romantic heart. Though really, for romance she need only think of her parents, who loved each other deeply and unconditionally. Rebecca wanted that, too.

She was on the verge of obsessing about mixed-religion relationships when their carriage reached a gatehouse that controlled entry to the army camp. One of the guards, a sergeant, she thought, shouted at the carriage to stop.

Allarde was dressed as a very superior footman to match the elegance that Cynthia had added to the carriage. Speaking flawless French, he announced that his ladies had arrived to entertain a very high official in the camp.

Rebecca bit her lip in an agony of tension. They could never have attempted this daring raid if all wellborn students at Lackland Abbey hadn't been taught French from the cradle so they were as fluent as she was. But what if something about Allarde was unconvincing? It was hard for him to look anything other than aristocratic. What if the sergeant liked being difficult and throwing his power around?

"And who might that high official be?" the sergeant sneered. He jerked open the door and stuck his head in the carriage.

While Rebecca froze in terror, Cynthia leaned across Rebecca and cooed, "The *very highest,* my handsome sergeant."

As he stared at Cynthia, whose gown was cut so low that she could raise the dead, Rebecca collected her courage and also leaned forward. Since she was closer to the soldier, she rested her hand on his wrist so she could read his emotions. He was dazzled by them both and inclined to pass them through just because they were pretty girls, but he didn't want to get into trouble with his superiors.

Time to practice her powers of persuasion. She smiled at the sergeant, trying to match Cynthia for allure. "Surely you do not wish for questions to be asked if we are delayed?" At the same time, she sent the mental message *We are harmless and necessary to the first consul. Let us pass!*

"Do you have papers?" he asked, his voice uncertain.

"Of course." Cynthia raised her hem and made as if she were removing papers tucked under her garter.

Rebecca's hand tightened on the mesmerized guard's wrist. *You have seen our papers and are satisfied. You have done your duty.*

The guard frowned in confusion, then said gruffly, "Very well, you may pass."

Rebecca straightened, letting her fingers drift across his wrist as she drew her hand away. "Thank you, *Monsieur le Sergant.* You are most kind."

His gaze lingered on her and Cynthia as he closed the door. "Straight along this road to the center of the camp, and don't wander onto any of the side roads!"

"We won't," Allarde assured him.

Then the carriage was rolling again, moving at a slower pace now that they were inside the camp. Endless lines of square wood-and-mud huts stretched in both directions, with occasional banners identifying different regiments. The tang of wood smoke was in the air as men sat around occasional fires. The elegant carriage attracted some attention, but in a casual way. No one suspected that British raiders had arrived.

The road began to descend toward the harbor of Boulogne. Rebecca gasped as she looked across the water. Ships' masts, hundreds of them. An endless forest of masts.

Tory sat in the rear-facing seat with Elspeth as a good maid should, but she craned her neck to look out the window. "Good heavens, look at the size of the flotilla! Seeing is very different from knowing how many ships are waiting for the order to invade."

"If the wards fail and their mages produce good weather, the Army of Boulogne will be knocking on English doors within a day," Cynthia said grimly.

"I've been monitoring the wards and sending what power I can spare." Tory leaned back against her seat, her face pale. "The wards might disintegrate at any minute. If that happens and we fail to change Bonaparte's mind, the army may be mobilizing and embarking on those ships by morning."

Rebecca pressed her hand to her heart, feeling almost unbearable pressure. In prison, she carried no particular responsibility apart from helping the other prisoners. Here—she felt the weight of all Britain pressing on her.

Tory said quietly, "Don't worry. We can but do our best. You've already proved that you have the courage to face anything."

Rebecca closed her eyes and prayed that Tory was right.

The carriage rattled to a halt in front of a long wooden building. A pair of bored guards flanked the main entrance.

Allarde opened the carriage door and bowed as if he really were their footman. "My ladies, we have arrived." He flipped down the steps and assisted Rebecca and Cynthia out, then their two faithful maids. Rebecca brushed her damp palms on her cloak. *Imagine yourself beautiful!*

Allarde approached the entrance, and the two guards crossed their rifles to bar his way. From their glances at Cynthia and Rebecca, they were no longer bored.

"Identify yourselves and state your purpose!" one of the guards demanded.

"My ladies are known as the Siren and the Rose," Allarde said as he bowed with a gesture that encompassed the guards and ladies. "Surely their purpose is obvious."

The guard who'd spoken smiled crudely. "Aye, 'tis." He swung his rifle out of the way and his companion did the same.

Allarde knocked on the door. After a wait that seemed long but wasn't, it was opened by a round-faced servant, probably Bonaparte's valet. "Why do you wish to disturb the consul at this hour?" he growled.

Allarde bowed grandly. "The Siren and the Rose have been sent by a friend of the consul to provide a bit of diversion at the end of the day."

Cynthia sauntered forward past Allarde, letting her cloak fall open to show her very revealing gown. "His duties are so difficult," she said silkily. "We have come to provide pleasure and relaxation."

The valet's eyes almost popped from his head, but he still looked uncertain. Time for Rebecca to go to work. She moved forward and touched the back of the man's hand. "We wish only to give him joy," she said throatily as she sent the message that the first consul would be very, very glad to see his visitors.

The valet's doubts dissolved. "Very well, you ladies may come in. *You* stay outside," he added to Allarde.

Allarde bowed again and withdrew to the carriage to stand on one side of the door. He looked like an obedient servant, but Rebecca knew that he wanted to be within call if there was trouble with Bonaparte. So did Nick, who descended from the carriage and took up position on the other side of the door from Allarde.

The valet frowned as Tory and Elspeth followed the strumpets in. "You've brought a whole harem?"

"If *Monsieur le Consul* wishes, indeed we have," Cynthia said sweetly.

One of the guards squeezed Tory's backside as the maids entered. She smiled flirtatiously and detached herself without missing a step, though Rebecca could sense how angry she was at the guard.

Inside, Tory and Elspeth stationed themselves unobtrusively by the wall while Cynthia untied her cloak and let it slither to the floor, revealing her sky blue gown. The valet swallowed hard, his expression glazed.

"Pray summon your master so that we may determine his pleasure," Cynthia said.

The valet bobbed his head and left the room. Rebecca took off her cloak and laid it on the large oval table. The chamber seemed to be used as both conference room and office, with paper and quill pens and an inkstand on the table.

Glancing around, Rebecca saw a huge map hanging by the window. She moved closer to see better. It showed a coastline but was so complex that she wasn't sure if it portrayed France or Britain.

"On a clear day, I can see Dover Castle through that window," a commanding voice said.

Rebecca whirled and saw that Napoleon himself had entered. She'd always heard him called "the Little Emperor," but in fact he was of average height. His white vest and breeches were splotched with ink, as if he wiped his pen on them. He was rather stout and would not have been impressive but for the mesmerizing force of his personality. She caught her breath, knowing that this was a great and terrible man.

Cynthia sank into a deep curtsy. "And surely someday soon you will stand in Dover Castle and observe Boulogne!"

He gave a bark of laughter and looked pleased. "It will not be long now. But what brings you lovely ladies here?"

Rebecca copied Cynthia's curtsy, rather badly. "A friend of yours said that you had been working very hard and needed amusement. We are here at his request."

The consul's brows arched. "Now who would that be? Soult?"

Cynthia rose from her curtsy. "We are pledged not to reveal his name. We are the Siren and the Rose, a fantasy created to fulfill your dreams."

Napoleon stared at her in fascination. "I had thought to work late, but perhaps I won't. Constant, leave us and retire to your quarters. I shall not need you again tonight." The valet bowed and left the room.

Cynthia had done her job. Now it was up to Rebecca. She glided up to him, grateful for the ballet lessons she'd taken for years. "Which is your choice, milord Consul? The blonde? The brunette? Both of us at once?" Fluttering her lashes and hoping she didn't look like a fool, she took his hand.

And was almost knocked backward by his intensity. Was he a mage? No, but a cold, ruthlessly ambitious man. *He burned to conquer the world, but most of all he must conquer the smug, superior English, who had defied and taunted him and forced him into war. He was a man of peace goaded by his enemies to take battle to their shores.*

Focusing all her uncertain magic, she sent the thought *Invading Britain will be your doom! You cannot cross the water. Turn away, turn away to the east. You cannot cross the water!*

Napoleon stared at her, his brow furrowed with confusion. Rebecca frantically repeated her message: *Turn away, turn away, Britain will be your doom! In the east you will find glory. Turn away, turn away!*

Cursing, he jerked his hand away. "You're a witch! You've been sent by the damned British to poison my mind! Well, it won't work, you traitorous slut!"

She couldn't do this, she realized with despair. The force of his mind was so great, his ambition so central to his nature, that she couldn't change him.

Napoleon swung a furious fist at her head. She dodged the worst of the blow, though he grazed her temple hard enough that she staggered. Instinctively she grabbed for his swinging arm, locking both hands around his wrist, because if she couldn't change him now, they were all doomed.

As the first consul tried to yank free, Tory grabbed Rebecca's shoulder, sending her own power and enhancing Rebecca's. Dizzily Rebecca poured all the magic into Napoleon. He stiffened and stopped thrashing as her energy flooded into him.

Stalemate. She had brought him to a halt, but she still lacked the power to change the fierce determination at the center of his soul. Rebecca had a tiger by the tail and she dared not let go. "I am no witch, but a healer sent to cure you of this madness. You cannot cross the narrows sea, my lord!"

Her magic and his will teetered in the balance. Then more hands touched Rebecca and she felt the essence of Cynthia's warrior spirit, Elspeth's strength and clarity. Rebecca blended their power with hers and Tory's and sent a cascade of searing light into Napoleon. *Invading Britain would be your doom, my lord hero! Turn away, turn away, for glory awaits in the east!*

The first consul's fierce gaze wavered. Then his face seemed to melt, furious intensity turning to bafflement.

It was working! His obsession with invading Britain began to dissolve. Rebecca sensed his chaotic thoughts as he tried to sort out his ambitions. *Why bother with that damp little island? The British are a bloody bedamned nuisance, but no real threat to Napoleon Bonaparte, the greatest soldier of this or any age. Leave them to rot on the edge of Europe, helpless to interfere with the glory of Napoleon's growing empire! Prussia, Spain, Italy, Austria, Russia—all would be his, and those spineless Britons would be unable to stop him! He was born to rule!*

As abrupt as the ricochet of a cut rope, the force that had been driving Napoleon to invade Britain vanished. He stared at Rebecca, his expression dazed. Magic churned through her like stormy seas.

Shaking and near collapse from burning so much power, Rebecca whispered raggedly, "It's done. Britain is safe from invasion. Elspeth, can you knock him out?"

As Cynthia wrapped a supportive arm around Rebecca's waist, Elspeth clamped her hand onto Napoleon's nape. A moment later, the first consul and future emperor of France went limp and folded onto the floor.

Mission accomplished.

CHAPTER 33

Rebecca stared at the dictator's motionless body. "He isn't dead, is he?"

"No, but when he wakes, he won't remember any of this," Elspeth said. "Quickly! We must move him into his bedroom and make it look as if he fell asleep naturally."

Tory looked through one door, shook her head, and crossed the room to peer through a different door. "Here is his bedroom."

Cynthia released Rebecca and grasped one of Napoleon's arms while Tory reached for the other. They started to drag him toward the bedroom but could barely budge his dead weight.

"Help us," Cynthia said through gritted teeth. "The little brute is heavy."

Elspeth took one leg and Rebecca pulled herself together enough to take the other leg. The colossus of France gave a snore, so he was definitely alive.

It took all four girls to get him into the bedroom, half dragging him. The room was very austere, as befitted a soldier. The bed was narrow, the coverlet plain, and the furnishings sparse.

Cynthia said, "We need to get his clothing off so it looks as if he has been amusing himself in the way his servant will expect. Rebecca, you're too young to see this. Rumple up his bed and make it look as if it's been used."

As Cynthia started unfastening Napoleon's breeches, Rebecca turned away hastily, grateful not to have to strip his clothing off herself. As she messed up the blankets and sheets, she heard the rustle of fabric and the thump of boots.

Behind her, Tory said, "Now we move him onto the bed. Rebecca, we'll need your help with this."

Rebecca turned warily and was glad to see that someone had draped a white towel over the consul's naked body. The bed was high and hard, and they were all panting when they dragged him onto the mattress.

Cynthia said, "The rest of you splash around some cognac or wine and do anything else that might make it seem he was carousing with strumpets. Quickly!"

Tory stopped, her fingers pressed against her temples. "The wards have been restored," she gasped with relief. "A little battered, but as strong as ever. With Bonaparte's will to conquer withdrawn, the mage corps's attacks have ended."

"Odd," Elspeth said, frowning.

"We'll think about it later," Tory said. "All those mages who were attacking the wards have had their powers freed up, and they might just notice us!"

The possibility was enough to send them racing about to create the scene of a pleasant, uncomplicated debauch. It was a relief to leave Bonaparte's residence, but Rebecca was as nervous as a cat, wondering if the guards by the door would be suspicious that the Siren and the Rose hadn't been there long enough.

Half expecting one of them to grab her, she clung to her stealth stones and tried to send the guards a mental message that there was nothing to be concerned about. Perhaps it worked. The four girls reached the carriage without incident. As Allarde swung the door open, Tory said under her breath, "Done! Britain will not be invaded."

"Thank God!" Allarde said equally softly. "Then we need to get out of here fast, because trouble is coming."

Nick helped Rebecca into the carriage. "Are you all right?" he asked in a worried voice.

She tried to smile. "I'm fine, but Bonaparte's mind was . . . not comfortable."

Looking even more worried, he said, "I'll ride inside with you. It's not like I'm of any use with the horses."

"It will be crowded," Cynthia warned as she climbed into the coach.

"We'll find the space," Elspeth said quietly.

They settled inside quickly. Nick solved the space problem by scooping Rebecca onto his lap, with one arm around her waist and his other hand locked on one of the holds on the wall to keep them steady over the bumpy road.

Rebecca burrowed into him, grateful for his warmth and caring after Napoleon's viciously cold ambition. Cynthia had dropped the illusion magic already, and Nick was his usual handsome self and wearing regular nineteenth-century clothing, not the elaborate footman's costume.

They were all silent until they drove out of the military camp. Nick exhaled with relief. "I'd like to see my mother's history book now. I'll bet the chapter for this time period now clearly reads that Napoleon decided against invading England."

"I certainly hope so!" Tory said.

"He won't invade," Rebecca said, sure of that in her bones. "He will find more accessible prey. In the end, he will be brought down, but it will be many years and many wasted lives until that happens."

Her words produced an uneasy silence until Cynthia said firmly, "Call me selfish, but the other European countries can fend for themselves. What matters most to me is that Britain is safe from invasion."

She got to her feet, grabbing on to a handhold so she wouldn't fall over in the swaying coach. "Since we're going to have to hike from the road back to the cave, I'm changing into my trousers. This gown was not designed for anything but simpering and drinking champagne. Nick, if you watch me, I'll turn you into a frog."

He laughed. "Surely you've noticed that I have eyes only for Rebecca."

Which was a silly thing to say—in Rebecca's experience, everyone liked to look at attractive members of the opposite sex, and Cynthia was very attractive indeed. But it was a very sweet thing to hear.

"I'll change after you finish," Tory said. "There isn't room for more than one of us to do that at a time. And to make sure Nick doesn't break his romantic vow, I'll throw your cloak over his head."

She did, too. Cynthia's long cloak settled over Nick and Rebecca like a tent. He whispered in her ear, "I like this. Very private.

A good place for me to tell you what a heroine you are, Rebecca. You took on one of the greatest conquerors in history, and emerged victorious."

She sighed against his shoulder. "I'm glad I didn't let my friends down, but it doesn't feel like victory to know that Bonaparte is soon going to declare himself emperor and that he'll be cutting a violent swath across Europe for years to come. Would the world be a better place if we'd assassinated him when we had the opportunity?"

He stroked her back under the cloak. "I don't know, Rebecca. As you said before, he did many good things for France, helping to make it a more just society, so it isn't as if his reign will be all bad. One of his generals would have taken his place and perhaps have been even worse. As for Europe . . ." Nick shrugged. "It isn't as if the Continent has ever been a particularly peaceful place. Look at our century."

Her mouth twisted bitterly. "Horror upon horror."

He pulled her closer. "There isn't much we can do except survive and enjoy life while we can."

"And be kind," she whispered. "We can always try to be kind."

"You don't have to try, Rebecca." He brushed a kiss on her forehead. "You're the kindest, most compassionate person I've ever met. And a heroine as well. Rest now, and shalom."

Shalom. Peace. Rebecca closed her eyes and slept.

CHAPTER 34

Tory's feelings of dread continued to increase as they rode through the night. Jack drove as fast as he could without risking a wreck or breaking down the horses, but even so, the few miles felt much, much farther.

Though she was tired, she couldn't sleep. Allarde was right: Trouble was coming, and it would almost certainly come from Colonel Levaux's war mages. They'd been concentrating on breaking the British wards to clear the way for invasion.

Now, like a hungry cobra deprived of its prey, the mage corps sought a new target. Tory sensed the mages' restless, confused, seeking energy. She wouldn't feel safe until they were through the mirror and back at Lackland.

Finally the carriage rocked to a halt and Allarde opened the door. "Jack has driven as far as the carriage can take us. Time to start hiking." He offered a reassuring smile. "Soon we'll be home."

Tory wondered if he believed that—there was a tense note in his voice. She took his hand and climbed down from the coach. Jack had driven off the road into the shadow of a steep hill where they wouldn't be seen by passing traffic. The path to the cave ran through the dark forest ahead.

Elspeth and Cynthia climbed out after her, then Nick. "Rebecca is changing to her trousers," he explained. "She didn't want to ruin Cynthia's gown crawling on her hands and knees through the narrow bits of the cave."

"For which I thank her," Cynthia said. "Not to mention that crawling would be beastly uncomfortable in a skirt."

Jack and Allarde started to unharness the tired horses. "You're going to turn the horses loose?" Tory asked.

"It's a good team." Jack stroked the sweaty neck of the rear wheeler. "I could use them at home, but I thought you'd object to taking them back through the mirror."

She laughed. "Not to mention the fact that they wouldn't fit through the cave. Someone will find and use them and the coach."

Cynthia had dropped the illusion of an expensive carriage as soon as they were out of sight of the camp. But the vehicle was still sound and someone would feel very lucky to find it. Tory hoped the horses ended up with poor farmers who needed them in the fields.

Rebecca emerged from the carriage, jumping nimbly down in her trousers. She looked stronger for her time with Nick. "I am so glad that is over!"

"You did splendidly, Rebecca," Jack said. "Without you . . . well, I don't want to think about what might have happened."

Tory slung her pack on her back. "Time to start moving. There are mages looking for us. I can feel them."

Elspeth grimaced. "I think I prefer the twentieth century. At least there, all we had to worry about was more dangerous weapons, not magic."

Tory had just started toward the woods when fierce, hostile magic exploded around her. The earth vibrated menacingly, and the steep hill to her right shattered. Massive boulders thundered down the slope and debris filled the air. The freed horses screamed and galloped away.

"It's Levaux!" Allarde shouted as he threw up a hand and grabbed at Tory's power to augment his own. "Run!"

The others bolted toward the forest while Allarde used his earth and lifting magics to shove the massive rock slide away from the Irregulars and toward the road. A boulder crushed the carriage like an eggshell.

Before Tory could run a dozen strides, a vast mage light appeared over their heads, illuminating them all. Directly ahead a huge tree crashed down, narrowly missing Cynthia and Jack. Jack swore viciously as he pulled Cynthia away, turning so the lashing branches struck his back instead of her.

An energy blow knocked Tory to her knees. Around her, she saw the same thing happening to her friends. She felt as if she were suffocating and realized that a magical suppression spell like the one at Lackland Abbey had been thrown over them. Only worse. Stronger. She felt as helpless as a kitten.

As she fought for breath, a tall, gaunt figure in black strode from the darkness into the circle of light. The master war mage. Eight rifle-carrying men in blue military uniforms emerged from the darkness to encircle the Irregulars at the edge of the light. All were mages connected to Levaux by threads of silvery energy.

Levaux's gaze swept across the Irregulars as they struggled to their feet one by one, stunned by the suppression spell. He blazed with power, far more than he'd had in Wales.

And not just his own power, Tory realized. Besides the magic he was drawing from the mages he'd brought with him, a multitude of other energy lines connected him to mages who weren't here. Most of the lines ran from him toward the caves. Levaux was drawing on the talents of dozens of mages, wielding their combined power like a great spider in an evil web.

Refusing to look away from his burning gaze, Tory said, "You weren't as strong in Wales."

"I wanted to see how much power I had that far from my base," he said. "Not enough, I found. I work better here." He gave a smile that showed too many teeth. "You vile children have delivered yourselves right into my hands. You'll add greatly to my power."

In a flash, Tory understood why the Irregulars had dreamed of slavery and hard labor when they spent the night in the painted cave. "You've enslaved your own people," she said through stiff lips. "French mages. You feed off the power of your mage corps to make yourself the most powerful mage in France."

"The most powerful mage anywhere, I believe. I know of no others who control so many powerful mages, nor any who have turned their slaves into a massive weapon under one man's control." His eyes narrowed as he studied Tory. "You have the same power I do, but you're too weak, too spineless, to use your magic to compel others."

Tory gasped with horror as his words resonated within her. She realized that if she wished, she could use her talents to blend and enhance the power of other mages as an instrument of enslavement. The thought sickened her.

"It isn't strength I lack, but wickedness," she said icily. "A quality you have in abundance."

He laughed. "How very moralistic of you. Why do I need morals when I have power? I have created an unstoppable force which will help Bonaparte rule the world!"

Jack made a sound of deep frustration. Levaux glanced at him. "You just tried to summon lightning to strike me dead, yes? A waste of time. The only magic that works within this circle of light is mine. But you'll be useful when I rebuild my weather group. The lot of you burned my best weather mages and they've been slow to heal. I like the idea that you and your blond trollop will calm the Channel for the invasion."

Cynthia looked ready to spit fire and Jack's expression was murderous, but before either of them could speak, Allarde snapped, "There will be no invasion, Levaux. Napoleon has changed his mind and is turning his attention elsewhere."

Face contorted, Levaux threw a bolt of furious energy that blasted Allarde to the ground, breathing but unconscious. When Tory instinctively moved toward him, the war mage barked, "Stop right there or I'll lay you out beside him!"

Though she yearned to defy him, Tory obeyed. They would need all their wits and strength if they were to have a chance of escaping this mad devil.

As Levaux looked away, Tory saw Allarde's eyes flicker. With the bond between them that was love, not magic, she realized that he was not as unconscious as the war mage thought. He was biding his time. Jack's eyes narrowed as he recognized the same thing. The Irregulars would not surrender tamely to this monster.

Levaux's gaze swept over the girls. "Somehow you changed Bonaparte's will. The rebound when you altered his mind disrupted my whole mage corps, and for that you will be punished."

His voice dropped to a blood-chilling whisper. *"Which of you little witches is responsible?"*

After a frozen moment, Rebecca said shakily, "I am. Do with me as you will, but release my friends."

Wanting to weep at Rebecca's courage, Tory stepped forward. "It wasn't her, it was me. She's too new and untrained to affect a man like Bonaparte."

"I was the one who brought down Napoleon," Elspeth said, her light voice clear as she also stepped forward. "Not either of them."

"We all did it, Levaux!" Cynthia said contemptuously as she moved forward. "We magelings burned out your weather circle, thwarted your invasion of Wales, and turned Bonaparte permanently away from Britain. We have defeated you!"

"Only for the moment. Once you are enslaved, my power will be even greater. But I will sacrifice the mageling who entered Bonaparte's mind. Perhaps her death will remove the spell she cast over him. If not, at least I'll have the pleasure of seeing her dead."

His eyes narrowed as he studied the girls. Then he said triumphantly, "You!" He pointed at Rebecca. "You I will *burn*!"

"That won't change anything," she said, her voice shaking but her head high. "I didn't cast a spell. I entered his mind and irrevocably changed his thoughts and goals."

"Why should I believe a barely trained mageling? When you're dead, I'll learn who was right!" Levaux raised his hand and a ball of fire formed on his palm.

As he hurled it at Rebecca, Allarde and Jack leaped simultaneously at the war mage while Nick tackled Rebecca. He threw her to the ground and covered her so that the fireball rolled over his back, setting his hair and clothing afire.

As Nick cried out in agony, Allarde and Jack grabbed Levaux

and wrestled him to the ground. Tory was farther away, but she sprinted toward them, giving thanks that while the war mage concentrated on his attackers, the flames burning Nick flickered out.

Jack threw a furious fist at Levaux's jaw, but the war mage managed to twist away from the full impact. Then he blasted both boys with a furious explosion of power that dropped them both in their tracks.

Swearing French curses with filthy words that Tory didn't recognize, Levaux scrambled to his feet. "I should have done this first!" he snarled as he threw a tangle field over both boys, Tory, Cynthia, and Elspeth. Because Tory was running, her momentum knocked her to the ground with bruising force when the tangle field hit.

All she could do was watch helplessly while he stalked across the circle of light to where Nick's blackened body still covered Rebecca. "If you're not already dead, witch, you'll wish you were!"

He grabbed Nick's limp body and yanked him away from Rebecca. And as he rolled over, Nick pulled a twentieth-century pistol from under his jacket and shot Levaux in the heart at point-blank range.

CHAPTER 35

The giant mage light vanished, blanketing the area with darkness. Rebecca screamed as Levaux's blood sprayed over her. An instant later, howls sounded in her mind. She struggled to get up, but she was pinned by the bodies of both Nick and Levaux and could barely breathe.

The war mage's death had ended all his magic, she realized dizzily. His mage light and his suppression and tangle fields were gone. No wonder he thought that killing Rebecca might restore Napoleon's desire to invade England. The anguished cries she heard in her mind were from the enslaved mages who had just been violently severed from their master.

Half a dozen smaller mage lights appeared, illuminating the

clearing again. The weight crushing Rebecca diminished and she guessed that Levaux's body had been unceremoniously jerked away.

A moment later, the rest of the weight vanished. As she gulped air into her lungs, she saw that Allarde and Jack had carefully lifted Nick away by his arms so they wouldn't touch his burned back. When they had him upright, Allarde asked, "Nick, how badly are you hurt?"

"Scorched but repairable," he gasped as he sagged between Allarde and Jack. "I think. Rebecca, are you all right?"

"Better off than you." Suppressing the desire to scream hysterically, she rolled onto her knees, then managed to clamber to her feet.

Half of Nick's blond hair was burned away and the clothing on his back was charred, but he managed to give her a lopsided smile. "I am not going to miss that fellow *at all*."

"Since magic didn't work here, a good thing you brought that Nazi pistol!" Allarde exclaimed, his face bruised but with no other apparent damage.

"I had a feeling a gun might come in handy." Nick swayed and sucked his breath in painfully when Jack shifted his grip on Nick's arm.

Rebecca caught Nick's face between her hands since his cheeks and jaw were unburned. Voice shaking, she said, "That was the bravest thing I've ever seen."

"Entering Napoleon's mind was braver." He tried to turn his head, then winced and stopped. "Besides, I was counting on Elspeth to fix me up. You can take care of a lightly grilled mage, can't you, Elspeth?"

"Yes," her calm voice sounded behind him, where she was already using her healing magic on his back. "But you'll be sleeping on your stomach for a few days."

Rebecca pressed her forehead to Nick's cheek and uttered a silent prayer of thanks before she stepped away. "Does anyone else hear screaming in your mind?"

"I do." Tory gestured toward the edges of the lighted area. "It's the enslaved mages who have been freed from their magical shackles."

Rebecca saw that the eight men were collapsed or folded in fetal positions. "Their minds have been burned as badly as Nick's back." She took a deep breath. "Perhaps . . . I can do something for them."

"I'll help," Tory said.

"So will I." Cynthia picked up the fallen pistol and examined it carefully. "I think I can handle this if anyone tries to hurt us."

Rebecca shivered. "It won't come to that."

Steps uneven, she approached the nearest French mage, a boy not much older than her. His hands were pressed to his temples, and he made little mewling noises as he rocked back and forth on the ground.

She knelt beside him and placed a hand on his forehead. "You're free now," she said gently as she touched his mind, finding the raw wound where Levaux's energy line had been connected. She sent gentle healing to soothe the injury. As the white light spread through him, she felt her own energy augmented by Tory's hand on her shoulder.

The young man's face smoothed out as the pain disappeared, and his dark, dazed eyes focused on Rebecca. *"Merci, mon ange,"* he whispered as he turned his head to kiss her hand. "I am Philippe. My friends . . . can you help them also?"

"I'll do what I can." A little embarrassed, she rose and moved to the next mage, an older man with white hair and a lined face. He was curled into a whimpering ball. This time she knew exactly how to proceed, and it didn't take long to heal his injured mind.

The old man's body relaxed and his eyes opened. "Bless you, child! I feel as if . . . a cloud has been lifted from my mind and a yoke from my back."

"I think that is exactly what has happened," Tory said soberly.

They moved on to the next anguished mage. Though the work was tiring, with Tory's help Rebecca completed her healing round fairly quickly. As the three girls returned wearily to where Nick was now able to stand on his own, the freed French mages conferred together, faces haggard but relieved.

Then the group approached the Irregulars. The white-haired man said, "I am Pierre Beauvallet, once Father Pierre and a priest before Levaux got his filthy claws into my mind. Who are you? How did you come to destroy that serpent?"

Allarde said, "We're English, and we came here to turn Napoleon's thoughts from invading our country. Levaux attacked us before we could escape."

Philippe sucked in his breath. "So that's what happened! The colonel had set every one of his enslaved mages to the task of bringing down the English wards. Day and night he worked us, like mules in harness. Then suddenly it ended in chaos. An hour later, he collected those of us you see here and brought us from the caves to attack you."

"Your headquarters are in the caves?" Jack asked, his brows arching.

"The war mage corps is there because of the great power concentrated in the earth." Pierre frowned as he looked inward. "We must return there quickly. Others of the corps are suffering as we did. Can you come with us, mademoiselle?"

Rebecca hesitated. She desperately wanted to return to the

safety of England, but she couldn't leave people in mental agony if she could help.

A tall, thin French mage said, "I can do the healings. I have a talent something like yours, mademoiselle, and after experiencing what you did, I can do the same."

Relieved, she asked, "You are sure?"

"I am sure," he said gravely. "There is no need for you to stay."

She sighed. "I want so much to go home."

"Then go with our thanks and blessings," Pierre said.

Allarde caught the former priest's gaze. "Will you use your magic to fight for France again?"

Father Pierre glanced around at the other French mages. Reading their expressions, he said, "Never. I would defend my country from attack as you have done, but I will not use my God-granted powers to harm others. My friends are of the same mind."

There were nods and murmurs of agreement. Face set, Philippe ripped the rank insignia from his shoulder. "I believe that within a day, everyone will have left and the caves will be empty. I don't think there is a single one of us who wanted to pervert his powers in the horrible ways we've been forced to do."

His opinion was supported by murmurs of agreement. "I'm glad to hear that," Rebecca said. "Go in peace."

Philippe bowed to her, and then his fellows did, too. Rebecca blushed and was grateful when Nick took her hand reassuringly.

The French mages filed away into the woods, moving in the direction of the caves. They made no attempt to take Levaux's body with them.

Staring at the limp corpse, Jack said, "Do you think we should bury him?"

Cynthia said, "I have a better idea. Stand back, everyone."

They did as she directed. Controlled fury in her eyes, Cynthia raised blazing fire around the fallen mage. The crumpled body burned swiftly. "Rot in hell, war mage!"

"Scourging out the evil," Rebecca said softly. "Let's go home now."

The others nodded. Jack said, "Nick, I have a spare shirt you can wear since your old shirt was half burned off."

"Thanks. Nothing heavier, though. My skin is awfully sensitive." Nick pulled off the old shirt, stuffed the remains in his sack, then donned the new one.

Rebecca tried not to stare but couldn't help admiring his lithe, muscular body. The body he'd put between her and being burned alive. His hair was still half-gone, but the skin of his back was smooth and unburned.

To keep Nick from freezing, Cynthia surrounded him with hearth witch warmth, and then they were on their way. Their route back to the caves was different from the one the French had used. Rebecca suspected that the caves were so extensive, Levaux hadn't even known of the painted cavern that held the mirror. If he had known time travel was possible, he surely would have used the power in some horrible way.

As they made their way through the woods, Nick took her hand. She clasped it tightly. "I don't think I thanked you yet for volunteering to be broiled in my place."

"The only way he could hurt you was over my dead body," Nick said flatly.

She shuddered. "Please don't say that! It could so easily have become true."

"But it didn't. We're heading home with our mission accomplished." A triumphant note entered his voice. "All alive and more or less intact. We're *good*!"

She had to laugh. "Indeed we are, and I'm profoundly grateful that I have helped our friends as they helped me. But I will be very, very glad to return to studying biology and mathematics and chemistry at Lackland Girls Grammar!"

"Peace and quiet, other than the odd bomb falling nearby," Nick agreed. "And . . . under the same roof."

His emotions were as easy to read as letters in flame across the sky. She said quietly, "To be of different faiths is a great challenge, but I no longer believe it to be an insurmountable obstacle. If we are both serious about building a bridge across our differences—I believe we will succeed."

His energy blazing joyfully, Nick swung around and embraced her, his lips meeting hers. She was shocked by how utterly right his kiss felt. How could she have resisted him so long?

She broke the kiss, shaken, and rested her head against his shoulder. "I'm afraid to put my arms around you for fear that I'll hurt you!"

He laughed. "I wouldn't mind, not after what you just said." He took her hand again. "But now we need to get moving. The sooner we reach the portal, the sooner we can go home."

Home. Together. Laughing and holding Nick's hand, she broke into a run to catch up with the others.

She'd never known life could be so good.

Tory was mentally drained and physically depleted by the time they reached the portal, but not so much that she considered resting before heading back to Lackland. She surveyed her friends, then lined them up with Elspeth at the far end in deference to the fact that Nick had suffered a major injury.

The way he and Rebecca were grinning, it was clear the two of them had reached some sort of understanding, so his state of mind was good even if his body wasn't fully recovered. "Say goodbye to the elephants and other painted beasties!" Tory called. "Is everyone ready?"

After a chorus of agreement, she turned to the mirror. Allarde squeezed one hand gently. The other she raised, concentrating on their destination. *Mirror, mirror, take us home, please!*

Once more they were dragged through chaos before returning to normal awareness, but everyone was so glad to be home that there wasn't a single complaint when they landed in Lackland. Since Tory was folded on the floor again, she used the opportunity to cuddle against Allarde. His arms went around her and they both simply rested on each other as mage lights were created.

"This mission began when you had a sudden foretelling about France invading England," she said. "What do you feel now?"

"That possibility is gone." He stood and helped her up. "We have a long war ahead before Bonaparte is defeated, but it won't be fought on British soil."

"Like Cynthia, I'm selfish enough to make that my first priority," Tory said with wry humor. Arms around each other, they headed back to the central hall, the last of the straggling group of weary magelings.

Mr. Stephens and Miss Wheaton greeted them jubilantly where the tunnel reached the hall. "You did it!" Mr. Stephens exclaimed. "The wards returned to normal just short of the point of total failure, and no one here feels any more threat of invasion!"

"And you're all home safely," Miss Wheaton said, her voice warm. "It's a miracle!"

"Not a miracle," Tory said, not removing her arm from Allarde's waist. "Just good teamwork."

Mr. Stephens's expression changed, his exuberance fading. "I'm sorry, Allarde, but I have bad news for you."

Allarde stiffened under Tory's arm. "Yes?"

"There is no good way to say this." The teacher hesitated before saying, "Your father is dying. You must return home immediately."

CHAPTER 36

Allarde had been expecting something like this, Tory realized. She felt his body stiffen but sensed no surprise when he said, "I'll leave first thing in the morning. Can you ask the headmaster to arrange for a post chaise?"

"Of course. And . . . I'm sorry," Mr. Stephens said.

"I'm going with you," Tory said. "I believe we've already established that I am not a frail flower to be left in the conservatory when life becomes difficult."

From his expression, she knew that this time he wasn't going to be noble and claim he didn't need her, but he did say, "You'll get into trouble with the school."

"Do you think I care about that?"

His mouth curved up on one side. "Not as much as you should. You might get locked into solitary confinement when you return."

It was a possibility and could be a serious nuisance. But she'd worry about that later. "We've sailed to Dunkirk under enemy fire, gone behind Nazi lines into France, and penetrated Napoleon's lair and returned safely home. School discipline doesn't seem terribly important just now."

Rebecca said hesitantly, "If I can be introduced to whoever is in charge—your headmistress?—I think I can assure you that she won't be concerned about your absence. When you return, she'll just nod and think that all is well."

"That could be convenient," Elspeth said. "No need to burn your bridges, Tory."

"Thank you, Rebecca." Tory smothered a yawn, suddenly so tired that she could barely stand. "But now I'll get some rest. We've a long ride ahead of us, Justin."

Though the trip was long, it was fast. Weather mage friends were very convenient at keeping storms away, so the roads stayed dry. Allarde was quiet but resigned during the trip. When they spoke, it was about their friends and adventures, not what they would find at the end of their journey.

When they stopped for the night, Allarde booked two rooms and referred to Tory as his sister. Since they both had dark hair, no one questioned that. But they slept in each other's arms.

The post chaise deposited Tory and Allarde at Kemperton Hall's front entrance well after dark on the second day of travel. As they waited for the door to open, Allarde said bleakly, "I don't know if I'm in time to see him. Foretelling ability is no good with something this personal."

Tory took his hand. "You did your best. And if he's . . . already gone, at least you'll be here for your mother."

"And she'll be here for me." His mouth twisted. "I wonder how long my cousin George will give her before she must move into the Dower House."

"Surely he wouldn't force her out!" Tory exclaimed. "A house this size should have enough space for the dowager duchess as long as she wishes to stay!"

"You haven't met my cousin George," Allarde said dryly.

The door swung open, revealing a stern-faced footman. His expression eased and he bowed them inside. "It's good that you're home, my lord."

"I'm no longer a lord, Griffin." Allarde handed over his hat. "Please have my luggage brought in and a room prepared for Lady Victoria. Since you're not wearing a black armband, I assume my father is still with us?"

"I believe so." The footman hesitated, then added, "To those of us who work here, you will always be 'my lord.' "

"Thank you." Allarde lifted Tory's cloak from her shoulders and gave it to the footman, then offered her his arm. "I imagine everyone is in my father's rooms?"

"Yes, my lord."

Allarde led Tory to the sweeping double staircase. He was doing an excellent job of keeping his composure like a proper English gentleman, but Tory felt how deeply he was strained. *"Courage, mon héros,"* she murmured in French. "At least you are here in time to say good-bye."

"For that, I am grateful," he said bleakly.

As they started up the stairs, Allarde stroked the polished marble curve of the railing. "When I was little, I loved sliding down these railings. My mother was always horrified if she caught me."

Tory could understand why since a fall might be lethal, but the thought of him as a dark-haired little boy swooping happily down the railing was endearing. "Now you slide between centuries."

That made him smile. "Only in your magical wake, my lady."

At the top of the staircase, they turned right and proceeded down a long corridor with high, molded ceilings above and rich carpeting underfoot. The hall was as magnificent here as it was on the ground floor.

When they reached the massive set of double doors at the end of the corridor, Allarde opened one for Tory and they entered together. The bedroom was as large and luxurious as one would expect for a duke, with a massive canopied bed in the center and fires burning in both wide fireplaces.

But though a duke was unlikely to die alone, Tory hadn't expected there to be so many people present. The only one she recognized was the duchess, looking pale and tired as she sat by the bed holding her husband's hand. More than a dozen other people were in the room: family members, she supposed, along with servants, a vicar, and men who might be physicians or lawyers.

The low murmur of voices stopped when she and Allarde entered. An edged male voice said, "So he's come!" The unwelcoming tone made Tory very glad she was here.

Another voice muttered, "Who's the girl, his mistress?"

"Lord Fairmount's daughter," was the reply. "Another damned mageling."

Tory kept her head high. Only Justin and his parents mattered, not these bigots.

"Justin!" His mother rose from her chair by the bed and crossed the room to greet him. "I'm so glad you made it here in time."

Tory stepped out of the way as Allarde and his mother embraced. The duchess's lovely face was haggard but resigned. In her son's arms, she found some comfort.

Allarde asked quietly, "How is he?"

"The end is very near." She stepped back and brushed at a loose strand of silver hair. "I think he's been waiting for you." She turned her gaze to Tory. "I'm glad you came, my dear."

There was a world of meaning and acceptance in the simple words. Tory replied equally quietly, "You know I will always do anything in my power for Justin."

The duchess nodded. Taking Allarde's arm, she led him toward the bed. A tall, dark-haired man around thirty stepped into Allarde's path. He looked like a rough sketch of Allarde, cruder and less refined. "Here to change his mind?" the man said, controlled anger in his eyes. "It's too late for that."

Allarde frowned. "I'm here to say farewell to my father, George. There is no question of changing his mind. Please step aside."

So this was George Falkirk, the heir, waiting hungrily for the title and the vast wealth of Westover. He looked as if he wanted to say more, but he had the sense to step aside.

Others drew back so Allarde could reach his father. The duke's eyes were closed and he looked as pale as death, but Tory saw the faint rise and fall of his chest.

"Father." Allarde took his hand. "You waited for me, as a gentleman should."

The duke's eyes opened and the faintest of smiles crossed his face. "Justin. I'm glad to see you one last time." The focus of his eyes shifted. "You and your lovely young lady."

Taking that as permission to move forward, Tory stepped to Allarde's side. "The feeling is mutual, sir." On impulse, she bent and pressed her lips to the parchment coolness of his cheek. "I wish I could have known you longer."

He smiled, his expression peaceful. "It's been long enough that I know my son is in good hands."

Tory bit her lip, moved that he accepted her even though she was costing Allarde his heritage.

The moment was interrupted when a brusque voice said, "Your grace, you must sign the papers *now,* before it's too late."

A man dressed like a prosperous lawyer thrust several papers at the duke, along with a pen dipped in ink. Behind the lawyer stood George, his face tight.

A drop of ink formed on the pen, then dripped onto the blue brocade coverlet in a black, spreading stain. Startled, Allarde said, "What papers are so important that they must be signed at such a moment?"

"The disinheritance papers, Justin," his mother said in a detached voice. "They have been drawn up, but your father hasn't signed them."

Allarde's confused gaze moved to his father. "You haven't signed? On my last visit, we discussed the matter and agreed that my magical abilities disqualify me for inheriting the title."

His father gazed back, his voice the barest thread. "Disinheritance is the accepted custom," he whispered. "A peer with magical abilities would face much criticism. It would be difficult."

Allarde looked as if he were barely breathing. "Difficult, yes. Not impossible."

"You *must* sign, sir!" George hissed, barely able to keep his voice down even though he was at a deathbed. "You owe it to our name, our family honor!"

"Do I?" the duke said reflectively. "What seemed so clear . . . no longer does."

His gaze moved from Allarde to his wife. He smiled again and then closed his eyes. The duchess took his hand, her expression stricken as her husband took a long, rattling breath . . . then breathed no more.

Tory gripped Allarde's hand as he closed his eyes in silent grief. She envied the love he and his father had shared, but that made this loss heartrending.

As the vicar began to pray in a soft voice, George said with barely suppressed fury, "Westover was going to sign! You all saw that! He intended to sign, but he was too weak at the end!"

A soberly clad man stepped forward. "Excuse me, Mr. Falkirk, but I am Hollings, his grace's personal lawyer for the last thirty years. He asked me to prepare disinheritance papers four years ago, when Lord Allarde entered Lackland Abbey. Yet in all that time, the duke never chose to sign them. I saw no evidence that he intended to do so tonight."

"I'm the true heir!" George said, his voice rising. "Not that wretched *mageling*! I'll take it to the courts! To Chancery! To the House of Lords!"

"Then you're an even bigger fool than I thought, George Falkirk." The duchess rose, petite but indomitable. "A whole roomful of witnesses saw my husband decline to sign the papers. Ever since Justin's magical talents manifested, the duke has been torn about whether or not he should disinherit his only son. A son who is superbly qualified to be the next Duke of Westover, and who loves this land as deeply as his father did." Her eyes narrowed. "He will be a far, far better duke than you could ever be."

George's fists clenched furiously and he took a step toward the duchess. Allarde instantly stepped between them. "You will not upset my mother," he said in a steely voice. "Nor are you welcome in this house. You will leave immediately." His gaze moved to a servant standing discreetly to the side. "Mr. Jenkins, see to it."

"Yes, your grace." The servant's voice was bland, but his eyes were jubilant. Here was another man who was glad that Allarde hadn't been disinherited.

Tory glanced around the room. Beyond sorrow over the duke's passing, she saw that some of those present looked appalled that Allarde would inherit, but more looked pleased. Only aristocrats hated magic. Average folk respected and welcomed it.

The duchess said, "The family would like to be alone to mourn, so all of you leave except for my son and Lady Victoria." The room cleared out at her order, and Allarde closed the door when everyone had departed.

The duchess sank into the chair by the bed. "This won't be easy, Justin. When you turn twenty-one and take your seat in the House of Lords, many members will give you the cut direct. Caricaturists will draw vicious cartoons, and much of what is wrongly known as 'polite' society will refuse to associate with you."

"I know," he replied. "I had accepted my disinheritance. Now I must rethink my future." He reached out for Tory's hand and held it tight.

"This won't be the easiest path," Tory said gravely. "But what is easy isn't always the best."

The duchess smiled. "What a very wise young lady you are. It's time that society changed its views about magic, and who better to convince them they're wrong than you two?"

Allarde hugged his mother. "As long as I have the support of you and Tory, I can face anything."

"I know." The duchess's smile faded. "Now, please leave me. I want to be alone with my husband for the last time."

Tears in her eyes, Tory withdrew with Allarde. After he closed the door, he said apologetically, "I'm sorry, I'm still in shock. I didn't expect this. I . . . I don't know quite what to do next."

"You need the strength of Kemperton," Tory said. "Let's go for a walk."

He nodded and together they went downstairs, collected their cloaks, and headed out into the cold night. Tory took his arm, grateful to be out of the suffocating atmosphere of the sickroom. As they walked away from the house, she felt Justin's tension begin to fade.

"I'm so sorry your father is gone," she said when they were well away from the house. "But he died peacefully at a great age and with those he loved best beside him. That is not a bad way to go."

"You're right, of course." He wrapped his arm around her shoulders and turned so they could see the towers of the great hall in the moonlight. "But I and my magic caused him great grief."

"Not so much that he stopped loving you." She studied how moonlight edged the strong planes of his face. "How do you feel about what happened tonight?"

He shrugged. "I never cared that much about the title."

"I didn't ask how you felt about the title, but about the fact that now Kemperton is yours for as long as you live." She made a sweeping gesture that encompassed the hills and fields and the great sprawling house. *"Yours."*

The glow that connected him to the land flared brighter, and he smiled. "That makes me happier than I dreamed possible. Almost as happy as having you." He turned and rested his hands on her shoulders. "I've never asked this formally and we won't be of age for years, but Tory—will you marry me?"

Her brows arched. "Of course. Was there ever any question?"

"Not really," he said, his gaze warm. "But I needed the words to be said."

"Now that they have been—let's dance on air in honor of your father, a great and good man." She put one hand on his shoulder and lifted his other hand in dance position, then let her magic flow out to meet his.

He summoned his own power, joining it with hers until they soared together into the air, swooping up toward the moon. Tory laughed aloud as they danced above the green hills of the land that was Justin's destiny.

"Did you know that there's a faint glow connecting you to the earth?" he said with an answering laugh. "Kemperton has claimed you as its own."

So this land was Tory's destiny as well as Justin's. "Perhaps someday you can create a sanctuary for lost magelings," she mused as he guided them back to earth. "A place where people like us but less lucky can find themselves and build a better future."

"That's a wonderful idea." They glided back to the ground and he bent his head into a kiss. "And you are the most wonderful girl in the world!"

As their lips met in a kiss of love and promise, Tory knew that his inheritance would not be easy for both of them. But together, they could face anything.

AUTHOR'S NOTE

The Dark Mirror series isn't real history—as far as I know, time-traveling teen mages have not been working behind the scenes to make events turn out the way we read it in history books! But the stories do use real history as the raw materials of the plot.

Between 1803 and 1805, Napoleon Bonaparte really did have a ferocious desire to invade England. He said, "All my thoughts are directed towards England. I want only for a favourable wind to plant the Imperial Eagle on the Tower of London."

So he built up a huge army concentrated around Boulogne and ordered a massive flotilla of ships to be built for the invasion. Needless to say, this upset people in Britain a great deal, and plans were laid to raise militias and even train volunteers to act as guerrillas if the French managed to land troops.

The French did attempt to invade Ireland and raise the Irish against the English, but none of the ships could land at Bantry Bay because of bad weather and rough seas. Weather mages, perhaps?

The invasion of Wales depicted in this book was based on a real invasion that took place in February 1797 near Fishguard in Wales. It's called "the last invasion of Britain" because the French did successfully land about fourteen hundred troops near Fishguard under the command of an Irish American colonel who had fought Britain during the American Revolution.

When the French troops landed, the local militia, the yeomanry, and many volunteers banded together to mount a defense. After a mere two days, the British commander, Lord Cawdor, managed to bluff the French into surrendering.

It's possible that the Welshwomen who lined up along the bluffs in their red shawls and tall black hats helped persuade the French to surrender because they looked like scarlet-clad soldiers. In truth, the local troops were many fewer until reinforcements arrived, but the French quickly realized their position was untenable. Surrender was a wise decision, and there were only a handful of casualties.

I used the real town of Carmarthen (which I've visited) to stand in for Fishguard, and I apologize for liberties taken. For more information, search "the Battle of Fishguard." I'm told there is a wonderful tapestry of the invasion exhibited at the Fishguard Town Hall.

Despite Bonaparte's massive preparations for invasion, in 1805 he dropped his plans to invade Britain and marched the Army of Boulogne, now known as the Grande Armée, east toward Austria. There was not another serious attempt to invade Britain until Hitler's Operation Sea Lion in World War II, but that didn't happen, either.

The English Channel may be narrow, but it's mighty!

Experience the magic . . .
the romance . . . the danger . . .
Step into the mirror.

Read all of the Dark Mirror novels by
New York Times Bestselling Author

M. J. PUTNEY

ST. MARTIN'S GRIFFIN
www.stmartins.com

Tory and her friends are celebrating the success of their second mission forward in time when an urgent summons calls them back to their own time: Napoleon is on the brink of invading England. Can a handful of young mages stop an army? In desperation, Merlin's Irregulars ask Rebecca Weiss, an untrained telepath from 1940, to come back to 1804 and change Napoleon's mind before it's too late. As Tory and Allarde make a commitment that will cost him his inheritance, Rebecca promises to do what she can to stop Napoleon even though she is unsure of her magical abilities. But Tory and her friends saved the Weiss family from certain death, and Rebecca will risk anything, even her life and her budding relationship with Nick Rainford, to repay them.

A daring mission takes Tory and Rebecca and their friends into the heart of the Army of Boulogne, where Napoleon is plotting invasion. But while their success may save England, they must still face the bittersweet consequences of their decisions when they return home.

"Absolutely riveting... Putney creates a vivid historical fantasy and delivers a page-turning read." —*RT Book Reviews* on *Dark Mirror*

"*Dark Passage* is hard to put down.... The characters will leave you thinking about them long after you finish the story." —Freshfiction.com

EILEEN BUCKHOLTZ

M. J. Putney is the YA alter ego of *New York Times* bestselling author Mary Jo Putney. The winner of numerous awards for her historical romances, M.J. is fond of reading, cats, travel, and most of all, great stories. Please visit her on the Web at www.mjputney.com.

$9.99/$10.99 CAN.

Cover design by Elsie Lyons

Cover photographs: girl © Emma Delves-Broughton/Trevillion; tree © Terry Bidgood/Trevillion; castle © Jill Battaglia/Arcangel Images

www.stmartins.com

St. Martin's Griffin
175 FIFTH AVENUE, NEW YORK, N.Y. 10010
PRINTED IN THE UNITED STATES OF AMERICA

ISBN 978-0-312-62286-2
50999 >
9 780312 622862